THE EMPTY WORLD

1

PORTAL THROUGH THE POND

DAVID K. ANDERSON

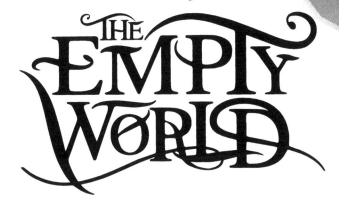

THE EMPTY WORLD

Book 1

PORTAL THROUGH THE POND

David K. Anderson

Magical Scrivener Press
22 Hawkstead Hollow
Nashua, NH 03063

www.magicalscrivener.com

Publisher's Note: This is a work of fiction. Names, characters, places, and incidents are a product of the author's imagination. Locales and public names are sometimes used for atmospheric purposes. Any resemblance to actual people, living or dead, or to businesses, companies, events, institutions, or locales is completely coincidental.

Ordering Information: Special discounts are available on quantity purchases by corporations, associations, and others. For details, contact the publisher at the address above.

David K. Anderson – First Edition

ISBN 978-1-939233-89-9

Printed in the United States of America

To my lifelong partner, friend, and wife, Patti.

PROLOGUE

Summer, *Ten Thousand Years Ago*

When they came to build their devices, they already knew of the world. They'd been studying it and many other worlds from afar for thousands of their own planet's rotations around its star. When they finally perfected how to cross over and not just observe, they had a reasonable idea what this geologically active, uncontrolled world would do.

Since they had been observing this world throughout its violent geological history, they knew that its last ice age was recently past, and what would later be known to the native intelligent species as New York, Vermont, Maine, and New Hampshire were very much like what they would be ten thousand years into the future. Of course, they didn't care nor would they ever know what the native species would call the land they settled on. They only cared that summers could produce hot, muggy, stale air that hung over the mountains and valleys, and, by late in the day, bring violent thunderstorms to the region. The prevailing winds were from west to east during those weather events and tended to sweep the hot electrically charged storms with them.

They had come to this region because they saw in it the best combination of power and predictability for their needs from the storms generated by the buildup of heat. Predictability being relative, they were desperate and time was short. They would rather have controlled the whole process from their world but they had found in this one an acceptable alternative— even if it was only for about one-sixth of the world's yearly cycle when the axis wobble brought the hottest temperatures to the area. Their own world had no such large swings in weather from season to season. They'd conquered and controlled their environment millennia ago, and that process was irreversible.

They knew that other, more appropriate areas closer to the planet's equator existed for the violent storms needed but they were too hot for the natural devices they were hurrying to construct. The water that was a major component of their hurried setups had to stay below a certain temperature that seldom was achieved where there wasn't a larger swing in seasonal temperatures than in the tropics or semitropical land areas. So they settled on the temperate zones, and especially areas in the temperate zones where there were sufficient landmass upheavals that helped channel the storms down into the valleys between. Ready-made funnels for electrical energy, so to speak.

Besides, their own world, or this emerging young one and the many others like it they had found, was really irrelevant. Shortly it wouldn't matter where they constructed the devices or where the power came from: they as a race would be gone and wouldn't care.

Eight Years and Ten Months Before the Present

Lillian was thin, almost too thin. She wore stiff dark blue jeans and a bright yellow, hooded sweatshirt that overwhelmed her frailness. To anyone watching her, the outfit would have seemed out of place on the hot, muggy evening. But she knew what she was doing. Her brown-dyed hair was tied back tightly and only added to her austere appearance.

She walked slowly, picking her way down the narrow worn path from her house. Erosion from frequent violent thunderstorms made the path a bit tricky in the summer. To keep her footing, she had to focus on carefully putting one foot in front of the other despite knowing the way so well.

The rolling hills and elegantly kept old house behind her were reflected in the gray water of the pond. She stopped only when the path ended abruptly at the weedy shoreline. There she waited, standing very still and facing the pond while the rising wind pushed at her back. A lone duck took exception to her intrusion and gracefully took off for parts unknown. The songbirds and the bullfrogs were silent, perhaps anticipating the storm along with her.

Lillian's alert green eyes gazed out over the murky water. They were her most arresting feature and, over thirty years ago, had helped to win her husband. She stared into the black depths below her, hoping those eyes would bring him back to stay.

After several minutes, she was dissatisfied standing on the shore, so she walked out onto the fifty-foot-long wooden dock, stopping halfway. Her husband had built it two years before for just these occasions. The new vantage point pleased her. She scanned the several acres of the pond she knew so well, her head weaving side to side slightly as she waited.

The pond was a natural body of water surrounded on three sides by the property she and her husband inherited nearly thirty-one years ago from his parents. They moved into the large Victorian house that her husband's great-grandfather had built in 1899, on the little rise of land they called a hill overlooking the pond.

She had come to that house as a new bride. Since that time, she and Jack had added the studio on the back of the house facing out toward the pond, as well as built the house down the hill for their daughter's family. The Jacksons' place had also been built across the pond on the piece of land that Jack's father sold just before he died those many years ago. She'd had many occasions to curse Grandpa Renfrew for that weakness in selling even that small plot on the other side of the pond. Since the Peters family had bought the house from the Jacksons six years ago, they were a constant irritation with their snooping and nosy meddling. Thankfully not much else had visibly changed in all those years. Lillian was now fifty-eight years old.

She frowned after her quiet reminiscing was over. Night was overtaking the hills, and that worried her. She turned from the pond and looked back up the path toward the house. The gray clouds raced overhead, outrunning the rumbling thunder not far behind. A big storm was brewing, the oppressive heat and humidity building toward the intense finish. Sometimes, though, the onset of darkness cooled things down enough that the gathering elements of the storm dissipated—defeated before ever getting started. That usually only happened earlier in the summer, before the really humid weather settled in. But you could never be sure.

Lillian allowed herself a smile at the thought that she was worried not because the storm was coming, but because despite the signs, it still might not come. The storm finally did arrive, though, building up gradually. She smelled it first, its distinctive odor being carried on the strengthening breeze. That smell did its best to trigger pleasant childhood memories, but she was focused on the problem at hand and resisted with an effort.

The rain came then, marching over the hills. It began as a soft buzz that grew louder on its way toward the pond. Then it came more swiftly in heavy sheets over the house and started dappling the pond before quickening into a pelting relentless deluge.

The wind picked up next, sudden and fierce, turning the water's surface into a million churning whirlpools. She swung back toward the pond, smiling again, ignoring the heavy wind and rain. She was grateful for her choice of clothes. Her only visible concession to the storm was to cross her arms over her chest and hunch up her shoulders a bit in a vain attempt to stop water from pouring down her collar. Finally she remembered the hood and pulled it over her head. Still she waited.

The lightning followed last of all. Sharp cracks of it lit up the darkening sky and forced her to flinch ever so slightly at its brutal power. Twice she leaned toward the water as lightning lit the pond. But both times, she wasn't satisfied with something, didn't see what she was looking for, so she relaxed slightly, straightening back up as the storm continued. A third crack sounded so loudly she put her hands over her ears. The pond seemed to glow for a second with the lightning strike. Eagerly she removed her hands from her ears. Finally satisfied with what she saw, she sighed and started counting down from one hundred.

At the count of sixty-three, a man's head popped out of the water a few feet from the dock. He swam closer and grabbed the dock with one hand while pushing a large watertight bag almost nonchalantly up and over the edge onto the dock with the other hand. Then he nimbly scrambled up, showing an easy familiarity with the process and surprising athleticism for his years.

Even though Lillian was only a few feet away, the sounds of the man's efforts were drowned out by the continuing wind and rain. She didn't offer him help, and he didn't expect it. They were both used to the routine. Once he was standing on the rough planks, he grinned at her.

"You're wet," he deadpanned, shouting to be heard above the storm.

"You're late, Jack dear, and look who's talking!" she replied just as loudly, smiling and hugging him.

"Let's get up to the house and dry off," he said, disengaging himself from her embrace. "I'll show you what I've done once we change." He indicated the watertight container with a gesture.

"How many?" she asked.

"I finished four and I have some more photos," he replied. "Now let's hurry!"

They started up the path toward the house. The storm began to let up just then, and she stopped in her tracks. Jack continued for two steps, then must have sensed she wasn't following. He slowed and turned with a questioning expression.

"Will you go back?" she asked.

Jack's shoulders sagged at the not unexpected question. "It's a chance of a lifetime, not to mention the place is exhilarating and inspiring. Yes, of course

I'll go back." He hesitated, then added, "You could come with me, you know."

It wasn't the first time he'd made that offer, not even the second or third time.

"No, I won't, I can't, and you know that."

It was the same answer, old now, all explained and argued out a dozen times over.

He nodded, neither accepting it nor outright rejecting it, and turned again toward the house. She followed more slowly so that he wouldn't see the fear and sadness on her face. But after thirty-one years together, she just knew he felt it all the same.

Two Months Later

Lillian was back at the pond, waiting as a storm gathered overhead. She was worried and it showed in her already lined face. *If Abigail's snooping keeps up much longer, I'll look a lot older than fifty-eight*, she thought. Mrs. Peters had been snooping once more with the binoculars just after Jack had jumped into the pond three weeks ago. He was going so often now, and Mrs. Peters was noticing the activity. If Jack didn't show up soon, she knew that Abigail Peters would tell her husband, Wendell Peters, who was a police officer in town. From there, it would get to Police Chief Lockhart. That wouldn't be good. She gave another mental curse to Grandpa Renfrew for selling the land.

Her next worry was that this storm could possibly be the last thunderstorm of the season, and Jack's final opportunity until next summer. Any rare January or February thunderstorm triggered by a nor'easter coming up the coast would find the pond frozen solid to a depth of at least a foot from the hard New Hampshire winter and would be useless to him.

The biggest worry, though, was that she'd seen her husband only fleetingly during the most recent thunderstorm a couple of days before. At that time, a lightning strike that seemed perfect had lit up the pond. But the moment passed and he was gone, and she didn't understand why. But then again, this was all beyond understanding anyway, so predicting an outcome to this amazing set of variables was futile.

The woman weathered the elements, deep in thought. She was so used to recognizing the right moment, despite its unpredictable nature, that she had time to reflect and play out the various scenarios that her growing fears imagined. The storm lasted longer than usual, which increased her fears to borderline panic. There were several false alarms. Just when it seemed the storm was abating and she was ready to give up, a final crack of lightning illuminated the sky and pond just right. She waited, counting as was her ritual. The expected happened right on queue as it had so often in the past—but again, Jack didn't surface.

Disappointed and afraid, Lillian was turning to leave when an object shot up out of the water and flopped on its side, floating with a slight bobbing motion, barely out of her reach. Deciding against jumping in from the dock after it, she walked back off the dock and entered the water from the shore to retrieve it. She was up to her waist when she reached the object that had drifted closer to shore while she walked off the dock. It was her husband's airtight bag. It had been inflated before being sealed so that it would float. She turned around and, using the dock for support, waded back out of the water. Once on shore, she opened the bag to the rush of escaping air. Inside was another finished canvas and a note. She took the note out and read Jack's strong, clean handwriting:

Dear Lillian,

It seems to be closing, narrowing somehow. I couldn't get through. I hope it changes back again, opens up some more. I will keep trying. If you get this, then you'll have my latest work. The storm must be almost over on your side, so I have to get the bag sealed and inflated before it's too late.

Love,
Jack

Ignoring the finished canvas and weeping uncontrollably, she headed up the path to the house, fearing she would never see him again and knowing that what she'd been dreading for the last couple of days was all going to come true.

CHAPTER 1

Christy Walker sat softly crying, staring out at the front lawn, her slim form cradled in the bay-window seat. The day was gray and heavy with rain. It was a miserable Saturday in more ways than one. The wind hurled the water in irregular sheets against the side windows that rattled at each new assault. Each time a new wave of water hit, the wind entered somewhere amongst the old window frames and whistled and moaned loudly throughout the room, the drapes flapping as if trying to hold back the intrusion. Christy used to think that sound meant the house was haunted, and her grandmother used to encourage the idea. Today the sounds were all but ignored by Christy as she waited for everyone to return from her grandmother's funeral.

"Now, now, Connie," Mrs. Pike had said to Christy's mom earlier, "you just go, and I'll stay and make sure everything is ready when you get back. I can't see any reason to see Lillian in there again. I said my good-byes to her at the wake last night. I can do more good here this morning."

Mrs. Pike had left Christy alone to cry all morning, only peeking in on her once or twice before continuing the food preparation for the day.

Christy still had on the sweatshirt and sweatpants and slippers that earlier had signaled her decision to stay home from the funeral. Realizing it was getting time for everyone's return, she went to change into the black dress her mom bought her just yesterday. She hated wearing dresses! But she knew that if she wasn't ready when everyone returned, she would be handed over to her dad. That happened only when her mom was too stressed to deal with her. Christy rightly figured this would be one of those times, if she wasn't dressed when they got back.

A little later in her new room upstairs—until recently, her grandmother's guest bedroom—she straightened out the dress and looked at herself in the mirror. Groaning with the realization that she wouldn't be able to hide the red and swollen eyes, she wished again that her mom would give in and let her wear some makeup. Not much—just enough to help. At least three-quarters of all the other girls in seventh grade were wearing makeup, and she was beginning to get self-conscious about herself being in the minority. School was almost through for the year, and maybe when she went to the big dance in two weeks, her mom would change her mind. She brushed her short blonde hair and tied it into a small ponytail (that would please her dad). She fidgeted with her pantyhose in front of the mirror, and despite the red swollen eyes, ponytail, lack of makeup, and the fact she really didn't like dresses, she thought she looked quite grown up.

The cooking smells drifted upstairs, and her stomach growled in protest. She suddenly remembered she hadn't eaten a thing all morning. If she could be hungry on a day like today, she began to feel she might survive it after all.

She heard the first of the cars pull into the driveway with a sloshing sound as the tires hit some standing water on the pavement. Then they made a very familiar crunching sound as they pulled onto the gravel beyond the paved driveway before pulling off onto the lawn. That would be her dad moving off the driveway to make room for the rest of the cars that were expected.

The gravel signaled the beginning of the driveway to her old house. When her parents and grandparents had begun to build the house down the hill, they had just extended the new driveway off the old one and covered it in crushed stone. The sound of that gravel driveway was unmistakable and lately brought a pang of sadness each time Christy heard it.

She went downstairs in a little better mood despite her reflections because she knew Trev would be there soon. Trevor Hanson was her best friend and had been for years. Actually she, Trevor, and Ginny Wentworth had all been best friends together since before even first grade, but Ginny had gone to private school in Maine for this past year, and it had somehow changed their wonderful, comfortable, crazy friendship. She hadn't seen Ginny or talked to her in months, not since at least Christmas, and neither had Trev.

Christy was waiting again on the window seat when her mom and dad walked in. Her mom handed her raincoat to her dad, and then, smiling a quick greeting to Christy, she walked through into the kitchen to find Mrs. Pike. Her dad took off his raincoat while nodding to Christy, then he came over and planted a kiss on the top of her head.

"How are you, sweetheart?" he asked, a smile of concern showing on his face.

"I'm okay, Daddy, thanks."

"Good. Well, I'll put these away," he said, indicating the coats over his arm. "You look nice in a dress," he added, heading upstairs to put the coats on his bed. "Nice ponytail, too!" he called down as he went, the old staircase creaking and groaning with every step, mixing with his rich, warm voice.

Christy's mom came back in and sat on the window seat beside her, giving her a little hug before speaking.

"My, you look very pretty. I see the dress fits you fine."
Taking Christy's face gently in her hands, she turned it
and stared into Christy's eyes. "Hmm," she said. "Why
don't you run up to my bedroom quickly and put just
a touch of my makeup on. You know which drawer it's
in?"

"Really, Mom?" Christy asked.

Her mom smiled. "Yes, really. I'd let you use what I
brought with me today, but I've used most of it myself."
Christy noticed her mom's own red and swollen eyes.
"And hurry back down," her mom continued. "Trevor
and his mom will be here shortly to help. Everyone
else, I suspect, is giving us a decent amount of time
before they show up. If your dad is still there, send him
down. I could use his help too."

Christy was still sitting on the edge of her mom
and dad's bed finishing up applying a little blush—she
hoped it wouldn't be too obvious—when Trevor walked
in.

"Your mom said I could find you up here." Then he
saw what Christy was doing. "Oh no! Dum da dum
dum—the first step!" he said.

"Oh, shush up. Does it look alright?" she asked,
turning toward him.

"Sure, it looks fine," he said as he plopped down
beside her. "Guess who I saw?" he asked as he loosened
his tie and unbuttoned his blazer.

Christy rolled her eyes at him. "Okay, I give up. Who did you see?"

"Ginny. She said to say hi," Trevor said, "and that she was sorry about your grandmother."

She turned toward Trevor, opening her eyes wide and dropping her jaw before smiling at him. "Well, I would have hoped she said hi! How is she?"

"Oh, she got fat!"

"Noooo," Christy said, bouncing up and down twice.

"Well, not really, but she did put on some weight." He grinned.

She punched his arm like she always did when he set her up like that. He grabbed her fist as she was starting to punch him again, but something in his face made her stop. His grin was gone. He released her hand, and she waited for him to continue. He avoided looking at her face.

"What is it, Trev? Like I said, spill it," she whispered.

He stared down at his hands again before continuing. "She also called your grandmother a loony toon, a nutcase, a complete whacko! Her words, not mine." Then, still not looking at her, he said, "I gotta tell you Christy, I wasn't impressed."

Christy's eyes filled with tears, and she gripped Trevor's arm. "Why would she say those things?"

"I don't know," he said, shaking his head. "I saw her and her mom at the mall. We started talking about this year, and of course she asked about you. Then Mrs. W butted in to say I should tell you how sorry she was about your grandmother. Mrs. W. walked off while we were still talking, and then Ginny said that she thought it was sad your grandmother was crazy."

Trevor looked up then, locking eyes with Christy, and continued. "I defended your grandmother, and she laughed at me and started saying how your grandmother wandered around the pond all these years since your grandfather drowned, looking for him as if he was still alive. She even refused the insurance money when he was declared legally dead. Did she really do that, Christy?"

"I ... I don't know," Christy said. "I remember when the lawyer came about the death certificate. That was two years ago, I think. He drowned almost nine years ago now."

"But they never found his body, did they?"

"No, but I don't ever remember her telling me she thought he was still alive," Christy said. "Why would she say those things about my grandmother?" Christy felt close to tears again.

"Don't sweat it, Christy. Maybe she listened to Mrs. Peters telling those old stories about his disappearance one too many times. This is a small town, and that was big news. We were only—what?—about four when he drowned?"

Just then, Christy's mom walked through the door and smiled at them. "There you are, you two. Come on downstairs. People are beginning to arrive." She looked at Christy's face and must have noticed both of their tense postures. "What's going on? Did something happen?"

"No, not really, Mom, but Trev met Ginny at the mall."

"Oh, that's nice! How is she?" she asked, focusing on Trevor.

Trevor squirmed. "Uh, she's ... she's okay, I guess."

Christy plowed through Trevor's uncomfortable pause: "Trev was telling me what she said when you came in. Ginny said Grandma was crazy. Do you think that's true?"

Christy's mom showed anger in her eyes for a moment, and then she sighed and gently pushed Christy aside to make room for herself between them on the bed. She sat down and put an arm around them both and squeezed. Then she said, "No, honey, your grandmother wasn't crazy. But when my dad, your grandfather, drowned, she did sort of fall to pieces a bit. But that was just denial. It was worse that they never were able to find his body in the pond. That would have helped to put closure on it for her. She did for a time act like he was alive but soon accepted that he was gone."

"But what about her constant visits to the pond like she was looking for him? Even I've seen her do that a million times. Why do that?" Christy asked.

Christy's mom looked first at Trevor then at Christy before staring straight ahead, frowning. It took her a few seconds before answering: "Haven't you ever seen someone, even if only on a TV show, go visit their loved ones in a cemetery and talk to them like they were alive? It makes them feel closer to them. I'm sure your grandmother was doing something like that. Remember, she didn't have a grave to visit, so maybe she went there to feel closer to him."

Christy and Trevor both nodded and leaned forward to look at each other for a second.

Christy's mom gave a final squeeze and stood up. "Some people can be insensitive, that's all," her mom said. "I'm surprised at Ginny, though. I wouldn't have thought it of her. But let's go downstairs. There is someone who wants to meet you, Christy."

CHAPTER 2

Mourners congregated in the front room and the central dining room. Mrs. Pike and Christy's mom and dad had spread most of the food on various tables throughout the two rooms and connecting hallway leading to all the rooms and the staircase. A few people were gathered in the hallway, nibbling on chips or neatly cut vegetable sticks, gazing at the half dozen or so paintings hung on the walls. Christy's mom went past everyone, nodding as she went, and Christy and Trevor followed.

Christy's mom led them to the kitchen, where a man was just turning to look at them as they entered. He was about to put a celery stick into his mouth but stopped when he saw who had come in. He was dressed in a nice gray suit, and under his left arm he had a fat manila envelope. His hair was jet black and very short, and he had a nice smile, which he turned on Christy when he noticed her staring. She wouldn't have called him short, maybe sort of stocky. He looked very familiar.

"Christy, do you remember Detective Lockhart?" her mom asked. "Of course, he was Police Chief Lockhart when you last saw him."

Christy hesitated until the memories fit the man and her mom's words made some sense. "Oh! Hi, yeah, I think I remember you."

The detective smiled and held out his hand. "Hi, Christy, nice to see you again."

Christy shook his hand, and he turned to Trevor.

"And this must be Trevor Hanson," Detective Lockhart said. "I remember you and your parents."

He offered his hand, and Trevor shook it with a bit more enthusiasm than Christy had shown.

"Yeah, I remember," Trevor said. "You were the cool police chief. My mom and dad liked you."

Detective Lockhart smiled. "I don't know about cool, but I certainly enjoyed my time here as police chief. Mrs. Walker?"

"Please, call me Connie."

"Connie, then. May I speak with Christy ..." He hesitated, frowned, and then with an exaggerated exhale of breath continued. "Umm, in more private surroundings?" he asked.

That caught them all by surprise, but Christy's mom recovered quickly. "Well," she said, then glanced out the window over the sink, looking at the porch. "It's just about stopped raining, but nobody else is outside. The love seat won't have been rained on since it's up against the house. We could take two folding chairs and go out there."

Christy watched Detective Lockhart. He seemed uncomfortable and about to say something, but instead he searched an inner pocket of his suit jacket and withdrew a letter-sized folded piece of paper. He took an unusual amount of time unfolding it.

Finally he shrugged and said, "Let me start at the beginning. Last week, I received a call from Morris and Quigley, the attorneys in town here. Paul Morris Jr. told me that Lillian Renfrew had passed away and that he had instructions from her that concerned me. I came up yesterday and visited their offices, where I received a handwritten letter from Lillian dated some six months ago. Apparently she had at that time just come down ill and wanted to make sure that what she had in mind would come to pass."

"Is that the letter in your hand?" Christy's mom asked.

"No," he said, talking directly to Christy's mom, "and that is why I hesitated when you suggested that we"—and he emphasized the "we"—"go out to the porch. This letter here is a list of the people that Lillian wanted to be present when I hand over this large manila envelope to Christy and tell the story of Lillian's and my little game. You're ... not on the list, Connie. I'm sorry." He sounded genuine in his apology. "In reality," he continued, "Lillian wanted Christy to have the final say as to who other than herself gets to hear my story and see what's in the envelope. But they must be on this very short list. Of course, you can ask me to leave now if that isn't acceptable to you. It was your mother's wish that it happen this way, but legally the lawyers couldn't or wouldn't do anything to force it ... and Lillian thought that her wishes would be enough for you, Connie."

He paused for a moment, shifting his weight from one foot to the other before continuing. "I will tell you this: if you say no, then I am to take this envelope and destroy it without opening it. And I for one hope you won't say no, since I don't know what's in this envelope, and neither does the law firm. Only Lillian knows what's in here. I think it would be a shame if it went to the grave with her, whatever it is in here."

He stopped and stared directly at Christy's mom, then slowly turned his eyes on Trevor before settling his penetrating eyes on Christy. She broke from his stare, uncertain what to say or do. A quick glance told Christy that the faces of her mom and Trevor were just as bewildered and confused as her own.

Christy's mom recovered first. "You are to know what's in there when Christy opens it, Detective?" She said it more as a question than a statement, and the hurt was thick in her voice.

"No," he said quickly. "Not if Christy chooses not to let me." He waved the envelope. "I am only to tell my side of the story."

Christy's mom stood there shaking her head. "I still don't quite understand. What story? What game?"

"What game?" Detective Lockhart repeated. "Your mother—Lillian—and I came to view my investigation of your dad's drowning as a game. She doesn't want me to say more, except to the people on that list, pending Christy's approval. But if you disapprove, Connie, then I leave now and throw this envelope into the fire."

Christy's mom stood mute, tears welling in her already red and swollen eyes. Detective Lockhart waited patiently, letting his information sink in.

Finally Christy's mom took a deep breath and, through her tears, said, "I suppose I'll have to trust Mom on this one."

Turning to Christy, Detective Lockhart said, "There are only three names on this list: yours, Trevor's, and Ginny Wentworth's. Is she here today? I certainly remember her family but haven't seen them here."

Christy frowned and said, "No, she isn't here. Trev and I will go outside with you. That's ... if you want to, Trev."

"Want to?" Trevor said. "I wouldn't miss this for a pair of box seat tickets to the Red Sox!"

CHAPTER 3

"**D**etective Lockhart," Christy said after the three of them situated themselves on the side porch overlooking Christy's old house, "do I have to open that right now?"

Trevor sat next to her on the wicker love seat, and the detective was leaning against the outer railing, his right leg up on the folding chair they had brought with them.

"No," the detective said. "As I've said, you don't even have to open it while I'm still here. I was to deliver it to you and tell you what your grandmother wished me to say. You can open it now, though, if you like. That is, if you don't mind that Trevor or I will see what's in it."

Trevor was fidgeting, obviously begging for attention. Christy shoved him gently and smiled.

"Okay, Trev, I'd know that squirm anywhere," she said. "What do you want to say?"

Trevor glanced at Christy and then the detective to make sure he had their attention. "I think we should hear Detective Lockhart first."

Detective Lockhart chuckled. "Trevor, my young friend, you are wise beyond your years. That is just what I was about to suggest that Christy do."

Both Trevor and Detective Lockhart waited for Christy's decision. Christy reached over and gave Trevor's arm a little squeeze, and she looked at the detective.

"Trev and I have been friends since I can remember—that's probably why my grandmother had him on that list—and I can't recall him ever giving me bad advice. So I think we'll listen to your story first, Detective Lockhart."

The detective gazed at their faces for a moment. "Trevor isn't the only one who is wise beyond their years, it seems. I don't know exactly why your grandmother wanted me to tell you all that's happened from my perspective, but I'm not nearly as afraid of it as I was when I arrived here this morning."

"Detective Lockhart, what did you mean when you said that you and my grandmother played a 'game'?" Christy asked.

The detective smiled. "We played a game called 'Cat and Mouse.' Now, you have to understand, we law enforcement people are supposed to be the cat in these games. That's the way we like it. Unfortunately, against your grandmother, I was the mouse and she was the cat. She was an extraordinary person. I visited her time after time during my investigations and spoke of my evolving theories, trying to catch her, get her to admit something." The detective chuckled again. "But instead she kept toying with me, enjoying every little moment that she kept me guessing and bewildered. Once I was satisfied she hadn't killed your grandfather, I warmed up to her."

"I don't understand what the game was about," Trevor said.

Christy nodded her agreement, and they both waited for the detective's answer. He smiled and cleared his throat. When he began to speak, Christy could hear admiration for his subject in his tone of voice.

"You see," he said, "I told your grandmother some two or three weeks after your grandfather drowned— or, more appropriately, I should say 'disappeared'— that I didn't believe he was dead and that she knew where he was. It was my trying to prove it over the next few years, until I left for Boston actually, that constituted our little game. I gathered a bundle of circumstantial evidence to prove my contention, but your grandmother never cracked. She never did tell me what I wanted her to tell me: what I suspected all along but have never been able to prove."

He took an audible breath before continuing. "I finally did get one little glimmer of hope that I wasn't crazy and way off base. Just after I accepted the job in Boston, I came here to visit with Lillian, to see how she was getting on." He smiled. "And I hoped that she'd tell me something. But she was as tight lipped as ever. Except she did say that when the time came for them to declare her husband legally dead, I was to check up on what she did."

"Did you?" Christy asked. "I do remember the talk of the death certificate. That was just a couple of years ago. I don't know much else except I think I remember my dad getting angry about something."

"I did indeed keep tabs on her, Christy," he said. "Your dad was probably reacting to the fact she refused to claim the insurance money due her. So, at least to my way of thinking, that was her telling me I wasn't all wrong, that in fact your grandfather was, or may still be, alive."

"But where is he? And why hasn't he come home?" Christy asked.

Detective Lockhart shrugged his shoulders and was about to say something when Trevor jumped in: "Why did he disappear in the first place?" Trevor asked. "I mean, what did he have to gain by it?"

Lockhart shook his head and smiled, staring at Trevor. "Would you care to be a detective?" he joked. "You asked the pertinent question: what did he have to gain? Actually what did either of them have to gain?" He looked at both Christy and Trevor in turn, then answered his own question: "The short answer, which took me a good three weeks to confirm, was ... nothing. They had nothing to gain. No hidden debts to run from, no problems with their marriage, no chance of becoming a famous dead artist."

The detective cleared his throat, then continued. "I thought for a time that the artist angle was a hot one. Your grandfather was a pretty good artist. I see that his paintings are still up all over the house. But in the end, I dismissed it. After all, he certainly didn't try to sell paintings while he was living here, and your grandmother didn't try after he disappeared, either. In fact, your grandmother took to hiding some of them. To keep them away from me, I think."

Detective Lockhart paused and seemed to lose himself in old memories before shifting his position against the railing.

"It was one of your grandfather's paintings that first made me think that he hadn't drowned in that pond," the detective said.

"Huh? I don't understand," Christy said. "I thought you said that they didn't try to sell any."

"Oh ... no, no!" Detective Lockhart said, shaking his head. "It wasn't anything like that. What I meant was that I saw a piece of art in your grandmother's hallway that was painted at least three days *after* your grandfather disappeared. You probably already know that your grandfather had a habit of putting the day, month, and year on a painting when he signed it."

Christy opened her mouth to speak, but the detective held up his hand to stop any questions.

"You see," Detective Lockhart said, "your grandmother called me and reported when your grandfather disappeared into the pond. But Abigail Peters swears that she saw him dive into the pond three weeks earlier than that, and he never came out and nobody ever saw him again after that. Your mother and dad didn't see him during that mysterious three week gap, either.

"Now, after a lengthy investigation, I pieced together that for the last two years or so before he disappeared, your grandfather hadn't been seen as regularly in his usual spots. But the absences were usually only for two or three days, or at most up to a couple of weeks. Always in summer, too, although that on the surface might not mean anything. It could have just been him taking time off in good weather. He'd given up working in his store also, and in fact even before he disappeared, he and your grandmother had been thinking about selling the hardware store. She finally did sell a year or so after he was gone.

"So," Detective Lockhart said, counting on his fingers for emphasis. "One, Mrs. Peters saw him go into the pond but not come out. Two, nobody else saw him after that night. Three, your grandmother had a painting on her wall dated three days *after* that date, a painting that was clearly done by the same person who had painted every other canvas in this house."

"But ... if he didn't disappear until the date my grandmother reported him missing," Christy said, "then the painting has no real significance, right?"

"True, but I researched those three weeks very thoroughly, and nobody but nobody saw your grandfather after Mrs. Peters saw him go into the pond. Even your parents didn't. It was bad luck for me that your whole family was on vacation for the first two weeks of that time frame. So I can't really confirm that your grandfather was in fact gone, only that he wasn't seen.

"Then, the third week, your mom was sick in bed for a few days. When she went back to work, she had to work late for a few days to catch up and didn't see him or try to contact either Lillian or Jack. Your dad was back at his usual work routine, so he didn't notice anything unusual, either. So because of all that, your grandfather not being around didn't click with your parents, which it certainly would have otherwise.

"Wherever he went, your grandmother wasn't worried about him, and it seems like she expected him to return. It was only three weeks later that she came to some different conclusions about it and called us. At that point, I thought she was grieving like anyone would be who had lost a husband or wife.

"At first, I thought this was a drowning, but then Mrs. Peters made her remarks to me about seeing your grandfather go into the water three weeks before. I put the three-week discrepancy down to some crazy motive of Mrs. Peters. I knew her well, and it wasn't out of character, I'm sorry to say."

At that comment, Christy and Trevor looked at each other and smiled.

The detective saw the exchange and said, "I didn't mean to criticize her; it's just that, knowing her personality hampered, or colored, my understanding of the situation, and I completely dismissed the fact that Mrs. Peters swore he never came out of that pond. She was adamant about it. That was ridiculous as far as I was concerned. I was certain that he had avoided her detection when he slipped back out of the water. She had a habit of spying on your grandparents, and they—especially your grandfather—delighted in fooling her.

"Once I pieced together all the evidence and realized that Mrs. Peters had in fact been the last one to see your grandfather, I began to wonder why your grandmother kept quiet for three weeks about his disappearance. Of course, the first thing I thought of was that she had killed him or at least been responsible for his disappearance in some way."

Christy opened her mouth wide to say something, but Detective Lockhart shook his head.

"No, but right away, I had to rule out anything like that," he said. "After all, if Mrs. Peters did see him go in and not come out, how could your grandmother have done anything to him? It was at that point I tried to piece together where he might have gone and why."

He smiled. "When I found the painting, I had to look at your grandmother's actions differently. It must have taken her the three weeks to come to the conclusion he wasn't coming back, and then she called us and told us a pack of lies. I don't know where he went, or why. But he didn't drown in that pond down there. And I don't know how he got that painting to your grandmother. It wasn't delivered by any postal delivery service. I double-checked that."

"Okay, but what has any of this got to do with it all?" Trevor said. "I mean, Mrs. Peters saw him dive in and he didn't come out again, right?"

"True, and that was the official ruling on this whole thing: a drowning. Then, seven years later, or about two years ago, your grandfather was declared legally dead. I was the only one who paid attention to your grandmother's peculiar behavior at that time. Seeing that painting really got me to thinking, so I couldn't let it go. As I said earlier, I first thought he might be hiding or running for some reason. But I couldn't find any possible motive."

Detective Lockhart sat for a moment, clearly deep in thought, before continuing. "The painting, the strange waiting to call us by your grandmother, the lack of a body, and the story from Mrs. Peters ... It all contributed to my taking a real interest in the disappearance. Mrs. Peters swears that your grandmother was at the pond on several occasions after your grandfather disappeared—usually during bad weather, just standing there, apparently waiting or simply looking into the pond. That was very significant too, as far as I was concerned. I didn't understand why at the time and even now can only guess."

"What if the painting was painted by someone else, even by my grandmother?" Christy asked. "Did you get an art expert to look at it and compare it to my grandfather's other stuff?"

"No, I didn't, and that's a fair question. But if that painting is still here, I'll let you decide for yourself." Again the detective hesitated before continuing his story. "Despite all the unknowns I ran up against and all the things that didn't add up, I was about to put this down as a disappearance or accept the official ruling of drowning and move on. But just because I was still curious and also interested in local history, I did an exhaustive search for any information about that pond down there."

He gestured toward the pond again and went on with his explanation: "I dug up some very strange accounts and stories that led me to believe that something was and probably still is very unusual about that pond."

Detective Lockhart paused to let his words sink in. When he continued, it was to ask a question: "Do either of you know what the Native Americans called that pond?"

"Uh, I've heard it before," Christy said. "The Indians had some real long name for it. I can't remember what it is, but in school, they told us it means 'water that empties the world,' I think. Now everyone just calls it Renfrews' Pond after my great-great-grandfather. They teach about the pond and its place in natural history in our grammar school. I always thought that was real cool that they talked about our pond in school. It is a good example to use for watersheds and spring-fed ponds."

Detective Lockhart nodded. "The word the Abnaki used for the pond is *Nebigipsigaki*. That's a mouthful. And who knows if I even pronounced it correctly." He smiled before continuing with his explanation. "And you're right: that's what the presumed translation is and has been since Colonial times. Several local history books use that as the official translated name. They use it as proof that the Native Americans were very ecologically minded and recognized that this pond was a watershed for the surrounding hills. It seems that nobody since the first non-Native American author in 1827 has actually translated that name for him or herself. The subsequent authors seem to have accepted that first author's account and just used his translation in their own work."

The detective shifted his weight again and was clearly enjoying his retelling of the research he'd done years before.

"Most people seem to think its name was meant to describe its ability to drain the land around it. If you look at the pond, that could be accurate. The Indians— Native Americans—had a marvelous way of naming things literally. Taken in that context, the name makes sense. The pond is an efficient drainage or runoff pond for the surrounding hills here. It's also spring fed, so it never dries up or fills up with sediment and disappears like a purely runoff pond might."

Lockhart stopped to gather his thoughts and sat down in the chair, obviously settling in for a lengthy explanation.

"If I hadn't come across no fewer than six different accounts of disappearances attributed to drowning since 1750, I wouldn't have looked any further into the history of the pond," he said. "Two in particular are interesting: one in 1816, the other in 1853. The earlier account was of an eight-year-old boy who was presumed drowned in the pond. He surfaced three years later and insisted that he had been to France ... and to another world through the pond."

Christy and Trevor took a quick glance at each other as the detective continued on. "His own family and the local community assumed he was either taken by someone or was lost and somehow returned on his own. He was institutionalized and died in his thirties, insisting to the end that he had visited France and another world for those three years. Strangely enough, he could speak French when he returned ... but he'd had no knowledge of the language before he disappeared."

"Weird," Trevor whispered.

Detective Lockhart nodded. "The latter account was of a young man in his twenties who disappeared and was also presumed drowned. He had been a troubled youth and owed a lot of money, and it was theorized that he took his own life by drowning. Ten years later, though, a man looking like him was seen in town. His own mother insisted that it was him, and so did several other residents of the town. This individual denied any connection to the missing man and avoided the woman who claimed to be his mother. Shortly after arriving and causing the stir, he left town. The mother of the missing man insisted till the day she died that the man who came to town ten years later was in fact her son."

"Wouldn't a mother know her own son without a doubt?" Trevor asked.

"Mmm, not necessarily," the detective said. "Remember, we're talking about 1853. Nobody around here would have had access to photography; it was very new and expensive then. She would have been relying on her memory, and a person can change a lot in appearance in ten years.

"However, there are no fewer than ten other accounts—all written down secondhand by local settlers—of Native American legends about the pond too. The first three are eerily similar. They mention travelers from other lands rising up out of the pond. The rest all mention people disappearing after swimming in the pond. Does that sound familiar?"

Christy just blinked and gave a small nod, feeling like she was getting more confused by the second.

"Well, those early settler accounts of the Native American disappearances and strange appearances all revolve around explaining away things as tales told around campfires to create legends to pass down.

I think they came up with whatever they could to explain what they didn't understand and couldn't really understand any other way.

"Ah, but then a very interesting thing came up after I read all these accounts. I sent the pond's name and the translation to an expert in ancient American languages who lives in Michigan—a Mr. Johansson if I remember. He corrected the translation for me. It's a Western Abnaki combination of words, and it actually means 'water into empty land,' not 'water that empties the land or world.' Similar, yes, but it can be interpreted very differently in light of the legends and old accounts. Without actually knowing what any of those old legends mean for certain, if you add your grandfather's disappearance into the mix, we have a very mysterious pond out there. I'm sure now you'd be able to research the Abnaki language on the Internet, but even nine years ago, that wasn't so easy."

Detective Lockhart paused and looked at the two young people facing him. Again he seemed to be gauging their reaction to his words. Christy remained quiet, as did Trevor, no doubt formulating opinions or grasping for some sense of what he'd heard, just as Christy was doing.

Before either had a chance to ask any questions, Detective Lockhart said, "Despite what I came to believe was the truth, I let the judgment of accidental drowning stand because I couldn't prove anything. All my investigations—except for the information on the mysterious pond disappearances—I included in my police report. And, of course, I never actually stated what I believed happened, at least not in the official report. I did speak many times to your grandmother about my theories, and she certainly got a kick out of them." He smiled. "Do you want to hear what I think happened?"

Detective Lockhart shrugged. "One, maybe two of them, you might put down to an overactive imagination, but so many of them? I don't believe so." The detective shook his head. "Look at it from this perspective. Go ahead fifty years. Christy, what will the story of your grandfather be thought of as? Will it be just another legend of the pond, conveniently catalogued as strange but unlikely to be of any substance? Just suppose that Mrs. Peters is right and he never came out of that pond. We never found his body. In fact, and this is somehow significant but I don't know how, nobody has ever found a body of anyone who supposedly drowned in that pond.

CHAPTER 4

Detective Lockhart stood and moved back a step to again lean against the porch railing, giving her room.

"I've told you all I came to say," the detective said quietly. "The rest is up to you, Christy—and your grandmother's envelope."

Trevor inched away from Christy, then he stood up and joined the detective.

Christy felt the silence around her and noticed the space her two companions on the porch had just given her. In that physical and auditory void, she began to hear the long unnoticed sounds of the mourners roaming throughout her house, along with the outside noises reawakening after the bad weather. A car door closed, and someone walked up the front steps just out of her view into the front room.

The envelope seemed to grow heavy as she realized she was on the spot for a decision. She patted it, validating the realness of it, then silently wished it would go away. The envelope represented all the pressures of the day thrown into her lap. It was too much, and she felt cornered sitting there. She stood up and walked to the back railing of the porch, feeling Trevor's and Detective Lockhart's eyes on her back.

Standing still, looking out at her old house in the distance, and hearing the remnants of the spring peepers down by the pond, she lost her composure and began crying. Crying for the loss of her grandmother, for the pressures of the funeral and her choice not to attend, and for the decision she was about to make— the decision that was going to hurt and disappoint two people she knew were probably expecting her to make a very different one.

Clutching the envelope to her breast, she turned. Avoiding the stares of Trevor and the detective, she bolted between the two of them and around the corner through the front door and up the stairs into her room.

She never saw Trevor's startled reaction or Detective Lockhart's sympathetic one. If anyone inside saw her distress, she didn't notice them, either.

Christy went immediately to her dresser and opened the locked drawer. Slipping the large envelope under some unused notebooks, she locked it up and sat on the edge of her bed and tried to stop crying. Once she gained control over her emotions, and a little embarrassed by them, she thought that she better go back out and explain to Trev and the detective. She hoped they'd understand, or at least forgive her if they didn't, but now that she'd acted, she wasn't going to change her mind.

What neither of them knew was that as the long story had unfolded through Detective Lockhart's narrative, little pieces of conversations between her and her grandmother over the last six months came rushing back to her. Christy had realized almost near the end of the detective's tale that her grandmother had been giving her bits and pieces of information—preparing her for this moment. As those bits of memory came back to her, she knew she was going to face the envelope alone.

Christy wished it could be some other way, but this was between her and her grandmother, despite what she'd just heard from the detective. The more she thought of it, the more she became afraid that he'd be angry with her. Detective Lockhart had spent a lot of time working on this problem, and he probably had a right to know what was in the envelope. She took only small comfort in the fact that her grandmother had said it was up to her to decide and that the detective knew that. But whatever the reactions, she had to go back to face them now.

The walk down the front stairs and out onto the porch was a blur, partly from her tear-filled eyes and partly from the fear of the detective and Trevor still waiting. When she rounded the corner of the porch and they came into focus, she smiled at them. Trevor got up and stood awkwardly, waiting for her to sit on the love seat. Detective Lockhart had moved toward the end of the porch and stood with his back to her.

He turned in time to see her weak smile. He nodded noncommittally and waited for her to make the next move. When she just stood there, he walked a step or two back opposite the love seat. Christy still didn't take the offered seat from Trevor, couldn't put herself at that emotional disadvantage. There was no way she was going to explain what she had to with the two of them standing over her. She stood facing the love seat and backed up against the railing.

Trevor spoke first: "What did you do with the envelope?"

Detective Lockhart spoke quickly to help as best he could: "You are in charge, Christy. Remember, that envelope has your name on it—nobody else's."

Christy let out a deep sigh and favored Detective Lockhart with a grateful smile before addressing Trevor. She knew then that she didn't have to explain or apologize to Detective Lockhart.

Her eyes welled up with tears as she began: "Trev, I'm sorry, I really am. I think I know why I have to look at that envelope alone—she wanted me to."

Trevor shook his head and dropped his arms onto his legs, his hands resting on his knees. "Christy, I ... I don't understand," Trevor said. "I thought you wanted me ... us ... to see the contents with you."

He turned to Trevor. "Trevor, go easy on Christy." He smiled. "I suspect her decision wasn't an easy one. She doesn't want to disappoint you or jeopardize the friendship you two have. Give her some credit that her grandmother's wishes are very important to her and they shouldn't come between you two. Don't let them, okay?"

Trevor nodded but still didn't look very happy about Christy's decision. He stood up and took the hand being offered by the detective. Then, when Detective Lockhart extended a hand toward her, Christy impulsively hugged the detective, ignoring the proffered hand.

When the detective had left and entered the house, Christy turned to Trevor. At first, he couldn't meet her eyes. Finally he did, but the look wasn't friendly.

"So much for my help," he mumbled and again turned his eyes away from hers.

"Trev, no, please understand."

"Yeah, whatever."

He shrugged, brushing past her and heading off the front steps and around away from her view.

She watched him go and began to cry in earnest again. She'd lost her grandmother, her house and bedroom, and now it seemed she'd lost her best friend, too, all in a few weeks.

CHAPTER 5

Christy walked around front and watched Trevor heading down the path toward the pond. She let him go and stepped inside the front door. Her mom was mingling with the Uptons and still talking with Detective Lockhart. The Uptons lived two houses down from Trevor in the biggest house in town. Rob Upton looked uncomfortable standing with his parents. He was a year behind her and Trevor in school, and Christy didn't know him very well. Plus he was a friend of the Peters twins, which automatically ruled him out as close-friend material. He saw Christy looking in his direction and nodded, his eyes pleading with her to come save him from the adults. His mother had her arm around his shoulders, and there was no way he could easily escape without appearing rude. Christy was in no mood, however, and ignored his silent plea, which turned into an angry glare as she walked past.

She headed around several groups of both children and adults. Christy walked into the kitchen and saw Mrs. Lake and her son Danny. She hadn't really met them yet, only seen the two of them moving things into her house—their house now.

The Lakes had lived in town for a year or so, in the apartments in the center of town, until Christy's dad put the "For Sale" sign up on their house a few months ago when it became apparent that Christy's grandmother wasn't coming back. Mrs. Lake had jumped at the chance for a nice home for her and her son when Christy's house came up for sale. The transaction had happened fast, and they'd finished moving in early last week.

Danny was a Cub Scout and Trevor, who was a Boy Scout, was Danny's den chief, whatever that was. Trevor explained it as being a baby-sitter for Cub Scouts, but Christy was sure it wasn't that; she knew that Trev was just poking fun at himself. All she knew about Danny was that Trev liked him and that he was deaf.

Christy had seen Danny and his mom signing to each other as they moved in over the last couple of weeks. They were doing it now as they came into the room. Danny was looking up at his mom, and she was bending over slightly, facing her son squarely so that the two of them could communicate more effectively. They paused slightly, then after a flurry of signs, put their hands down by their sides and faced Christy.

Mrs. Lake straightened up. "Hello, this is Danny, and I'm Katie Lake. You must be Christy."

Danny reached and found his mom's hand, and she took his into her own. Christy's mom entered then and smiled at them all.

"Good, I see you've met each other," Christy's mom said.

"Danny and I were just introducing ourselves to Christy," Mrs. Lake said.

Christy's mom nodded and smiled. Danny let go of his mother's hand and stepped apart slightly from her. Then, to Christy's surprise, he spoke clearly while signing and looking directly at her.

"Hi, Christy, it's nice to meet you."

Mrs. Lake smiled. "You didn't expect him to speak, did you?"

Christy shook her head.

"Danny speaks very well and reads lips too, which we call speech reading," Mrs. Lake said. "He wasn't born deaf and had speech well before he lost his hearing. It makes it easier for him to communicate, and he always speaks as he signs to be polite. That way, you can understand him without knowing sign language. If you make sure you look directly at him when you talk to him, he has an easier time understanding you, even if you don't know how to sign."

Christy nodded and realized that it was a prompt for her to reply to Danny. She nervously made direct eye contact with him, and once she saw that he was returning the stare, she began.

"Hi, Danny, it's nice to meet you too." Impulsively, she asked, "Was that the real sign for 'hello'? And can you show me 'Nice to meet you' again?"

Danny grinned and nodded yes, showing off his dimples and sparkling blue eyes clearly visible behind his silver-framed glasses. Closing his thin nimble fingers, and turning his open palm out, he made the sign for "hi" again by touching the side of his temple and extending his hand out. Then he signed "Nice to meet you" again. It was a series of quick gestures that he slowed down for Christy to see more clearly.

Christy tentatively mimicked him. The first attempt drew a smile from Danny and Mrs. Lake. But the second time she tried it, she felt it succeeded. Danny nodded, grinning, and then replied by speaking and signing again.

"Yes, nice job," he said, stepping back closer to his mom and reaching for her hand.

Mrs. Lake smiled and began speaking again. Danny looked up at her to follow her conversation since he wouldn't let go of her hand and she couldn't sign for him.

"Christy, your mother told me you might be interested in making a little money this summer. I wouldn't have asked today of all days, but Danny needs a babysitter while I'm at work, and unfortunately I need someone starting Monday. Being next door, I thought of you. Your mom said it was okay to mention it now."

Christy knew that she was supposed to respond, but she was still reeling from all that had happened so far today. Her eyes teared up again, and she avoided looking directly at anyone.

"Christy?" her mom said gently. "Are you okay?"

Christy turned away from her mom's stare and tried to keep her composure, but was losing the battle. Through the tears, she saw the open kitchen door behind the Lakes and the escape it offered. So for the second time in under a half an hour, she bolted past startled onlookers up to her room.

Christy slammed the door closed behind her and plopped down on the bed. Shut up in her room without the eyes and expectations on her, she began the slow process that, if she'd recognized it, she'd have known it for what it was: grieving. Even without her knowing what it was, it held her in its grip with emotions she couldn't contain.

She cried and thought about how unfair it all was. How could her mom spring stuff like that on her today? Why did today even have to happen? Why did her grandmother have to die? Was nothing ever going to be the same again? Even Trevor had abandoned her. Now they wanted her to babysit Danny all summer. What a drag that was going to be! Didn't anyone care that her grandmother had just died and she was hearing strange stories about her and even hurtful things from the Peterses and Ginny, too, of all people?

Just when the tears were almost ending out of sheer exhaustion, her mom entered quietly and sat down next to her, enveloping her in a warm, comforting hug. Christy held on in silence for a few minutes, content with the closeness.

"Why, Mom, why did it happen now?" Christy finally asked.

Her mom thought for a moment. "I don't have an answer for you, Christy. I just know that we were very blessed throughout these last couple of months. We got a chance to say good-bye and tell her how much we loved her, and she got the same chance. She wanted us back in this house, and she got to see that, too. Some people never get the chance that we had. Sometimes a loved one is gone in an instant and you never get the chance to say good-bye or whatever it is you need to say. I never got the chance to say good-bye to my father—your grandfather—and I miss him and that opportunity almost every day. So in many ways, we were very lucky these last months. I know you probably don't see it that way, but someday you will. I promise you that."

With that promise, her Mom released Christy from her tight grip.

"Detective Lockhart stopped to talk to me before he left," her mom said. "He said that you needed time to digest your grandmother's death and that you'd look at the contents of the package in your own time. He wanted me to make certain you keep your promise to him about the package. He wouldn't tell me what he meant, but he said you'd know."

Christy nodded but kept quiet.

After a slight hesitation during which Christy's mom seemed to be judging Christy's capacity to process anything further that day, she said, "Christy, honey, I'm sorry about springing Danny on you like that, but Mrs. Lake is in a real bind and it seems so perfect with them living in our old house. You would get the chance to be there as well as here this summer. And you'd make some money in the process. I'm not going to force you to take the job for the summer, but I am going to make you watch him this coming week after school because poor Mrs. Lake has no alternative. It's only a couple of hours a day after school, and then once school's out for the year, it would be all day long. By Wednesday, you can tell me how it's going and if you wouldn't mind continuing or if you only want to do it for this week. I won't force you to continue if you don't want to, and I think that's more than helpful to Mrs. Lake. I will tell her to keep looking beyond this week for someone, in case you don't want to continue."

Christy was emotionally exhausted and had no fight left in her so she just numbly nodded agreement. Her mom smiled at her and hugged her again. Then Christy noticed a thin hardbound book that her mom had placed on the bed as she came in. She reached for it.

"What is this?" Christy asked.

Her mom smiled. "It's a sign-language book. I thought you might need some help, and Mrs. Lake recommended it—in fact has let you borrow it."

Christy looked at it warily. It was a thin volume that said *Sign Language: A First Book*.

"Mom! This is for first-graders or kindergarteners!"

"Christy!" her mom said. "Do you know anything about signing?"

Christy shook her head.

"Well, then, I think this should be perfect. Look, honey, you don't have to study this unless you want to. This isn't going to be like school, but if you find yourself wanting to know how to say something ... then this can help. And you saw how helpful Danny is willing to be, so I think you'll be fine."

When Christy showed no signs of making a comment, her mom took the opportunity to wrap up their conversation: "You don't have to come down again unless you want to, but I have to get back to the guests and help your dad and Mrs. Pike start the cleanup as everyone leaves."

She gave Christy another hug and landed another kiss on the top of the head, then was quickly gone, leaving Christy to herself.

Christy looked at the door her mom had just exited through and then down to the book on her lap. She heaved the book at the closed door and, still totally miserable, buried her head into her pillow and tried to bring the tears back. There truly were none left, though, so all she did was drift off to a sorrowful and very self-pitying sleep.

CHAPTER 6

Christy woke the next morning and the envelope was all she could think of, so she retrieved it and set it on her bed. The flap had been sealed with cellophane tape. She gently pried it loose, rolling up the tape between her fingers. She opened the flap and peered into the envelope. There were several smaller, letter-sized envelopes, a loose piece of folded paper, and a small bundle of what looked like photos tied with string.

Her grandmother loved string; she'd used it all the time, claiming that it wasn't used enough anymore. Christy smiled at that thought, then was amazed that she hadn't cried, that the string had only prompted a pleasant memory, not more tears.

She dumped all of the contents onto her bed. One of the smaller envelopes was bulging in the middle. She lifted it and immediately noticed the heavy feel of metal in it. Ripping the end off, she dumped two keys onto her bed. They were labeled in her grandmothers' neat printing. *Attic storage room* was written on both of them! Christy had no doubt that these two keys were the missing keys to the locked room. One was a small key and looked like most padlock keys she'd seen, and the other was similar in style to what the rest of the doors in the house had for keys.

That they were here filled Christy with anticipation and added weight to the tale told to her by Detective Lockhart. Her first impulse was to sneak up to the attic and use them, but her curiosity about the rest of the contents overpowered that urge, so she set the keys aside and reached for the loose piece of paper.

It was a long scribbled note to her from her grandmother and was dated only three weeks before. Her grandmother must have added it to the packet just before she became too ill to do anything.

She smoothed out the folds and began to read:

Dear Christy,

I'm writing this from the hospital. You all have moved into my house at my urging, and your parents have sold the place Jack and I built for them before you were born. I'm relieved and comforted that you now own the pond and Jack's great-grandfather's house. I will have Paul Morris add this to the packet I prepared for you months ago.

I am so sorry that I never let you in on this amazing story while I was alive. I guess it was because I was mortally afraid of losing you like I lost my dear Jack. Plus you were so young. But it was selfish and unfair of me not to put the facts before you and to let you decide. By the time I felt you were ready, we weren't quite as close anymore. I miss our tea-and-toast sessions that we had for so many years.

You and your friends are just now beginning to assert your independence from your parents and other family members, and are spending less time with them and more time with each other. That's as it should be. That is how we all learn about relationships. And I have to say that I think you are doing a marvelous job of it. But that drifting apart and my sickness coming now as it has, sort of delayed my confiding in you.

Why did I not bring this all to your mom and dad, you might ask? Well, I feared for whatever is on the other side. I feared it would be lost to greed. Adults can be very close minded. Not that I think your mom and dad are the least bit greedy, because I don't. I'm just not certain they'd think this through like Jack and I did.

A child's mind is needed here. Or at least a very mature adult's mind (you can think I mean "old mind" here if you want) that has gone beyond the scientific discoveries available and world implications, not to mention the financial possibilities, and can go back to that simple childlike acceptance. Jack and I had that, but your mom doesn't yet, and you haven't lost it yet, I hope!

If you have reached for this first, and I assume you will, then you may not understand what I am saying despite what I hope Detective Lockhart has told you.

If that is the case, then I want you to open the envelope with the metal in it. They are keys to the attic room. Since she hasn't to this point, I'm betting that your mom won't have let your dad pry the door open and that the room is still undisturbed. Go when you won't be seen, and if it is at night, take a flashlight. And remember that what was my bedroom is right below the attic room, and your parents are in there now.

After you see what's in there, come back and open the envelope with the red dots on the seal. In there is the whole story—well not the whole story. I put everything in the big envelope that I could think of, but I get so tired so quickly now that I've had to rush things in my explanations. I'm sure I've left things out, and I am sorry for that. I'll try to add things as I think of them, if I am able to.

I also put in many of Jack's letters and descriptions that he sent back to me while he was there. There are a few letters with his thoughts on the place that I hope will give you some sense of it.

If you are alone when you are reading this, I want you to know that I primed you to decide that as best I could but gave you the option of having your friends and

Detective Lockhart there as well. You need to understand what I'm asking and what you are up against. Then, once you grasp what this all means, you can choose to tell others as you see fit.

If you are not alone, I want everyone to think very long and hard before making any statements to others or to your parents. It could mean the end of this wonderful place we've discovered and also the end of your (our) quiet home and town. So please, please go slowly and think.

I love you,

Grandma

The feeling that her grandmother was speaking directly to her made Christy shudder from the reality of her death. Her eyes welled with tears, and she fought against the ache of wanting to talk to her again. Waiting to open the envelope with the red dots, she searched for more current letters or notes, hoping for the further explanations her grandmother mentioned, but didn't find any.

Christy didn't understand what her grandmother was talking about, at least not entirely, but she had some sense from the long discussion yesterday with Trev and the detective. And she was thrilled that the attic probably contained the missing paintings spoken of by Detective Lockhart: the paintings that supposedly depicted strange landscapes unlike any the detective had ever seen.

Putting down the letter, she set her watch for a ten-minute reminder so she wouldn't be caught in the attic and have to explain herself. Then she quietly opened her door, determined to do what she'd been directed to do: check out the attic! Silently moving into the hallway and tightly clutching the keys from the envelope, Christy tiptoed past her parent's bedroom and opened the doorway to the attic stairs. She winced as it creaked slightly. After a short pause to make sure the sound hadn't been heard, she slipped through and closed it behind her.

The stairway was gloomy, lighted by one small oval-shaped window, but it was enough to see her safely to the landing and the attic doorway above. Fumbling clumsily with the padlock key, she eventually had the heavy lock off and resting on the floor at her feet. The lock in the door itself proved to be more difficult. It was an old brass doorknob, and the corrosion gave her a momentary fear that she would snap the key off in the lock without it opening.

Removing the key to regroup, she decided to try once more and inserted the key again. This last effort worked, and she smiled at her good luck. In a second, she was through the door and stood inside the attic room.

CHAPTER 7

Streaks of light poured through the dormered windows as Christy stared at the room for the first time, barely breathing to try and control her excitement. After all the hundreds of times she'd been in her grandmother's house, even slept in the guest bedroom that was now hers, she'd never been up to the attic before. The windows were narrow, but there were enough of them so that Christy could see the room with no artificial light. The splashes of bright light and deep shadows revealed the beautiful contours of the room and its architectural highlights.

The room smelled of old paint and dust and something like mildew that reminded Christy of mushrooms. It wasn't a pleasant-smelling place, but the cheery light coming through the windows invited her to continue in. The walls were sloped inward between the dormers, and the ceiling was low. She had no trouble standing tall.

She glanced all around the room to take in its features and what was stored there. The old magazines her mom had mentioned, piled high in irregular crooked stacks, were directly illuminated by the strong rays of the morning sun and looked very much like a city skyline in silhouette. On the far side of the room, stacked on their edge and leaning up against the wall nestled between two dormers, were more than a dozen canvases. A dusty yellowed sheet was thrown over the top of them. Because of the stacking, only the front one was partially visible, with its vibrant colors and odd shapes catching a ray of light that had found its way through the magazine piles.

Even from a distance, Christy knew the canvas showed no Maine village or New Hampshire mountain scene. She'd never seen colors in one of her Grandfather's paintings quite like what peeked out at her from beneath the sheet. Heeding her Grandmother's warning about her parents' bedroom being directly below, she inched slowly along the floor, leaving scuffling footprints in the dust but making no noise.

She crouched down next to the stacked paintings and pushed the old sheet off the top of them. It collapsed in a heap, throwing dust in the air that was clearly visible in the strong rays of sunlight. Christy immediately regretted pushing the sheet, as she sneezed before she could catch herself. The next few minutes were spent completely still, listening for any signs of her parents awakening. If she had known just how late they had stayed up last night cleaning, she wouldn't have worried so much.

Satisfied that nobody was stirring below her, she carefully separated the front painting from the stack. She placed it on her lap and tilted it up to catch the full sun. It took her breath away.

Dominating the scene was a large rock formation—or maybe a mountain—with a hole right through it showing the light—almost reddish—sky behind. The bare rock features were alive with yellows and blues and swirls of green color.

At the foot of the mountain stood a series of objects that resembled trees but had lollipop-like tops instead of a crown of leaves. Those round, flat-on-edge crowns were bright orange and looked to be one solid piece.

To the left of the grouping of lollipop trees was a lake glowing with fire. Large islands of floating coals burned brightly, giving off great plumes of green smoke.

To the right of the lollipop like trees was a figure standing on a hill in the foreground. It was a four-legged animal somewhat like a cow, but Christy's grandfather had apparently painted it like a cartoon figure that had been flattened by a steamroller, because it was facing front but looked to be only a few inches thick. Its legs looked like ribbons. Its head was more normal looking in thickness and was twice as wide as the animal's body. It had big ears and wide nostrils that probably gave it the cow-like appearance. Instead of a tail, it had a long, thin, and very wide appendage that was held up in the air over itself and seemed to be billowing out as if catching a strong wind. The color of its skin, which her grandfather had done a nice job of capturing as a fur-like texture, was silvery blue and very shiny.

Filling out the skyline behind the large rock formation and receding into the distance was a series of mountains painted with what looked like traditional glaciers sliding down their slopes.

Christy studied it intently, finally deciding she didn't know if the rock formation was the size of a mountain or a molehill, or if the tree grouping was the size of redwoods or toothpicks. The lake of fire could just as easily be the size of a puddle or raindrop. All the features were so strange and different, with no recognizable scale, that she had no idea of the scope of what she was seeing. Only the animal in the foreground had any common recognizable scale, and it was drawn to be overlooking the rest of the scene so was of little help determining the scale of the rest of it all.

Christy's phone vibrated silently, and she turned it off—her ten minutes were up. Better to be safe than sorry, although she regretted her decision to set the ten-minute limit. There was so much to look at, but once she had determined a course of action, she never wavered from it. It was one of her strengths.

Silently putting down the painting, she stood up and made her way to the door and out just as quietly. She locked the door with the padlock, and holding her breath, she made it down to the second floor door that opened to the hallway. Remembering the creaking of the door when she entered on her way up, she opened it in slow motion. It barely complained, and she began to breathe again. From there, it was easy to slip back into her room.

Christy next did as her grandmother had suggested by opening the envelope with the red dots. She unfolded a typed multipage letter, again addressed to her from her grandmother. It took her over half an hour to get through the letter, and then she reread it twice before finally putting it down and looking at the rest of the manila envelope's contents. She untied the string around the photos, and all of a sudden, the scale of what she'd seen in the painting came to life for her. She gasped in wonder at each of the three dozen or so photos.

Finally she heard her parents stirring in the room down the hall, so she quickly gathered up the contents strewn all over her bed and put everything back into the large envelope. She had just enough time to put it back and lock her drawer up when her mom poked her head in and smiled sympathetically.

"Feeling any better today, honey?" her mom asked.

"Yes, a little bit, but I'm drained and my eyes are sore," Christy answered truthfully, smiling to cover her fear at the close call.

"We're all drained. This has been an emotional few days. I'll leave you alone now, but I wanted to say that I think you handled everything that was thrown at you yesterday very well. Even that thing with the envelope and Detective Lockhart went okay considering the strangeness of it. I won't pressure you about it. You can tell me what you want, when you want, or not at all, as the case may be. It's entirely up to you. I trust your grandmother. Just make sure whatever you promised the detective, you do it. Okay?"

Christy was surprised at the little speech but smiled and nodded. "Sure, Mom."

Her mom blew her a kiss and winked before closing the door.

The rest of the day, Christy wavered between sadness at her grandmother's death and the burdens put on her from the day before, including starting to watch Danny Lake tomorrow after school, and the eagerness and excitement of the contents of the envelope.

It couldn't all be true, could it? She wondered.

CHAPTER 8

As much as Christy wanted to verify if the pond really was a portal to another world, she knew it was still only May, and thunderstorms, which according to her grandmother's information were vital to the process, were still not an every-week occurrence, like they would be in the heat of July and August. She therefore made the determination that she would wait till after school let out for the year in three weeks' time. Any thunderstorm after that would be fair game for the test!

For the next three weeks, Christy busied herself with preparation as if she were really going and not just testing. Forgotten were the dance and her resolve to ask to use makeup for it. Also forgotten was any talk of not watching Danny for the summer. By the end of that first week, she was actually having fun watching him.

The day after her exploration in the attic Danny had charmed her to no end and that set the tone for their budding friendship. From then on, she increasingly enjoyed her struggle to learn while Danny delighted in teaching her sign language, and Christy constantly had to laugh at herself. She had always wanted to learn a second language but never thought it wouldn't be French or Spanish. But with Danny's guidance, she was slowly learning ASL and enjoying the challenge. Danny also made it a point to walk every day they could around their two properties, showing her all the plants and wildlife that he had been learning about from Trevor.

Trevor was a problem, though. Neither had yet spoken to the other since the funeral day. Christy hated the silence, but in a way, it helped her resolve. She knew that if she got back on good terms with Trev, he would try to worm out of her what she was up to. She didn't want that to happen.

She also reasoned that if they were back to normal and Trev began to squeeze her for answers to what she was up to, she might refuse to tell him. Then he'd get angry again, and they would be right where they now were. That scenario made it easier to let things stay like they were for the time being. But she didn't like it. She missed her best friend—and the good advice he would undoubtedly supply. Her resolve to stick to her grandmother's wishes held, though, and she kept Trevor at a distance.

The night before the last day of school, Christy was up in her room with the door locked while poring over the contents of the envelope like she'd done almost every night since the funeral. Several things were now apparent to her after reading and rereading all her grandmother's and grandfather's letters and descriptions and theories of the mysterious world. Particularly enlightening were the letters that her grandmother had included from her grandfather. He had not only painted and photographed the world, but he had also written about some of his experiences and especially about his impressions of using the portal, all of which were very detailed. He also tried to explain why and how it worked, but that explanation was vague, full of only theories and guesses.

What was apparent to her was that her grandfather believed that there were other portals to this world and back. He didn't know where any were but had heard rumors of at least one. He was always upbeat in his letters and was determined to solve the mystery of why the portal was closing from his side but was still working fine from the pond side, or to find another portal and get back. He constantly beseeched her grandmother to join him, but since any reply was probably in what her grandmother called the "Empty World"—based on Grandma's letters—Christy didn't know what her grandmother answered. Christy could only assume that she had said no time and time again.

Another apparent fact was that the portal from the other side was completely closed off now and had been since about a year after her grandfather had sent the last painting across—the painting that had interested Detective Lockhart. Since that time, nothing except letters in small packets had come in this direction according to her grandmother. And the dates on the notes and letters corroborated that. Even after the portal had completely closed, her grandmother had continued to send things over to him, never knowing if he got them, of course.

Christy's grandfather wrote as if there were other people in the Empty World but never mentioned anyone specifically, and none of the photos or paintings ever showed any other humans. Christy wondered why.

The most heart-wrenching letter of the whole packet was the one that her grandmother labeled: *I just don't know.* In it, she said that she wasn't sure if the portal was really closed from the other side (how could she know for sure?). She was only assuming based on the fact that it was narrowing, getting smaller over time, and suddenly nothing from Jack was coming through. She hoped it was because the portal was closed and not because something had happened to him. That something may have happened to Jack had been her worst fear and the final argument to keep her from crossing over. She didn't want to go across and find him gone or dead, because then she would be alone without her family or Jack and with no way of getting home.

Some things weren't too clear. It was as if her grandmother and grandfather hadn't needed to say certain things, like some things were understood that they discussed in their correspondences from world to world. They must have talked about these things in the many times that he came home, and then all they had to do was make a reference to them in their letters. It made many things they talked about back and forth unclear and hard to follow.

For instance, he continually said that he had his ear guards on to alleviate her constant fears about something. But nowhere in their letters back and forth, or in her letters and explanations to Christy, was it mentioned what the ear guards were about.

Christy was certain that if her grandmother hadn't been so sick when she started the manila envelope for her, it would have been better organized and many things would have been explained more fully. As it was, Christy was forced to guess at a lot, and she was left to wonder about way too much that was only hinted at in one form or another.

She was organizing a list of supplies to take with her, and she agonized over the ear guards mentioned so often. When she found a dusty set of ear guards tucked in an old fishing tackle box she'd almost ignored up in the attic, it thrilled her. She now had everything on her list mentally checked off. Then it dawned on her. She was planning like she was really going! Not just doing a test. Then her promise came back to her and she realized that she couldn't—wouldn't—break it.

That night, she drifted off to sleep knowing she was only going to do a test to see if the portal really existed. The next thunderstorm, she'd get ready like she was leaving and go see what happened to the pond. She knew just where to stand and generally what to look for. It was scary ... and exciting.

The next thunderstorm proved to be too soon, though, as she was away with her mom, who had taken the day off to take Christy and Danny to Boston for the day. Christy was antsy about it but resolved to have a good time in Boston anyway. She and Danny were getting along great, and she certainly appreciated the money she made every week.

One thing led to another, though, for weeks on end, and Christy wasn't ready or wavered between believing and not believing the story, so she hesitated and missed several opportunities.

By the middle of July, she could almost follow Danny's signing without listening to him speaking. It took that long for her to also firmly determine to go ahead with her plan to test the pond.

The month was well along before a powerful enough storm came through that Christy thought would produce the right conditions. Fortunately for her, it came on a Sunday afternoon, so she wasn't watching Danny. She had spent a good amount of time preparing, and it looked like the storm would hit their town about dusk, when she could hide what she was doing from her parents and any other prying eyes, such as the Peters twins. They, like their mom, often used a pair of binoculars to watch the goings-on around the pond, as they were so quick to always tease Christy about.

The afternoon crawled by slowly. Christy logged onto the internet several times to check on the current weather reports and would have scanned the TV channels but was afraid her mom would wonder why she was so focused on the weather. Instead she dragged her backpack out from under her bed and checked her packing job against her list. She hadn't forgotten anything. Even though it was only a practice run, she placed the backpack in a large zippered vinyl bag that she found in her closet packed with blankets. Once she had taken the blankets out, it was the right size for her pack.

Christy declined to go when her parents wanted to go out to eat as they usually did on Sunday. When they left early to do some shopping before dinner, it left her alone with more time than she had hoped for.

The day was darkening, more with the coming storm than with nightfall yet. Christy pulled out the backpack and her poncho. She headed toward the kitchen and sat at the table, staring out at the studio and the pond beyond. Her focus changed to the refrigerator, where she smiled at a series of small square magnets with

American Sign Language signs on them, which her mom had bought to help in her learning.

She was having doubts but kept reminding herself that her grandmother must have been telling the truth. Could her grandmother have made up all of it out of grief over the loss of her husband? Christy argued the pros and cons one last time in her mind.

It was the research done by Detective Lockhart that again convinced her of the truth of it all. Without that supporting information and dozens of long-ago legends of the pond's strangeness, Christy would have dismissed her grandmother's story, and all the paintings and photos, too. Photos could be faked, and paintings and stories dreamed up out of nothing. The loss of a husband to drowning just could have been motivation enough. But people had been disappearing from that pond for centuries, and if the stories were to be believed, people had also been appearing out of that pond for centuries.

Christy fought down the doubts one last time while donning the poncho, and headed out the back door. She made her way along the walk between the house and the studio, then started down the path.

It wasn't dark enough for her liking yet, and the storm hadn't really arrived. She heard distant thunder, and way off to the west, she saw where lighting was flashing on a regular basis. She didn't want to be exposed to prying eyes while she waited, so she walked fifty feet down the shoreline from the dock toward a small peninsula that jutted out almost thirty feet into the pond. It was in the direct line of sight between the Peters' house and the dock, and afforded some privacy by shielding the activities from view.

There were a dozen young poplar trees about twelve to fifteen feet high that her grandmother had let grow on the small point of land. Growing up between them were small hazelnut bushes. Christy headed toward a thick clump of hazelnut bushes and crouched down amongst them for protection from the wind and to keep prying eyes off her. Until she met Danny and spent those afternoons wandering around the pond and land, she hadn't known the names of any of the trees or plants. Now she recognized them without thinking.

She suspected the concern for privacy was why her grandmother had let the peninsula become overgrown in the first place. The need to hide her activities from the snooping Mrs. Peters would have been just the right motivation.

Christy waited, braving the worsening weather. She had hoped the storm wouldn't really pass overhead till darkness, and it at first had looked like that would be the case. Unfortunately for her, the wind and rain picked up before dark, and then she knew the thunder and lightning were going to hit before dark as well. She stood up and walked off the peninsula and out onto the dock. She stood waiting, hoping that the descriptions given her by her grandmother were accurate and that she could interpret the signs correctly.

Huddled with her back facing the wind, Christy stared across the pond. Finally the thunder and lightning caught up with the rain, and she knew it wasn't going to be much longer. Suddenly, above the almost deafening sounds of wind and rain mixed with the thunder, Christy felt as much as heard something vibrating the dock behind her.

Christy turned at the vibration. To her shock, she saw the Peters twins and Rob Upton coming her way. Cory had a vicious grin on his face. Brad was bareheaded and just seemed uncomfortable in the rain. Rob was running on at the mouth to the twins as they came toward her.

Anticipating the teasing to come, Christy leveled a cold stare at the three interlopers. Rob took a breath as they stopped just short of where Christy was standing, and he started to speak again but Cory stopped him.

"Turn it off pipsqueak, will you?" Cory said.

Rob fell silent and just stared.

"Boy, this is great!" Cory said. "Picking up where the old crazy lady left off, are we?"

Brad gave a nervous little laugh, and Rob shook his head to get some of the rain off.

Christy stamped her foot, gritted her teeth, and looked up at the approaching storm. She turned on the three interlopers and said, "Cory, you and your zombies get out of here! You're trespassing on my property."

"Ohhhhh, really?" he said. "Why don't you call the police chief? Oh, yeah, that's right, he's my dad. Too bad!"

Christy eyes narrowed as she stared at him.

"What are you up to?" Cory asked. "What's with the backpack in a baggy? Going somewhere?"

"Loco, like her grandmother!" Rob said, and the three all laughed.

Just then, the storm produced a violent flash of lightning and an immediate boom of thunder, which told Christy that it was moving directly overhead. The time was getting right, only now she didn't want it to happen. She turned toward the pond, hoping to see nothing, and when the signs mentioned by her grandmother didn't materialize, she turned and faced the three boys again, relieved that they wouldn't see anything.

Cory was studying her, curious about the whole situation. He had followed her gaze out over the pond and back. Then he dropped his gloating tone as his curiosity got the better of him: "What were you looking at, Walker?" he asked.

Christy hesitated before replying and then lied, "Nothing. I just like it out here in a storm."

"Loco," Rob said, "just like I said."

Brad spoke for the first time: "Cory, can we go? I'm cold."

"Shut up, both of you," Cory said. "I want to know why she's here ... and lying about it."

Christy resolved to just keep quiet and leave instead of trading insults with them. At least they wouldn't see what she came for. She started back down the dock, but since the boys were in her way, Cory took advantage and blocked her from passing.

"Get out of my way, you jerk!" she yelled, tears beginning to well up.

"No!" Cory said. "You're here for a reason, and I want to know what that is."

Brad whined, "Come on, Cory, let her go. She's upset—and let's get out of here. I'm wet and cold."

"Me, too," Rob said.

Cory didn't move, just kept staring at Christy like he was trying to pick up some kind of sign as to what she was up to.

Christy was about ready to shove him out of the way, even if it meant pushing him into the pond, when she cringed at another brilliant flash of lightning followed right behind by a deafening thunderclap. She turned again toward the pond.

"Come on, Cory," Brad said. "Let's go." His arms were wrapped around himself and he was visibly shivering.

Cory looked to be wavering and about to give in when Rob pointed and yelled, "Guys! Look at the pond!"

Even as he said it, Christy gave a startled little cry. Just beside the dock and out a little bit past where Christy was standing, the pond took on a yellow glow from beneath. Christy gazed at the glow, transfixed with wonder and forgetting all about hiding this moment from the three boys.

The boys, meanwhile, grouped around just behind Christy. Rob peeked over her shoulder. The light swirled and coalesced into fluid patterns of light and dark. Christy thought she saw things sparkling, along with walls that glowed and formed some sort of a tunnel with a pale red color at the end of it.

"Walker!" Cory whispered. "What's going on here?"

"I don't know," she hissed.

"It … It looks like the pond is … It's transparent," Rob said in a hushed voice. "And … there's a cave under there … and I think … I think I see clouds."

Rob squeezed around Christy, and she felt too enthralled to say anything to him. Cory pushed past Christy too and moved up behind Rob, who now bent down closer to the water.

"Oh, wow!" Rob said. "It looks like there are diamonds or crystals in there. You can almost touch them!"

Cory grinned viciously again. "W-Well … why don't you, wimp?" Cory said.

"Not me!" Rob shook his head and started to rise up and back away.

Right behind Rob, Cory blocked Rob's path almost without thinking. Rob tried to get by, but Cory's attention was now on him, not the pond. The two faced each other in an uneasy confrontation.

"Come on, Cory!" Rob said. "Let's go!"

Christy watched as Cory's lips twisted into a sneer.

"No way, wimp!" Cory said. "I think you're going to take a closer look."

Then Cory grinned and, with a quick motion, pushed Rob off the dock.

"No!" Christy cried.

She watched as Rob's startled face and muffled exclamation were swallowed up by the pond ... and then he was gone.

CHAPTER 9

Christy screamed.

"Why did you push Rob in?" Brad asked. He shifted his eyes back and forth between his brother, Cory and the water where Rob had just disappeared. Then he added, "He could drown."

"Nah, he's a great swimmer," Cory said, not taking his eyes off the water. "Besides, I didn't hear any splash as he hit the water, did you?"

Brad squeezed his hands together and starting to pace the dock, looking down at the water where Rob had fallen in. His lips were moving like he was talking to himself.

The strange glow was gone along with Rob. If they hadn't witnessed it, there was no way to tell it had ever been there.

"Christy, where is Rob?" Brad asked as he stopped and stared into the now black depths of the pond.

Christy was speechless with the horror of what had just happened. She stood silently, seething with anger as the storm lessened around them.

"Yeah, where is he?" Cory said, facing Christy. "Come on, Walker, tell us!"

"You moral degenerate!" Christy screamed.

She turned on Cory, and, whipping her backpack around suddenly, she took him by surprise and hit him with it. He stumbled into the water with a startled expression on his face. He submerged momentarily but bobbed up immediately, sputtering and looking at the water around him with frightened eyes. But the water truly had returned to normal. Brad looked first at Christy then the water. Then, while keeping a wary eye on Christy's backpack, Brad helped Cory onto the dock where he soon sat panting and dripping. Christy stood over Cory and stared down at him.

"I wish you'd have sent yourself instead of Rob!" she yelled and then started to walk down the dock.

Cory jumped up and started to follow her. "Hey! You aren't going anywhere till you tell us what just happened."

She stopped in her tracks and whirled around facing Cory, who halted suddenly to avoid bumping right into her. He stepped back slightly but stayed facing her. Christy took a half step forward, closing the little distance between them, and poked a finger into his chest.

"What happened?" she said. "You want to know? Well, you might just as well have let him drown because he's not coming back in any case. And you caused it!"

She was holding back tears as she yelled at him—and getting more angry and frustrated with each passing second.

Cory seemed momentarily taken back. "I-I-I didn't know what would happen. It's not my fault. In fact ..." His face slipped back into its usual expression. "In fact, it was you who pushed him in, Walker! Right, Brad?" He yelled, turning momentarily around to address his brother. "We saw it, didn't we?" When Brad just ignored him and continued to stare at the water, Cory turned around to face Christy again.

Christy screamed at him. "Why, you lying weasel! I could probably take you down myself, I'm so pissed off right now! You had better own up to what you did."

Brad stood up then and almost ran the few steps to Christy and his brother. Stepping between them, he tugged on Christy's sleeve. "What do we do now? Is he really gone?"

Not waiting for Christy to answer, Brad dropped his grip on her arm and turned to Cory, grabbing him by the sleeve too. "What do we do now? How do we tell his mom and dad?"

"Shut up!" Cory said, slapping aside Brad's hand.

Christy's mind was racing in a hundred different directions. She calmed down enough to think out some of the ramifications. She was always good in quick decisions under duress and had been the leader of her clique of friends ever since she had been old enough to have friends. Most of the clique had drifted off over the years, except for Trevor and Ginny, but Christy still was the one they turned to when a decision needed to be made quickly. Trevor, with his common-sense rational approach to problems, was the better at reasoning when he could examine everything from every angle with the benefit of time, but he was no good in a panic. That's where Christy shined. She needed that talent now more than ever before.

"If I were you," she began through her sobs, "I would lie, which I'm sure you're good at."

"Why should we lie about what happened to Rob?" Cory asked as he used both hands to lift the front of his shirt up to clear his eyes of rain. Then he fixed a hateful stare onto Christy as he waited for her answer.

"Because nobody will believe you if you tell the truth!" Christy shot back.

Christy took a deep breath to calm herself down. She didn't like getting so angry at people that she called them names out of frustration. She continued in a calmer voice, speaking through the crying and the dread of what had just happened and what it would mean.

"Listen," she said, "Rob is in another world right now. That down there," she said, pointing at the water, "call it a portal or doorway or whatever, leads to that other world."

"Yeah, right!" Cory said. "A magical doorway to another world? Come off it, Walker!"

Christy shrugged her shoulders. "See, you saw it with your own eyes and even you don't believe it. How do you plan on convincing anyone else it's true? But it's not magical. It has something to do with the electricity generated during a thunderstorm. I haven't figured it out yet."

Brad was listening to the exchange while still staring back and forth between Christy, Cory, and the water below. "If it's a doorway," Brad said, "then ... he can come back, right?"

"No," Christy said. "It doesn't work from the other side. It used to but doesn't anymore."

Cory stood staring at her, seeming to gauge whether to believe her or not. Brad turned from Christy and his brother and stood on the edge of the dock, staring into the water as if he was waiting for Rob to appear any second.

"This is your fault, Walker!" Cory said with stronger conviction. "If you hadn't kept this a secret, this would never have happened."

Despite the apparent absurdity of his claim—after all, Cory pushed Rob in—his claim was part of the reason Christy was so upset. Some of the blame did fall on her. After all, she had caused the twins and Rob to follow her by her secretive behavior at the pond not being secret enough. If only she'd been more careful. If only she hadn't tried to see the portal at work. If, if, if ... Unfortunately, there were no do-overs.

Knowing that Rob was alive was the only thing that kept her from falling completely apart. She made one of her best attempts at pulling herself together and began to form some plan of action while the twins stood there in silence, watching her cry.

"We're going to have to agree on a course of action, and do it right now," she finally said, barely able to get it out between her sobs.

Brad looked up from the water and whimpered slightly. He nodded his head in agreement.

Cory shoved his brother to show his disapproval. "We ain't agreeing to anything you have to say, Walker."

Christy had calmed down enough to not lash out at him. She wiped her eyes from the tears and the rain, and composed herself as best she could. She then shook her head side to side and folded her arms across her chest.

"Okay," she said, her voice thick from the sobbing. "Call your dad and tell him that Rob has drowned in the pond. Tell him you saw Rob go in and he never came out again. Then go tell his parents, too!"

"From where I stand, that's exactly what happened," Cory replied.

"Right!" Christy nodded, trying to end her sobbing enough to make her point to Cory. "Don't forget to mention that you pushed him in and laughed about it while you did it," she said. "So, at the very least, you caused his death. Don't forget to tell the Uptons that, while you're at it."

She measured the effect of her words on the twins, especially on Cory.

Then she spoke directly to him, making eye contact: "Or go ahead, tell them what we just saw. See if anyone believes you. They'll only think you had something to do with his disappearance at that point anyway. I mean, why would you make up a crazy story like that if you weren't hiding something?"

Christy paused to let her words sink in.

Cory was sharp, she knew, and looked like he was thinking rapidly, coming to the same conclusions that she had. Finally, without any letup of his derogatory attitude toward her, he nodded to her.

"Okay, Walker, what's your idea?"

Christy paced the dock from side to side, thinking before answering. She was in control now and knew it.

"You've seen your dad handle missing kids before, haven't you? When Sandra Fernandez went missing for those two days last year, what did he do? Did he call any outside help in?"

Cory thought for a moment, his attitude obviously softening with his fear and his dawning understanding of what Christy was getting at.

"No," he said. "He was about to call someone from Concord who has bloodhounds, but by that time, she turned up at her cousin's home in Bangor." He paused to think, then continued. "He would have used the bloodhounds right away, I think, but her mom was pretty sure she'd run away, not gotten lost or abducted."

Christy nodded, absorbing the information. "Then everyone has to be convinced that Rob has run away. It will buy some time till I can think of something else. And since you guys are his friends, you'll have to do it, not me. But I'll tell you what to say."

Cory snorted his displeasure. "I'll handle our dad. I know what to say to stall him so he doesn't go whacko with this. We have to convince the Uptons that he's run too, or Dad won't have any choice but to pull out all the stops." He started walking off the dock, calling over his shoulder as he did: "Come on, Brad, let's get out of here before we're seen. I'm cold."

Brad shrugged, made a face, and was about to follow when Christy stopped him by grabbing his arm. He pulled away from her touch but stayed, staring down at his own feet, waiting for her.

She spoke in a whisper: "Don't let him get out of hand, Brad, please! I'll find a way to get Rob home.

"You better," Brad whined then paused for a second and glanced at Cory, who hadn't noticed yet that Brad wasn't following along. When Brad continued, he did something he never did: he looked Christy straight in the eye. "Rob must be scared to death! I would be," he whimpered.

Despite the rain, Christy could see he was beginning to cry.

Christy squeezed his arm in sympathy. "I know, Brad. I would be too. But I'm hoping my grandfather is there to find him and keep him safe. Don't say anything to Cory about that part, please!"

Brad's eyes opened wide at the comment, but he just nodded his head in agreement and ran to catch up with his brother, leaving Christy alone in the darkness.

CHAPTER 10

The next day was horrible. People were asking all sorts of questions of the twins. Christy saw the activity at their house and silently hoped Cory would do what he said he'd do. More than once, the chief peeled out of his driveway with his lights flashing and raced off. It wasn't until Christy was asked by her mom if she knew why Rob Upton would run away that she breathed a sigh of relief. Cory must have stuck to their plan. And at least for now, they believed his story.

Christy went shopping with her parents early in the evening the day after. When they drove up their driveway, they saw Trevor sitting on their porch railing, gently tapping his foot.

"I haven't seen much of Trevor this summer so far," Christy's mom said as her dad parked the car. "Did that envelope thing cause you two problems?"

Christy was startled by her mom's perceptive comment, but she just grunted. "No, we're okay. I've just been busy with Danny, and Trevor had scout camp for a few weeks, that's all."

"Hmm!" her mom said as they got out of the car. "If you say so, honey." She left the comment hanging in the air.

As they walked up the steps, her parents both waved to Trevor, and he waved back. Usually her mom would have stopped to talk, but she clearly sensed something hadn't been right for weeks between Trevor and Christy, so she took Christy's dad by the arm and walked inside quickly.

Christy walked over and sat on the love seat opposite Trevor. They sat in silence for a moment, both feeling awkward.

Finally Trevor spoke: "I'm an idiot."

Christy smiled slightly. "Yes, you are."

"I guess I get too angry and hurt over things."

"Yes, you do," she replied. She was enjoying this!

Trevor smiled back and slid down from the railing to stand in front of her. He went to give her a high-five, but she kept her hand down.

"Come on," he said.

She shook her head and stood up. "Nope, come here."

"No! Come on."

She ignored his protest and enveloped him in a bear hug. Then she clung to him for a few extra seconds. Neither of them saw Christy's mom smile as she turned away from the window overlooking the porch.

Trevor tolerated the hug in silence till he felt Christy sobbing on his shoulder. Then he hugged her back before gently pushing her down on the love seat. He stood over her, watching her reactions.

"What is it?" he asked. When Christy didn't immediately answer, he sighed. "It's Rob, isn't it? It's true about the pond, right? Somehow Rob got into it, didn't he?"

Christy wiped tears away and nodded silently, staring into his eyes. "I ... I saw it with my own eyes and Cory pushed Rob in just as the portal opened up."

"This is unbelievable! It's really there?" He shook his head in disbelief. "But how come they were there when it opened up?"

Trevor seemed to have accepted the truth of the pond almost without missing a beat.

Christy explained what happened as Trevor shook his head at each incredible detail.

"Were you in on the 'running away' story that Cory is spinning?"

"Yeah, we decided that was better than trying to tell what really happened. Nobody would believe the truth, and then they'd dive in the pond or drain it, looking for him, thinking he'd drowned or something. I know he's alive, though—just not in the pond."

"Are you sure?"

"Trev ... I know what the twins and I saw. I'll show you the stuff from my grandmother and grandfather now so you can understand it as much as I do. I need your help."

Trevor nodded and then asked in rapid succession: "What's the plan? You have one, right? Is there a way to get back?"

"I don't know for sure, but in the letters from my grandfather, he mentions rumors of other portals, one in particular that he thinks is working. Remember Detective Lockhart said he thought that maybe this pond is a doorway to France because of the French-speaking incident with the kid over a hundred years ago? Well, this doesn't empty out into France, I'm certain of that, but that just means there may be another portal that is in France that also leads to this strange world. Hopefully it goes both ways, unlike this one."

Trevor nodded again.

"The letters also mention a colony of French-speaking people that my grandfather has heard of over there—another clue that there may be a portal from France to that world."

"That's a good clue."

Now Christy nodded. "I just wish I could figure out why this portal stopped working from the other side. If we could figure that out, we'd have no trouble. My grandfather used to travel back and forth at will, or at least only at the whim of a thunderstorm. More times than not, the correct conditions are generated when a thunderstorm goes overhead. I actually think that this pond may attract the lightning, sort of like a lightning rod. How it does that, I don't know. I don't think it's random, though."

"What do you mean?"

"Well, how come so many thunderstorms come right overhead? And how does it happen that when a thunderstorm does come overhead, lightning always, or almost always, strikes the pond. Doesn't that seem odd to you?"

Trevor shrugged.

"Trev, you can't believe how beautiful it is. If we weren't so scared when it happened, I might have been able to look more closely at what was there."

Trevor shook his head, looking like he was thinking about the things she'd said. "I can't believe that anything can control the weather, like creating or attracting a thunderstorm for instance, but maybe like a lightning rod, something can channel the lightning to the pond once a storm is overhead. I can at least believe that much."

They spread the contents of the envelope on Christy's bed, and Trevor looked at everything for two hours. He read everything, all the letters and descriptions, and examined every sketch and small photo and asked a lot of questions, most of which Christy couldn't answer. Then Christy sat him in front of her computer and showed him some photos she'd taken with a digital camera of the paintings in the attic room, promising to show him the real ones whenever they could get up there without being seen or heard.

When he had seen all of the photos, they sat and she told him the plan she had indeed thought of just as Trevor had reasoned on the porch she would have.

After Trevor left, Christy sat for some time more wondering how she was going to go about doing what she knew she had to do—and if Trevor would ever forgive her for taking him into her confidence then deceiving him!

Time was short. Christy was worried and figured that they had only days before either the twins slipped up or someone started asking more questions about Rob's disappearance. Hopefully they wouldn't call in the bloodhounds to try to trace his steps, because that might lead right to the pond and too many questions.

Long forgotten were her promises to Detective Lockhart. Since Rob had disappeared into the Empty World, things had changed for her. She had to go get him. Cory was right: it really was her fault, at least partway.

She felt better now that Trevor was back as her confidant. She didn't feel so alone with the monumental secret. At least for now, she felt she wasn't doing it alone. She had even given Trevor a short list of things she hadn't been able to acquire yet and knew that he'd take care of getting them. Most things were already packed and waiting, though.

CHAPTER 11

For the next few days, Christy lay low with her plans and just enjoyed watching Danny during the daytime. Trevor was making a little money helping his dad around their house, so he wasn't often stopping by, but she chatted with him every night online. It seemed safer than risking being overheard on the phone.

Christy made a mistake and sent Trevor the whole list of things she'd packed. He asked about the ear protection, and she hated to do it but she had to have Trevor buy his own pair. She and Trevor couldn't figure out why it was so important but didn't dare ignore her grandfather's warnings and comments about them.

Finally they were ready. The upcoming weekend looked promising. Thundershowers and oppressively hot, humid weather were forecasted for the whole weekend.

That Saturday afternoon the breezes were few and far between. Christy and Trevor sat on her porch trying to stay cool. They had packed everything down to two backpacks, one for each of them, which were safely stored under the porch hidden behind the bushes, ready to go at a moment's notice.

They were just now catching up on the two months during which they hadn't spoken to each other. The last week had been too busy with preparation for such small talk.

Christy was grinning at what Trevor was saying when she remembered something.

"Oh! Trev," she interrupted. "You didn't tell me you knew all that neat stuff about plants and knots and other things. I had to learn it from Danny."

He laughed. "I didn't know you'd be interested. It's just typical scout stuff, that's all. Danny's really interested, though, and he's going to be a great Boy Scout next year. How are you getting along with him?"

"Great!" Christy replied. "He's really amazing. He loves putting two and two together. He can infer the most incredible things from the tiniest clues. You should see him look at footprints and other small disturbances in the ground like broken branches or things knocked out of place and come up with plausible explanations for what took place."

Trevor grinned. "I have seen it. He's better at it than most every scout in our troop. I call him Sherlock. And he's still just a Cub Scout. Oh, have you learned any sign language yet?"

"Yes, I'm getting pretty good at it. And he is really helpful." Christy frowned slightly as she thought of something. "That's another thing. I never knew you were learning sign language from him. Why haven't you ever mentioned that?"

"I have," he said. "You just haven't listened real well, I guess." He grinned back at her.

A rumble from behind the house way off in the distance interrupted their talk. They both sat up and smiled at each other with determination.

"Looks like one is coming," Trevor said matter-of-factly.

Christy nodded and gave him a nervous thumbs-up.

Just then, Mrs. Lake and Danny drove by, heading for their home, and waved to the two on the porch. Christy and Trevor waved back, watching the car meander down the long driveway and pull in front of their house.

Trevor's eyes followed the Lakes' car. "Do you miss your old home?"

Christy sat silently, thinking before answering. "Not as much as I thought I would. It helps that I'm over there a lot with Danny and that I spent almost as much time here when my grandmother was alive. I probably slept here in the room that's now mine when it was my grandmother's guest room as much as I slept at home ... at least until the last couple of years. I just didn't come here to see her as much as I used to."

Trevor nodded and listened as more rumbles disturbed the quiet around them. The day was getting dark also as the clouds moved in and obscured the scorching sun.

"The weather forecast has severe weather warnings across the state through 11:00 p.m.," Trevor said. "Do you think we should wait till dark?"

Christy nodded. "It showed the last bands of showers coming through our area as late as 10:00 p.m., so I think we can wait for darkness. It gets dark around 8:15 to 8:30 this time of year, so that gives us a good chance."

Trevor nodded back at her. "Did you write the letter of explanation we're going to leave behind?"

Christy hesitated for a second but then pulled a folded envelope from her back pocket. "All in here," she said.

"Can I read it?" Trevor asked.

Again she hesitated before finally putting it away. "No, better not, just in case my parents come out. It says just what we discussed anyway. It was a good idea of yours for us to write one. I might not have thought of it."

Trevor accepted her statement, and the two of them sat through one band of severe showers that hardly produced any lightning at all. Around eight o'clock, Christy's mom poked her head out the window.

"You two coming in out of the rain?" she asked.

"No, Mom," Christy replied. "It's so hot, I think we'll stay outside as long as that's alright."

"Sure, just don't walk off the porch if there's lightning, okay?"

They both nodded, secretly knowing that's exactly what they had planned to do. A few minutes later, Christy heard her parents walk upstairs. Shortly thereafter, she heard their bedroom air conditioner start up.

"That's great!" Christy said. "It looks like they're staying in their room to keep cool. We're good to go anytime it looks right."

They both fell silent as the import of what they had planned set in. Christy couldn't look Trevor in the eye, but he didn't seem to notice anything wrong. If he did, he likely attributed it to general nervousness on Christy's part. For her part, she was silently rehearsing her speech, which if conditions proved ideal, she was soon going to have to give.

The wind picked up as the darkness descended. It brought little relief as the temperature and humidity still hovered around oppressive levels. At around 9:00 p.m., they heard more rumblings, and the sky was routinely lighting up in the distance: sure signs that another band of thundershowers was coming through.

Christy leaned over and pushed off with both hands, bouncing up off the love seat.

"We better get going," she said.

Trevor nodded and followed her off the porch. They dug around under and behind the bushes, then dragged out their backpacks, covered with waterproof-sealed garment bags, then silently headed down the path to the pond.

The lone streetlight, far off up the steep slope on the side of the pond facing the road, reflected off the water and gave a faint illumination to the wooden dock. They didn't dare risk using a flashlight so were grateful for any light they could get. They both pulled on ponchos in anticipation of the next round of heavy showers as they quietly walked out to the proper vantage point.

Once there and waiting, Christy took the letter Trevor had asked her to write and sealed it inside a sandwich baggie. She then duct-taped it securely to the dock. Trevor nodded approval silently. Someone would be sure to find it.

The wind was picking up, and the choppy water was black save for the single dancing line of illumination from the streetlight. Christy pointed to the spot they would be concerned with, and Trevor's eyes darted over the area then stopped.

Christy saw his attention go toward the poplars. "What, Trev? Did you see something?"

"No, I guess not. I thought I saw something moving in the bushes below the poplars over there, but I don't see it now."

The sky regularly lit up far behind the house and over the hills. The distant muffled rumbles that followed made their way down and echoed off the Peters' place before being absorbed by the trees across the road.

Knowing that now was the only time she had, Christy pulled Trevor close to say something to him as the wind and rain began in earnest and the thunder became louder with the approaching storm.

"Trev! I need to say something to you, and I don't want you getting upset."

He frowned at her tone but nodded, looking unsure.

"Trev ... I have to go. I caused Rob to be there, and it's only right that it should be me."

Just then, a sharp crack of lightning startled them.

"I know," he said, nodding. "Of course you should go with me."

Christy looked at him, and her eyes softened. She wiped rain from her eyes, stalling momentarily. "No." She shook her head. "I mean I should go alone, not with you." Then with more conviction, she said, "I am going alone, not with you."

"What!" Trevor shouted. "What are you talking about?"

He spun around in a full circle and faced Christy again, stamping his feet and throwing his hands up in the air. Christy grabbed at his flailing hands and took them in hers. Then she leaned her head close to his to be heard over the building storm.

"Trev, we both can't go. You have to stay here to explain that I'm okay. No letter will be able to do that as well as you can. You have to get Detective Lockhart here and be the one to show him the packet and be an eyewitness to the fact that it's all true. If we both went, the Empty World would be exploited without one of us here to keep the packet of my grandparents' stuff hidden from everyone but the detective. Once the stuff was found, they'd begin to believe that we weren't drowned, and someone would figure it all out. You have to stay to stop that from happening."

Trevor listened and just scowled. He tried to pull his hands out of Christy's grasp and turn away, but Christy held on and wouldn't let him.

"You never intended me to go, did you?" Christy squeezed tighter as she saw the hurt on his face from that realization. Then she saw his face flash anger again and he said, "You can't go alone! I won't let you! You need me to help you! We had this all planned!"

She hated this, but she had no choice. "I have to go alone, Trev. I just have to. I need you to help me here by keeping the Empty World a secret, if possible, from the whole town. If we both disappear, there's no way this remains a secret. You have to stay to get Detective Lockhart up here, and then the two of you can decide who needs to know. Without you staying, there's no way we can control who decides that."

"How?" he yelled. "How am I supposed to do that?"

"I ... I don't know," she replied, sobbing now as he tried to turn away again.

Christy held on till he stopped struggling. Then, letting go with one of her hands, she used it to gently but firmly pull his chin back so he was looking directly at her.

"Trevor, I'm going alone, and you're going to find a way to help from here. There isn't any other way. Please understand that! If you don't say 'yes,' we'll leave this dock and I'll find a time to go when I'm alone. It's me now with your help, or me alone some other time."

"I'll watch for you and follow you anyway!" Trevor said.

"No you won't, Trev. You can't watch for me all the time. I'll just make sure I'm alone."

Trevor dropped eye contact by glancing down at his feet as best he could with Christy holding his chin. The wind swirled around them, and the rain pelted their ponchos as they stood together at odds with each other.

It took several seconds, but Trevor finally nodded in acceptance of it. His whole body relaxed in resignation, and he made eye contact again. But the anger flashed in his eyes, and when Christy relaxed her grip, he pushed her hands away. She mentally breathed a sigh of relief, and her eyes held empathy for his feelings. She knew it must be tough for him to take all this in on such short notice. But she also knew that this was the only way it would have worked. He would have found a way to follow her if she'd told him her real plans days ago. Hurting so badly herself because of her actions, she swore silently that she'd never ever betray her best friend like this again.

They just stood there, facing each other, and she also finally relaxed. In that moment, they both accepted the other's role. Then she smiled. The anger momentarily left Trevor's face, looking like it had been replaced by fear.

"I don't know where to start," he said with a thick voice.

She hugged him quickly and then let him go. "Start by calling the detective, and tell him the truth. He'll know how to proceed. Now step off the dock so you won't get any ideas."

He nodded and picked up his pack to leave. Christy quickly tore the duct-taped envelope off the dock and handed it to him.

"Trev?"

"Yes?"

"You are braver than I ever will be for doing this. You know that, don't you?"

He just stood there, waiting, staring at her, clearly not wanting to answer her, not wanting to verbally give in as he'd already physically done. Christy waited for a few seconds, the rain hitting and dripping off both of them.

"I know what I have to do, but you have a harder task," she said after a strong gust of wind passed. "It's one that I could never do. But you'll find a way. I know you will."

He continued to say nothing, just stared at her with tears in his eyes now. She accepted the silence.

"You're my hero, buddy," she said.

He smiled slightly at that and managed a wink. Christy then gently pushed him to get him started off the dock. He turned to go with a backward glance. Christy waved.

"Tell my mom and dad I'm okay," she said. "Convince them, please?"

"I will," he stated flatly. "Take care of yourself, okay?"

"You, too."

She watched him walk off the dock and head a few yards back toward the peninsula. Then she turned toward the pond and gave all her attention to it. The storm was now producing loud thunder and occasional lightning that seemed almost right overhead. Christy picked up her pack and cradled it in her arms, waiting. It wouldn't be long now.

Over by the peninsula, Trevor felt confused. He'd let Christy talk him off the dock and into not going. He stomped his feet and kicked at a clump of cattails encroaching onto land from the pond's edge. He turned to watch Christy as the lightning illuminated the scene like it was daytime for a split second. In that second, Trevor saw a small form hiding in amongst the hazelnut bushes about twenty-five feet into the peninsula. He waited, staring at it, but without the direct illumination of a lightning flash, it was difficult to tell what it was. It looked like a person, though.

Within seconds, the form moved, and Trevor saw clearly it was human. Glancing quickly to make sure Christy wasn't watching, he walked toward whoever it was. When he had gotten within ten feet of the person, the form stood up—and Trevor saw it was Danny!

Danny signed that he had seen the two of them on the dock and wondered what was going on. Along with a flourish of hand movement, he said aloud, "You're not happy about something, are you?"

Trevor, without really thinking it through, all of a sudden thought of a way to help Christy. Maybe if Trevor didn't know Danny as well as he did, and if he hadn't been involved with him through scouts, Trevor might not have decided on such a course of action, but because he didn't think of Danny as a typical nine-year-old, he motioned for Danny to come to him.

When Danny was beside him, he motioned for him to kneel down beside him and face across the short distance to the dock where Christy was waiting.

He turned toward Danny and said, signing as he spoke, "Christy needs our help. I can't go with her because she needs me to stay here. That's why I'm not happy, plus I'm worried about her. I want you to go with her and help protect her and bring her home again. She's going looking for Rob Upton, the boy who ran away. Do you understand me?"

Danny nodded then asked, via signing and saying, "I don't know what you mean by go with her, though. Go where?"

Trevor smiled grimly, then said and signed, "You'll see. Watch! You can't go on the dock till the last second or Christy will not let you help her, so I'll tell you what to do. Okay?"

Danny nodded.

"Good!" Trevor signed and spoke. "You are going to see something pretty amazing in a few minutes, and then Christy is going to jump in the water. But it won't be water for a few seconds—it will be a doorway to somewhere else ... a place Christy calls the Empty World. Rob is there now and needs help. You have to jump in too, just after Christy does. Can you? Will you?"

Danny smiled and said while signing, "Be prepared! Right?"

Trevor grinned at him and said, "Always, scout, always." He lifted up his covered pack. "You take this; it has the stuff I was going to take with me. It will get you through anything, I hope."

Danny nodded and accepted the pack. They both waited and watched, tolerating the storm as it barreled overhead. It was only a couple of minutes before a lightning strike hit just right. The loud clap of thunder almost rattled their teeth.

The pond glowed, and just beyond where Christy stood and below the dock, the water coalesced and turned light yellow. Trevor was fascinated watching, but he pointed out to Danny what he wanted by making gestures. Christy was waiting for the right moment and could tell when that was better than Trevor, so he had to wait for her to make her move before sending Danny.

Trevor made it clear that when he said "Go," Danny was to go immediately and jump in after Christy.

Then Trevor started to remove his poncho to give it to Danny, who barely acknowledged the gesture since he was too intent on watching Christy. It was fortunate that Danny was watching, because suddenly Christy jumped with no warning.

Trevor hadn't anticipated just how the events were going to happen, how little warning they would have, but he didn't have to say anything. Danny was off, clutching the pack and fumbling to remove his glasses. He headed for the dock, his small legs churning as fast as could be. In an instant, he had taken a running leap before Trevor knew what was happening. Trevor didn't get the chance to give Danny the poncho. No sound of a splash reached Trevor ... but they were both gone.

Trevor stood up, suddenly alone and unsure of whether or not to believe what he'd just witnessed. Even though he was cold and wet, he slowly walked out onto the dock and looked down. All he saw was black impenetrable water. Any signs that there had been anything other than water and mud down there were gone. He looked up at the still-strong storm and, readjusting his poncho, walked off the dock and started up the path.

When he got to Christy's grandfather's studio, he stopped under the floodlight. Again he thought about Christy talking him off the dock with her argument about his role being to stay behind. Even if she was right, he realized that he shouldn't have conceded the point so easily. Was it because he was afraid and really was looking for an excuse not to go? If that was true, then he'd involved Danny because he was afraid, and that fact didn't sit too well with him. He could hide behind Christy's well-thought-out reasons for his staying behind, but in the end, he knew in his gut that he should be there with her now.

Shaking off his angry thoughts at himself for being so compliant and at Christy for deceiving him, he opened the envelope Christy gave him. No long explanations like Trevor had asked her to write, instead it said:

Dear Trevor,

I'm sorry to do this to you. You'll think of what to tell everyone, I know you will. Look in the crawl space under the studio. I put all the stuff from my grandmother's packet there. Take it and show it to Detective Lockhart. There also is my cell phone. I won't need it so you use it to call the detective as soon as you can.

Luv, Christy

CHAPTER 12

Christy's knees buckled under her as she hit the ground hard. She dropped her backpack and tried to cover her ears as her head seemed to explode. Sound like she'd never imagined! It filled her whole being and overwhelmed her. With her fast-disappearing rational thoughts, she took her hands away from her ears and tried to claw her way into her pack through the plastic protection.

Her hands didn't seem to respond to her thought processes, and she moved them back over her ears, abandoning her attempt to open her backpack. Within seconds, the sound wasn't just inside her head: it seemed to take over her whole body. Then she gave up and curled into a ball before she lost consciousness completely.

Danny stumbled as his legs gave way under him. He hit solid ground and rolled over, still clutching Trevor's covered pack. His senses were on overload as he entered the so-called Empty World. He was vaguely aware and surprised that he didn't come out underwater. Immediately all else was forgotten as he felt his head begin to throb. Reaching in to his breast pocket, he pulled out his glasses and put them on quickly. Then, still clutching the pack, he stood up and looked for Christy.

It was nighttime, but there was light enough to see a short distance. Christy was ten feet away from him, curled into a fetal position, her hands pressed tightly over her ears, her eyes closed and head swaying. Her pack was next to her. Danny got up and, ignoring his throbbing head, ran and knelt down next to her.

Christy had apparently tried to get into her pack by ignoring the zipper on the garment bag and just ripping into it. She had partially succeeded in getting into the pack, and something was protruding partway out of it. Danny glanced quickly at Christy and then looked around to see their surroundings. The wind on his back was stronger than he'd ever felt before. Even through his clothes, his back was stinging from windblown sand.

Understanding came quickly, and he reached in and pulled out what Christy had started to retrieve before abandoning the effort and curling up into a defensive position. He momentarily had some difficulty but twisted the earpieces and then, without hesitation, fit the ear-protection device over Christy's ears, gently pushing her hands away to do it. Then he lifted up the poncho hood onto her head again. It was large and loose enough to fit over the sound-damping ear protectors.

Then, even though all he felt was a strong pressure, he opened Trevor's pack. Finding a matching pair of ear protection in it, Danny slipped the device over his own ears. The soft heavy-padded ear cups were a little too big for his small ears, but they helped. At once, the pressure that was making his head throb stopped. Something was making noise like he'd never imagined before, and it had incapacitated Christy.

He sat waiting. Christy appeared almost unconscious, but her slight rocking continued, so he knew she was at least partially conscious. Danny took stock of their surroundings. The area they were in was almost bare rock. No vegetation was visible at all for what seemed like a hundred yards in all directions. He couldn't hear it, but he could feel the strong wind. Other than the sand stinging him in the back, he couldn't see any signs of the wind. It was a barren area they had come into: they were in a round depression about fifty feet across that Danny thought reminded him of a crater. No trees, no plants or grass, no large structures, nothing at all to be blown by the wind and give a clue as to how strong it was except for the pressure of it on his back, along with the stinging from the tiny invisible sand particles.

Danny didn't dare turn into the wind without eye and nose protection, and he wasn't wearing a poncho. He had snuck down to the pond out of curiosity to see what Trevor and Christy were up to, and hadn't properly prepared for the rainstorm back home. All he had on was his very soaked sweatshirt, and he was beginning to feel the chill as the wind cut through the saturated cotton fabric.

Hoping that Trevor would have packed a backup poncho or at least a cheapo plastic foldable second raingear, he rummaged through the pack again. Smiling at Trevor's preparedness, he found a new three-dollar, clear plastic poncho. He tore open the case and, despite the difficulty with the constant wind, quickly put it on. He also found Trevor's scout neckerchief, so he temporarily removed the ear protection and tied the bright red cloth around his nose, mouth and chin like an Old West bandit to help keep out the stinging sand.

Once he had all his gear on, Danny looked back down at Christy. He knew he couldn't move her, so all he could do was wait for her to come around.

Soon she stirred and sat up. Touching her ear protection, she realized what it was and then she looked at Danny in surprise.

He gave a wave and signed, "It's me ... Danny. Are you okay?"

She nodded and then, obviously hurting from the stinging sand, reached into her pack and brought out two pairs of safety goggles. She handed one to Danny and put the other on herself. They were large enough for Danny to fit them over his glasses.

"How?" she signed to him.

"Trevor asked me to follow you. I was spying on you two from the hazelnut bushes," he signed.

Christy shook her head in the negative. She hadn't understood his signing too well, Danny knew. Without his speech, which was impossible with their ear protection and his mouth being covered, she couldn't follow his signing. She'd learned a lot in the few weeks that she'd been watching Danny, but probably not as much as she'd thought. His pantomimes and added speech had surely bridged the gaps in her signing skills.

Instead of trying again, Danny looked around for a place out of the wind. A cluster of low rocks was visible a few yards distant in the pitch blackness of the night. Their only light to see by was cast by the strange stars up above, but it was enough to see where they were going for the few yards needed. He got up and, taking Christy's hand, led her to it and the relative shelter it provided. Crouching down out of the strong wind, they tried to communicate. Without the use of speech, it was difficult at best. Finally they resorted to scratching words into the hard-packed dirt they were sitting on, but darkness made even that very difficult.

Sitting on the leeward side of the cluster of rocks was only marginally better than sitting directly in the fierce wind. Soon Danny was just as frustrated as Christy and started looking around more at their surroundings.

Even with the eye and ear protection, they couldn't look right into the wind. The small stinging sand was dangerous enough that they were worried about their skin. Christy's hastily rigged nose and mouth protection wasn't nearly as effective as Trevor's scout neckerchief was for Danny. She had only a small handkerchief that barely covered her nose and mouth.

Danny looked around at the small window of direction that the conditions allowed. With his back to the rocks, he could only look ahead. He had no clue as to the real direction on a compass that it was, and since it was nighttime, there was no other way of checking. The stars and their strange configuration, so different than home, gave him no help, either.

They huddled together for warmth for the rest of the long night, not communicating since it was so difficult with Danny's deafness and the strong wind. The morning came while they were both dozing uncomfortably. The wind never let up.

Christy woke up to Danny shaking her gently by the shoulder. She came to, staring at the bright day, and they looked around at their surroundings as best they could. The wind still made it almost impossible to look directly into it, so they concentrated on looking downwind. Christy knew Danny was in for a big surprise since he didn't have the benefit of the paintings back in Christy's attic to prepare him for the strangeness spread out in front of them. Even though she was prepared, the reality still amazed her.

The immediate vicinity was bare of anything except a rock outcropping rising into the sky, which had been just out of their sight in the dark. It dominated the view in front of them and was about the only feature in their vicinity except small clusters of stony rubble spaced irregularly around where they had rudely landed the night before. They had used one of those clusters of rubble to shield themselves during the night.

That they were on a hilltop of some stature was evident by the way the landscape lay in front of them. They were on a gentle slope that spread out downhill, giving them a view of the distance that they would have been able to see much more of except for the intrusion of the rock outcropping. Off in that distance, they could see strange lavender- and bluish-colored vegetation, and the sky was more red than blue. Water sparkled like a ruby ribbon way off in the valley below.

Danny was still taking in the distant sights when Christy nudged him and pointed to the outcropping of rock. It was close, not over a quarter mile away. It stood out from the barren landscape in the immediate vicinity like the pyramids of Egypt stood out from the surrounding desert. There was what looked like a manmade carving in the shape of an arrow chiseled into the surface directly facing them—which would have been almost invisible except for the shadow cast into it by the angle of the morning light. Below the arrow was a darker shaded area shaped like a sliver that looked like it could be the entrance to a cave just out of direct sight and continuing around the other side of the rock formation. They were too far away to really guess what it was.

They nodded to each other and gathered up their things, then cautiously headed toward the outcropping. The wind was not quite strong enough to blow them forward on its own accord, but it definitely made walking a tricky maneuver. They came up to the dark depression and saw that it was in fact an entrance to some sort of cave or hollow in the rock. Quickly entering, they found themselves sheltered from the strongest of the wind. The light only penetrated fifteen or twenty feet into the cave before a sharp bend shut off most of the outside. Christy took her flashlight out—wishing she'd thought of it the night before when they were writing in the dirt—and Danny nodded his approval. Once lighted, the tunnel revealed itself as having smooth walls and a ceiling some ten feet above them.

Hand in hand, they crept forward. The cave, or tunnel, seemed to go on forever and angled slightly downward, like it was heading into the ground. Within a hundred paces or so, they went around another bend in the tunnel, and light slowly began to illuminate the way for them. Christy looked around in all directions, including toward the ceiling, but couldn't find where the light was coming from. The shadows it cast were very faint and in several directions at once, so they were no help to her in figuring out the light source.

After going for what seemed like an hour, they saw that around another bend it was becoming lighter the more they walked. Somewhere ahead was a strong light source. They walked toward the source of the increasing illumination because it seemed like the best place to go.

Taking a final turn in the tunnel, they came out into a large room-like cavern with light coming down through a shaft in the ceiling. The expanded tunnel was now a large enclosure that had to measure fifty or sixty feet wide, and the ceiling rose twenty or so feet high. The shaft that spilled light into the natural room was eight or ten feet wide, and they could see that it was ten or fifteen feet above the opening that the shaft finally ended at the daylight. They were thirty or forty feet deep under the hillside.

Directly in front of them, and barring their further progress, was a pool of water, which gently rippled from the downdraft of wind through the shaft. The light from above danced off the ripples, reflecting the strange red color of the sky. Beyond the large cavern they had entered, and on the other side of the pool out of their reach, was an opening like the one they had just stepped out of. It looked like the continuation of their tunnel. But they had no way to get to it.

They had removed the kerchiefs from the faces early in the tunnel but were still wearing their protective ear gear, and Danny gingerly removed his as Christy watched.

He waited a few seconds and then signed, "I don't feel pressure; it should be safe to remove yours."

Christy thought she understood enough of what he meant that she tentatively started to remove the bulky ear guards. Danny nodded approval as she lifted them off her head. She felt only the slight downdraft from above, but off in the distance above her, she could hear the wind still raging across the opening of the shaft. The strange noise that had incapacitated her during the night was now just a distant wailing coming down the shaft.

The pool in front of them was almost as wide as the large cavern they were in. Not sure how to proceed, they signed and talked to discuss their situation. The walls and floor of the cavern met in an angle at the water's edge that was too steep to walk on. It appeared that they were stuck on their side of the pool of water with no way to get across.

On the other side of the pool, directly opposite from them, was what looked like a drawbridge pulled up into an inaccessible position. While they were discussing ways to get across, they suddenly saw the drawbridge begin to lower itself down by a series of pulleys attached to the ceiling and threaded with ropes secured to the bridge itself.

The bridge slowly lowered till it was within inches of their shoreline, then slammed down the final distance with an audible creaking of the timbers.

They stood together not knowing exactly what to expect. Christy heard footsteps beyond the large room—coming from the continuation of their tunnel on the opposite side of the pool of water. She nudged Danny and pointed in that direction.

Out of the tunnel stepped a man dressed in old jeans and a plaid flannel shirt. A hooded sweatshirt was tied around his waist. He was carrying a walking stick that looked to be carved from a tree limb, all gnarled and worn from long use. On his back was an old canvas backpack, and his belt had several items attached and dangling from it. The man smiled and waved, then shouted a greeting.

"Sorry for the rude banging! The rope slipped through my hands there as I was lowering the bridge. Come on across and introduce yourselves. I'm Jack Renfrew. Who are you?"

CHAPTER 13

Christy held Danny's little hand tightly and looked at the grandfather she barely remembered. It may have been her amazed expression, which included an open-mouthed stare and appraisal of the man opposite her, that made him begin to smile and start to say something. But just as he was about to talk again, Christy let go of Danny's hand to rub under her nose with her index finger as some dust or something tickled her. It was the same mannerism that her mom had. Christy had instinctively picked it up from her over the years.

Her grandfather's eyes narrowed then became wide, and with a startled sharp intake of breath, he dropped his walking stick.

"My God!" he said quietly. "You are so much like your mother. Christy? Is that really you?"

Christy nodded slowly, nervousness setting in. How was she now to greet him after all these years? The answer was given to her, the choice taken away from her. Once she acknowledged who she was, her grandfather extended his arms and enveloped her in a bear hug. Danny moved aside and watched their faces, hoping to read lips and follow anything they might say.

Christy's grandfather held tight, pressing her head to his chest. She felt him sobbing silently and let him cling to her without comment. Tentatively she returned his embrace and found herself crying, caught up in the moment.

After several moments, he released her, backing her off and stroking her hair before wiping his eyes. He looked at Danny standing silently by.

"Who have we here?" He smiled. "You can't be a brother of Christy's; she doesn't have one. Lillian would have mentioned a grandson in one of her letters she was able to get to me. Bless her." He paused, looking sad. "She didn't—couldn't know if I was receiving them because I couldn't reply, but she kept sending me updates anyway. The last pictures I got were several years ago, though. And the letters have stopped coming." His shoulders slumped visibly as his comments ended.

Christy answered him while he was deep in thought: "This is Danny Lake. He and his mom Katie have bought our house."

Christy's grandfather was staring at the reflections of the rippling water on the cavern wall, when all of a sudden, it must have registered what she'd said to him.

"Bought your house? Where did you move to?" He looked down at her.

"Into your house, Grandpa." She took a deep breath and said, "Grandma's … dead. She died of cancer over two months ago now."

"Lillian … gone?" Her grandfather gasped. "Child, I … I have to sit down."

He leaned on the bridge railing and shook his head in disbelief, then he slowly sank down to the tunnel floor and buried his head in his hands. His whole body began to shake in silent sobs. They let him be with his pain and grief. Finally it was Danny who approached him again. He took the grieving man's hand and held on. Christy's grandfather smiled at Danny.

"It's a pleasure to meet you, Danny," her grandfather said.

Danny let go of his hand and signed while saying, "It's nice to meet you too, sir."

Christy's grandfather's eyes went wide, and he surprised them both when he signed and finger spelled his name: "Please, call me J-a-c-k."

Danny smiled, and Christy was about to ask how he knew signing when her grandfather said and signed,

"With the deafening wind out there, I learned a little signing shortly after I started coming here. You have to wear those infernal ear protectors, so often it's a necessity to use signing. There are small groups of people who come through here from time to time, and all of them need to know some basic signing or they can't communicate. I am by no means good at it but it comes in real handy, as you can imagine."

"Danny saved my life, I think," Christy said. "When we got here, I passed out from the horrible-sounding wind before I could pull the ear protectors out. It was Danny who put on my protectors before it got any worse. He felt the pressure and figured out what was bothering me."

Her grandfather nodded and looked at Danny with new respect.

"Very quick thinking, son. You most certainly did save her life. In a little while, she would have been deaf and possibly brain damaged and would have died from the elements," he signed.

"Thank you, Jack," Danny signed and spoke at the same time.

Jack smiled in acknowledgement to Danny, and then, picking himself up and reaching for his walking stick, he said to both of the newcomers: "Let's go to my home here and talk. I have a million questions, as I guess you probably do too. It's quieter there and more comfortable. Besides, this pool isn't going to open up anymore."

Christy and Danny both looked at each other. From their startled expressions, her grandfather no doubt realized that they hadn't known the pool was the portal back, or used to be, before it stopped working.

"I don't understand it," her grandfather said, "but in this world, the portal to here is out there in the wind where you came through, but the way back is here through this pool of water—at least it used to be. Back home, both directions are through our pond. Why there isn't one exit and entrance, so to speak, on this side, I haven't figured out yet. I should have waited outside for you, but it's less hostile in here to wait for someone to show up, as I expected someone to do."

"You expected us?" Christy asked.

"Yes, I found a youngster about a week ago. He wasn't so lucky as you two. He really was seriously hurt by the wind and noise, but he's alive, although his hearing is almost completely gone. I thought that someone would come after him. He's frightened and almost non-communicative. That's understandable since he can't hear me, but I did get bits and pieces of information from him. I was hoping a rescue attempt might be made. But let's get going. I'll take you to him."

"Rob! He's alive!" Christy exclaimed.

"Yes," Jack said, smiling at Christy. "So let's go!"

He extended his hand to Danny, who took it. Then Danny reached out his other hand, and Christy took that.

Hand in hand, Jack led them deep into the rock outcropping. They walked a good mile or so, Christy guessed, all underground through the smooth-walled tunnels. On the walk, Jack asked Christy all about her grandmother and the illness that had taken her life. He was clearly still in shock about it and choked up each time he tried to say Lillian's name or asked about something particular. Jack's sad questioning ended just as the floor of the tunnel climbed upward again and they slowly came out into daylight.

"You won't need your ear protectors here," Jack stated as they emerged from the bowels of the hill. "We're insulated enough from the sound for it to be only an annoyance. Most of the area around here is horribly affected by the strong wind and the sound of it. This small acreage directly beyond the tunnel we walked through is well protected from the force of the wind and its devastating sound. I can't be certain, but I think that this whole setup is by design. This area is protected deliberately from the sound. At least, that's what I think because these tunnels look manmade, but again, I can't be sure."

"What causes the sound, Grandpa?" Christy said. "I never heard wind so loud before. And the wind is real strong, but it doesn't seem to be as strong as a hurricane, for instance, so I don't understand how it can be so loud."

Jack nodded, then said while signing, "To the north of here is a range of mountains. You may not have seen them since looking into the wind would have been very dangerous. They consist of various granites and, curiously, a lot of sandstone. There is one formation almost directly north of here about five miles that has weathered out all the sandstone, and only the more permanent granite remains. The mountain is over nine thousand feet high, and up on the slope about six or eight hundred feet from the top, a major section of sandstone was wedged in between the more permanent granite when the mountain was apparently pushed up by the pressures of the plate tectonics thousands or millions of years ago.

"Over time, the sandstone was weathered out by the wind and rain till there was a hole right through the mountain that must be over four or five hundred feet high and almost that wide. Who knows how long it took to weather out? The hole must be miles deep since it extends straight through the entire mountain."

Christy was hanging on every word her grandfather was saying, and at the description of the hole in the mountain, she almost mentioned that she'd seen the painting of it but didn't. She didn't want to interrupt him.

He continued while Christy and Danny listened and followed his hands and lips.

"North of the mountain range is a field of glaciers. Those glaciers send cold air down toward the mountains, causing incredible winds. When those winds hit that formation, they make a deadly sound. That hole is acting like a large deep-bass whistle. The sound is almost crippling for anything or anyone who is within a fifty-mile fanlike area this side of the mountain—except for us here in this little protected area almost directly in the middle of the affected area.

"That sound must have been going on for thousands of years because I've seen plants and animals that have adapted to it—with protective earflaps and strange shapes, taking advantage of it. Hopefully over more time, the rock will weather even more and stop making the whistling sound, or at least diminish and not be a problem."

Jack became silent for a moment, and Christy and Danny let it pass without comment or questions, taking in all he'd told them.

Finally he continued. "All I've said is really just conjecture about how the mountain became a deadly sound device, since I'm no geologist. I think that, however it happened, many years ago something else happened that was really terrible. There are signs of holes blasted in the ground. Possibly bombs being the cause, and there is scarring on many hillsides from some intense heat devices. I've dug down into the ground in a couple of places and found rusting metal devices that could only be pieces of huge ground assault weapons or vehicles, sort of like tanks but of a very different design.

"The caves, or tunnels, we came through really look to be almost carved out or blasted out somehow, so they're definitely manmade. Plus the light throughout most of these tunnels is untraceable. I can't figure out where it is coming from. So that's another point for these all being manmade, and based on the level of sophistication of the mysterious lighting, whoever made these tunnels had some very advanced technology. A few of the tunnels have no light, like the opening part of the one with the portal. I think they probably used to have light in them but for whatever reason, they don't anymore.

"The strong wind is broken up as it travels south through forests and over other mountains, so that, too, diminishes the farther from the glaciers you get. Over the last eleven years of my time here, first coming and going and then being stranded here for nine years, I've talked to many people about the sound and wind. A few people whom I've met have said that in other areas of this world, there are other dangerous sound- and wind-generating phenomenon. If they exist, then it is too much to assume that they all are natural. One freak formation causing a killer sound is maybe within the realm of possibility, but more than one? I don't think so."

They had stood just outside the tunnel going back into the hillside they'd come out of. While listening to Jack, Christy and Danny had not really looked at the scenery around them—Christy, because she was so curious about the sound mountain and had some prior knowledge of the place, and Danny, she knew, needed to concentrate on Jack's signing and his lips. When Jack paused and it became clear he was through with explanations for the moment, they took the opportunity to stare at the wonders they'd come out into.

It was warmer with the strong sunlight from the reddish sun burning overhead than it had been on the barren hilltop. The sunlight cast a ruby glow on the landscape before them. This was no barren hilltop like the spot where they had emerged from the pond. The wind was still too strong to tell if there was any insect life making sounds, and they couldn't see or hear any birds or animals, but the area was alive with all sorts of plant life. Here, the intense dangerous sound coming from the mountain was just a fluctuating, low-pitched moan or wail that could be ignored. To Christy, it sounded almost like a gathering of walruses.

The landscape was familiar to Christy from Jack's paintings, but she knew that Danny was looking upon it for the first time. Jack, meanwhile, stood silently while Christy and Danny looked around.

"It is so much more beautiful than your paintings make it to be," Christy said. Then, realizing how that must have sounded, she added, "Oh! I didn't mean it like that!"

Jack smiled. "I understand what you mean. So Lillian showed you the paintings? She said she was going to hide them."

"She did. I only saw them after she died," Christy said.

Jack shook his head. "I have so many questions to ask you. But since this place must be a big surprise to you, my questions will wait till you've satisfied yourself with what you want to know."

Jack pointed southwest toward what looked like a tall stand of trees, although trees unlike anything that Christy or Danny had ever seen before.

"Beyond those jibs is my home," Jack said. "We're about a half mile from there."

"Jibs?" Christy asked.

She saw that Danny nodded his approval of her question since Jack had spelled the word with his hands, having no sign-language equivalent.

Jack let out a belly laugh that they would come to know well. "Just my name for those particular trees," he said. "They look a lot like a jib on a sailboat. Must have adapted to the wind by flattening out and turning so that their narrow edge was into the wind. You'll see a lot of that type of adaptation to this wind here. A great number of plants and animals have flattened themselves out to avoid the major brunt of the wind."

"Grandpa?" Christy said.

"Yes, honey?" he responded, looking directly at her and stopping for a second.

"Rob ... is he going to be alright?" she asked.

Jack hesitated before answering: "He isn't in danger now of dying, but I'm not sure if his mind is what it was, because I don't know him. Also, he's afraid still, and I can't get much out of him." He started walking again, saying as he went, "Let's get to my place."

CHAPTER 14

Jack led the children down the slope and into lush growth that swayed and rippled with the constant wind. The noise was tolerable for Christy and her grandfather, so they didn't use their ear protection. They moved southwest along a well-worn path that was spongy underfoot. Within a few minutes, they came to another rocky hill protruding out of the lush growth. Christy saw immediately that there was an opening that faced away from the strong wind. When they came up to the opening, Jack stopped and let Christy and Danny enter ahead of him.

Inside, the walls were just as smooth as in the tunnel with the pool. The tunnel here was straight and well lit by a shaft cut—or weathered out—overhead. Thirty feet or so into the tunnel, they passed under the shaft of light, and just beyond, the tunnel bent to the left and then opened up abruptly into another large chamber. This chamber was dry, unlike the other large chamber they'd been in with the pool of water.

The chamber was also dark. Some light from the shaft made it to the entrance, but it petered out quickly into blackness. Jack took a wooden torch wrapped at the head in oiled cloth and placed the handle between his knees. Then he produced a small piece of quartz and a strip of steel from beneath the folds in his clothing and deftly struck them together. The spark immediately caught the oiled cloth, and Jack blew on the smoldering ember. Within seconds, the cloth lit up brightly. He placed the torch into a cradle cut out of the solid stone of the walls. The light barely reached the far walls of the chamber, and Christy and Danny saw what looked like a dead end.

"This chamber, tunnel, or cave, or whatever you want to call it, doesn't have that strange lighting that all the other tunnels or chambers have," Jack said. "Whether it ever did or not, I don't know."

"Grandpa, where's Rob?"

Jack smiled. "He's probably outside exploring. We've come to an understanding: he knows how far he can go and be safe, so I let him roam around. It may help him come around if his mental state is the result of shock from his entrance into this world. To be truthful, most of the time he just cowers over by his sleeping mat, so the more he ventures out, within reasonable distances, the better I think it is." Then Jack waved his arms in an all-encompassing motion. "So ... this is my home. Welcome!"

Christy looked around as curiosity pushed Rob's plight into the background for the moment. The chamber was filled with her grandfather's things: canvases, an easel, a canvas cot, various shelves that looked like they'd been brought from back home, and wooden crates, some closed and some open. One of the open crates had jars and bottles packed tightly within. Another open one had tubes of paint just thrown in randomly and a paint-spattered wooden artist's palette. In the back of the chamber was a cooking spit made of steel and hovering over a neatly arranged circle of stones, blackened by fire. No fire was in the pit at the moment. There were car batteries in a corner with cables attached, along with a long extension cord that trailed out of the mass of cables and snaked across the floor into the dark recesses of the cave.

Christy was awestruck with what she saw on the shelves. They were piled high with crystals, like the ones her grandmother had on display back home. But here, there were dozens if not more, and they were just stacked on their sides, creating piles of them sometimes as much as four and five high.

Danny, though, hadn't seemed to notice the crystals. Christy saw that he was grinning from ear to ear at the whole setup in front of him, and then he signed to Jack: "Can you show me how to use the flint and steel?"

Jack smiled but shook his head to say he hadn't quite followed what Danny signed. Danny pointed at Jack's belt and mimicked his striking of the steel on flint, then pointed at himself and again at Jack with a questioning expression.

Jack nodded his understanding, then said and signed, "Yes, I'll let you try it. It's quartz, though, not flint. Haven't seen any flint yet, but quartz works just as well. I see your neckerchief, but you look a little young to be a Boy Scout."

Danny nodded and signed while also speaking, "The neckerchief is Trevor's—a friend of Christy's and also my den chief. But I am a Cub Scout. I'll be a boy scout next year," he said, and Christy could hear the pride in his voice.

Jack nodded, replying with clarifying gestures: "I was a scout too when I was your age. Hmmm, I can see I'll have to brush up on my signing skills if we're to communicate effectively, won't I, Danny?"

Danny smiled in reply and then looked up to the ceiling area above the fire pit. A puzzled expression came over his face. He signed rapidly but also spoke out loud so Christy and Jack both could follow his conversation: "Where does the smoke go? Doesn't it get too smoky in here when you cook?"

Jack smiled and ruffled the boy's hair. "You're pretty sharp there, Danny. Actually I don't know where the smoke goes. It doesn't head up the light shaft. The draft is too strong coming down the shaft. I think that there are some hidden cracks up in the ceiling area.

The smoke just drifts up there and then disappears. I've lit a fire and tried to follow it by climbing all over the outside of this hillside but can't find where it exits this chamber I call my home.

"That I can't find where the smoke goes, but that it certainly goes somewhere, is another curious factor about the tunnels, chambers, or whatever you want to call them. That both this one and the pool have shafts going up to daylight is also stretching coincidence, don't you think?"

Christy, who had started listening to the conversation, signed some of what Jack had said, and Danny nodded his understanding again. Jack thanked her with a wink.

"And why is it that this area is spared the brunt of the wind and noise?" Jack said. "I've traced the pattern of where the sound is on a map I acquired. If you start at the source of the sound, the mountain, you can draw a fan shape with the handle of the fan being the sound mountain, and the fanned-out edge being over forty miles south of the mountain—and that farthest edge is close to fifty miles across.

"Inside that imaginary fan shape, the wind and sound have altered the plants and animals over thousands of years, maybe longer. Except for this small area, and we're smack dab in the middle of what should be the worst sound. And this small protected area just happens to have several chambers like this one. I've found four so far within an acre or two. Why? Was it planned that way? And if that's so, why is the pool not protected? Right outside that, as you've seen, it's very dangerous wind and sound. It isn't till you travel underground through the tunnel beyond the pool that you come out to the protected area that we're in here."

"I don't know from personal experience if there are any other areas in this world with these strong killer winds and sounds, but as I said on our way here, according to others, there are. I haven't gone too far beyond what I've just described, but I've had some contact with people from other areas of this world. Not much, since this area is dangerous, but a few have come through here. They all talk about similar areas with the same problems of sound created by winds. It's interesting, though, that nobody mentions another mountain with a large hole in it like the one that generates the sound north of here."

Danny had been staring at Jack, trying to follow his words by lip-reading, but was now shaking his head in frustration. Christy had only been able to sign every few words and then only if she knew them. Poor Danny was caught not knowing where to look.

Christy got Danny's attention then slowly signed and spoke: "I'm sorry, Danny. We'll have to be more aware of you. I'm just not fast enough to interpret while Grandpa is speaking."

Jack nodded and, looking right at Danny, said, "Yes, I'm sorry too. Just from the little I've seen so far, my signing is not as good as Christy's. Or, at the least, I'm out of practice. We'll work something out, though, I'm sure. You speech-read pretty well too, don't you?"

Danny nodded, and Jack smiled.

While Jack was talking and holding Danny's attention, Christy moved around toward the shelving and picked up a few of the crystals, absently fingering them and turning them over in her hands.

Her grandfather watched her for a few seconds, then commented, "Beautiful aren't they?"

"Yes, they are," Christy said. "Grandpa, where did you get all these? Grandma had a couple just like them on display in the living room."

"They were mostly scattered around the ground and in the portal pool cave. Most I've just collected from around the pool of water, but over the years, I've got the ones in the water by setting down the drawbridge and lowering myself over the rail into the water. When the portal was working, you couldn't get them if you were jumping in to get back home. They seemed to just not be there, but the water seemed to be gone for the few seconds that the portal was working too. Your grandmother told me about the two crystals the divers found while looking for me." He grinned. "They're just quartz crystals, although extremely beautiful and probably valuable to the right collector. I suppose I collected them because I thought that when I got home, I could sell them for something without giving away where I found them. I know that crystals of this purity are fairly rare and may have brought a nice chunk of change from a collector."

Jack sighed slightly and added, "I never thought I wouldn't get back home."

Christy saw that Danny was watching Jack closely, trying to follow everything he was saying but having a hard time of it. Jack, too, noticed Danny struggling to understand. He smiled at the boy and gestured at Christy, who signed a recap as best she could.

Danny nodded his thanks. He gestured for Jack's and Christy's attention. When they were watching, he signed and spoke, "How do we begin our search for another portal?"

Jack chuckled, seeming to admire Danny's grown-up attitude.

"Well, Danny, we start by talking to Clacker, an acquaintance of mine. I was already planning to take Rob if nobody came for him after a couple more weeks. I guess I should really have hoped that nobody would come since it now means that there's more than one person missing back home. But ... it's what we have to deal with," Jack said sadly. "Still, if anyone would know how to proceed, Clacker would. He knows or hears just about everything that happens in this part of this strange world. And you kids, especially you Danny, will like Clacker, I think. We first need to pack some food and things. It's quite a few miles to where we need to go. I'd rather not take any of you with me because it is always dangerous, but I don't see much choice."

Christy felt a surge of butterflies in her stomach and blurted out, "Dangerous? How?"

Jack smiled grimly again. "We don't have time for me to tell you all about what I've seen and surmised about this place. For now, just take it on good faith that there are people and things here that are not friendly. Mostly outside of the noise areas, though. And the good thing is that for the most part, this world is very sparsely populated. Christy's grandmother and I started calling it the 'Empty World' because there're so few people.

"The areas around here and by the pool are very deadly for some creatures, intelligent and otherwise, who would try to hurt us, so we're fairly safe here in the fan-shaped area that defines the noise area. Anyway, I'd leave you here, but I need to find you kids a way home, and that may mean a long trip in the other direction from Clacker's place. I will tell you, though, that the map I acquired some years ago came from a man who spoke French and swore to me that he came through a portal like the one we know about."

Christy felt her eyes grow wider at the mention of a French-speaking man, but she said nothing.

"It's somewhere beyond the Dead River, which empties into a massive swamp, and beyond that is a large sea. There is supposed to be an island just off the coast. I think that island has the portal, but I don't speak French and he didn't speak English, so we had considerable trouble understanding each other. It's a long journey from here, and as I said, it's very dangerous, but we have no choice if I want to get you back home. But let's save any more questions and explanations for the long walk and start getting ready to go.

"When Rob wanders back in, we'll see how he takes seeing you guys and what his reaction will be when he learns we're going on a trip."

Christy sat on her grandfather's canvas cot while Danny was learning the ins and outs of using quartz and steel to start a fire. She was looking at all her grandfather had carried from Earth to the cave over the dozens of times he'd come through the portal before it stopped working. Danny and her grandfather were crouched over the fire pit with their backs to her when she felt a tap on her back. She turned and there stood Rob, wild eyed and crying when he saw her.

Christy started to stand up as she shouted out in surprise, "Rob!"

Rob grabbed her in a bear hug. Through his tears and with his face pressed tightly against Christy's shoulder, his voice came out muffled: "Can I go home now, Christy?"

Christy didn't know what to do. She just let him hold her tight as her grandfather and Danny got up and came over to them. Jack put his hand on Rob's shoulder while smiling grimly at the young boy's question to Christy.

"Well," Jack said, "we'll have to explain to Rob the situation hasn't changed and you're stranded here like him till we find another portal. He'll be upset, that's for sure."

With Rob still hugging her, Christy spoke to her grandfather: "Let me try to explain to him."

Jack nodded agreement and gently pulled on Rob's shoulder to get him to let Christy out of the bear hug. Rob reluctantly let go and turned his attention to Jack, and then noticed Danny for the first time.

"You're the kid who moved into Christy's old house, aren't you?"

It came out as a shout, and Christy and Danny flinched ever so slightly at the loudness of his voice. Rob noticed their reaction and frowned.

"I'm sorry," Rob said. "I can't hear anything, including myself talking, but ..." He hesitated and turned toward Jack. "... I think it's coming back. I can hear a noise when I strike a rock now."

Looking directly at Rob, Jack said, "Good! You may be getting your hearing back."

Rob responded with a bewildered expression, and Jack gave him thumbs-up and smiled. Then, looking more at Christy, Jack said, "That's more than he's spoken in a week here. I think he's going to be okay."

Christy touched Rob on the sleeve to get his attention again and spoke gently, "Danny and I jumped into the pond, and got here just like you did. We have to find a way back home. I'm sure my grandfather told you the portal doesn't work from this side and we need to find another one."

Rob threw his hands up in frustration and shook his head side to side indicating that he hadn't understood what Christy said.

Christy looked up as her grandfather produced a pen and a small pad of paper from within his clothing. He handed it to Christy. It had pages and pages of short scribbled sentences, and Christy understood that this was how her grandfather had been communicating with Rob for a week now. She quickly flipped to a blank page and wrote what she'd just told Rob, then handed it to him.

Rob read it and stomped his foot in frustration then turned away from the three others and put his hands over his ears and began to sob silently.

Jack shook his head and said, "That's what he's mostly been doing since he got here."

As Jack, Danny, and Christy made their preparations for leaving in the morning, Rob ignored them. He only occasionally glanced at them as they stuffed things into packs and discussed what the day ahead would bring. But he wasn't the only one who was mostly silent.

Although she spoke with Danny and her grandfather enough to get things done, Christy was deep in her own thoughts as she again and again went over the events that had happened—and her culpability in first Rob's and now Danny's predicament. She could blame Cory all she wanted, but the truth was, only she was really to blame. With the excitement and nonstop new sights she and Danny had been experiencing since their arrival now leveling off, her thoughts kept coming back to the blame. There was no way to get around it. Everything that had happened and would or could happen on this search for a way home could be laid directly at her feet.

CHAPTER 15

"**B**eautiful, isn't it?" Jack said as they broke into the open overlooking a series of deep valleys. "Let's take a short rest."

They had been walking for hours through more lush overgrowth that was swaying in a now increasingly familiar way. Christy noticed that the farther they got from her grandfather's place, the more the wind caused the larger treelike vegetation to move and, in some cases, bend over dramatically. If the wind wasn't pushing against their backs, they may not have been able to make any headway against it. Despite the boost from the wind, Christy had struggled to keep up with her grandfather and Danny but had steadfastly refused to ask for any breaks. Rob was the only one who seemed to be having as much trouble as she was. But he was vocal about it, and her grandfather had to sternly admonish him a couple of times about his whining.

As she came up beside her grandfather and saw the land spread out before her, she agreed with him and was silently grateful for the short rest. Danny's hands were flying in a nonstop stream of questions for her grandfather.

"Slow down there, Danny," Jack said and signed with a chuckle. "Christy can't keep up with you, and if she can't, I certainly can't, either." He held up his hand to stop Danny from signing anymore. "I've taken us almost directly southeast along the path of least resistance, so to speak. Now we have to head a little bit more northeast out of the safe area and back into the noise. We may have to travel for a day or so in the bad noise areas, so I want to caution both of you to keep your ear protectors on no matter what."

They walked without stopping again for several hours. There was always something for Christy and Danny to marvel at as they trudged on. Rob kept his head down and didn't participate in any of the interactions between the others and didn't seem to notice any of the amazing scenery spread out before them. No matter what marvels they saw, the wind never let up. It relentlessly pushed at their backs for the most part, but as they began to alter their course, it blew sideways at them, making it more difficult to proceed.

Taking advantage of the relatively quiet conditions of the areas they were traveling through, Christy asked her grandfather numerous questions. He in turn asked her about her grandmother and mom and dad, and then finally got around to how she had come to be there. When Christy mentioned how Rob had been pushed into the pond, Jack swore several times and then apologized for the outburst.

As the shadows lengthened, Jack found a stand of bushes growing up behind a huge boulder. The plants had grown and flourished, protected from the worst of the constant wind. He stopped and set down his pack, groaning as he slipped it off his back.

"Ah! That was getting heavy. We're going to stay here tonight. It should be protected enough for us."

He helped Christy off with her pack, and she nodded her thanks. Danny had already slung his pack off and was looking around. Rob just sat down with his pack still on and closed his eyes, clearly exhausted.

Danny waved at Christy and her grandfather for attention, and when they were looking at him, he said and signed, "How far have we traveled?"

Jack signed and spoke: "We've traveled about fifteen or sixteen miles."

"That far? Really?" Christy asked.

Danny also couldn't believe it and signed so.

Jack grinned. "You'll find that you can do a lot more here than back home. I wonder if the oxygen level is higher here. That could be one thing that is contributing to us being able to do more. Plus you may or may not have noticed, but I think gravity is somewhat less here than on Earth. Those packs I packed for you would have crushed your spirits after a few miles back home, but here, you can walk amazing amounts of distance carrying a lot more weight than you could on Earth.

"Where you came through into this world is a good example. I think that the barren hilltop and circular depression or crater where you come through was once a pond. You come through several feet above ground and fall when you get here. If gravity was the same as back home, it would hurt a lot more than it does.

"I also think that where you come out into this world used to be a chamber like the one where the portal back to home is. All the rubble and broken stone in a circular pattern around the depression could be all that's left of a collapsed tunnel. With the strong wind there, it's possible that most of the debris may have over time blown downhill along with the water from the exposed pool." He smiled. "I can jump higher, and I feel much lighter than back home on Earth. How about you?"

Christy nodded. "Yes, maybe I do, now that I think of it."

Danny nodded his agreement, smiling.

"You mentioned the lightness in one of your letters to Grandma," Christy said.

"So I did, so I did," Jack said, smiling.

"I tried to remember everything I read and saw in the packet Grandma left for me once I understood what it all meant," Christy replied.

Danny signed a quick comment and scuffed his foot in frustration. Jack smiled sympathetically at him, and Christy answered his comment.

"I couldn't have told you about this, Danny," Christy said. "My grandmother asked me not to say anything to anyone. Trevor was wrong to ask you to follow me. Now I am also responsible for you being here as well as Rob."

She kicked the ground and fell silent, tears of frustration and responsibility welling up in her eyes, all the blame she'd heaped on herself earlier coming out as tears and sobs.

Danny hugged her as Jack looked on.

"I could have said no, but I wanted to help," Danny said.

Christy managed a smile. "I'm glad you're here, even though you shouldn't be. You saved my hearing if not my life when we got here."

Jack nodded his agreement with Christy and then added, "Danny, what you did just to come here was very courageous. Christy knew what she was getting into, sort of, based on all the information Lillian gave her and the photos and descriptions I sent. But you, young man, you made a quick decision to jump into a pond during a storm, following Christy here to help keep her safe, after only a short explanation by Christy's friend

Trevor. You took Trevor's word for everything and made that decision within seconds. That took guts."

Jack ruffled Danny's hair in admiration, and Danny smiled his thanks. Christy wiped her eyes and nodded at Danny, smiling her appreciation for her grandfather's statement. Christy noticed that Rob only minimally paid any attention to them, perhaps because of his inability to read sign language, or maybe it was his continuing anger and shock at his situation. Christy looked over at Danny, who was still grinning from her grandfather's praise, and then at her grandfather, who, after ruffling Danny's hair, had kept his arm loosely across the boy's shoulders. Seeing those two making the best of the situation, she started to become annoyed at Rob for his foul mood. Since they were on a mission to find a way home, she felt he should at least have brightened up some. It was that moment more than any, seeing the contrast between the attitudes of her two companions, that started her on her way to forgiving herself for their situations.

As she slowly came out of her self-pitying mood, Christy practiced some signing while she watched her grandfather making the spot he had found into as comfortable a camp as possible. Danny was in his glory helping the older man who seemed to enjoy the young boy's attention. Christy, for her part, was grateful to just be sitting, watching and trying to remember more of her signing. She knew that when she spoke, it was much more difficult for Danny to follow it. Her grandfather seemed to be very good at signing and talking at the same time for Danny's benefit, but she was still learning to sign and wasn't as proficient at it as she'd have liked to be. She glanced at Rob who sat alone, not helping, and he didn't seem to be noticing any of the activity around him.

Christy shifted her weight and winced in pain, her muscles screaming in protest. Despite the lesser gravity, the walk had taken its toll on her. Her legs and feet were aching, and she suspected that tomorrow they'd be aching even more than now.

Darkness came quickly. Because of the strong wind, they couldn't build a fire for extra warmth. They were still too out in the open. The bushes and the carefully constructed wall of deadwood that Jack and Danny had built afforded them enough protection from the wind to be fairly comfortable for the night, but there was no way they could risk a fire, even if they could get it lit and keep it lit.

Just before they settled down for the night, Jack told them what to be prepared for the next day. They were sitting facing one another, wrapped in the warm blankets Jack had brought. He started by pointing off into the dark. When Danny and Christy looked where he gestured, he began.

"Just about three more miles in that direction, the sound begins in earnest. We're going to have to be wearing our ear protection when we get there. So I will tell you guys what to expect. Danny, you may not really need the protection, but with your description of the extreme pressure you felt, I think you should keep them on."

Danny nodded his acceptance of the suggestion, and Jack continued.

"The wind isn't much stronger and shouldn't be any more difficult to walk in than what we experienced today, which was bad enough. But make no mistake about it: the noise is deadly."

Jack looked from Christy to Danny, and after they both nodded understanding, he continued.

"Good," he said.

Glancing over at Rob, who had his head down ignoring them all, Jack said, "I want you two to help me keep an eye on Rob. He's going to be a problem if he doesn't come around and become more involved with us as we travel." After nods again from Christy and Danny, he said, "Other than the well-worn trail, you haven't seen any signs of anyone else, or any manmade structures, except possibly the tunnels and portal. That will change quickly in the morning. We'll see plenty of signs of people but hopefully avoid actually seeing anyone. I call this the Empty World, but there are pockets of settlements and random groups of people roaming this land, and none of them will be friendly for the most part.

"But because we will be pushing to get to Clacker's place, we won't stop for explanations or even to sign anything unless we need to. There will be one exception. You don't want to come up to Clacker's place unannounced, so I have to send a message to Clacker when we get to the post office."

Danny laughed, and Christy looked surprised.

Jack chuckled at the reactions. "Well, it's not really a post office; more like a postal delivery service, somewhat more primitive. Although, if I do say so myself, it is more ingenious and elaborate than anything I've ever seen. It puts carrier pigeons to shame.

"Anyway, the terrain we'll be going through is for the most part flat. More strange plants are everywhere. Trees, or what passes for trees here, are all altered by the wind, and any creatures we see will probably be altered in some way by the wind or the noise. Remember, if I tell you to do something, you do it, without any questions—spoken or signed. Your life depends on it. Okay?"

Both Christy and Danny agreed in unison.

"Good," Jack said. "If there's some danger or any type of crisis, I'll grab Rob; you guys worry about yourselves and follow my directions. Now let's get to sleep. Keep the blankets on. With the wind, it can get pretty chilly at night even though it's technically summer here all year long."

Christy picked a spot and settled down with her head up against the log-and-brush windbreak. Then Danny settled down next to her left side for the night, and her grandfather next to Danny. Rob stayed a little apart but also within the meager protection. Christy woke up several times during the night as her muscles began their protest of the long hike the day before. Toward morning, as she shifted her position to get comfortable through the aches, she felt a body on her right side. Rob had crawled close and fallen asleep.

Christy woke up early the next morning with Danny shaking her by the shoulders. He grinned at her and held out a handful of what looked like dried apples and a cup of water. She took them gratefully, and while she munched on the rubbery fruit, she watched her grandfather rolling up the blankets and securing them on their packs.

"Grandpa, are these really apples?" she asked.

"Yes, I've found several apple and crabapple trees in the more protected areas around here. I assume they've come through somehow with someone and seeded themselves; or maybe they were deliberately planted. I can't be sure. There're blueberries and blackberries, too. Probably a lot more plants native to Earth are here also; I just haven't seen many yet. Or maybe these fruits aren't native to Earth. Maybe they came from here and were introduced to Earth. Who knows? One thing I've seen a lot of is bamboo. Maybe it can grow here so well because it can withstand the wind. It is all over the place in isolated areas, even this far north. You'll see some shortly after we get going. But enough talk; we have to get started. Finish your fruit and let's go."

Christy did what she was told and stood up to get her pack. Her legs protested with shooting pains as she limped, grimacing over to her pack. When she hefted it onto her back, she turned and saw her grandfather looking at her, smiling.

"We'll start off slowly so you can warm up your stiff muscles," Jack said. "I'm sorry we had to push it so hard yesterday. But in truth, it's not going to get any easier."

"I understand," Christy said. "In a couple of days, I should be okay. This happened to me at the start of soccer season in the fall. I won't slow us down."

Jack grinned and patted her on the shoulder. "I know you won't. I watched you yesterday. I pushed it as fast as I could, and you took it without complaining. You're a lot like your grandmother. She'd be proud."

Christy took in the compliment gratefully as she shifted her pack slightly to get the best balance. Jack warned them again about having their ear protection ready and pointed toward the trail, letting Danny start off first. He nodded to Christy to go next, then gave Rob a gentle nudge to follow Christy. He trailed the three of them out into the worst of the wind.

After only a mile or so, Jack stopped and made them put on their ear protection. The sound was getting intense. They continued on for several more miles when Jack stopped again. He signed for them to gather around him. He made it clear that he was going to take the lead.

The terrain was flattening out and they were following a winding path worn into the spongy ground. The foliage growing up did not vary much, but all of it was rubbery. Nothing larger than the height of a tall man could be seen anywhere in sight.

Christy began to notice that the scenery was looking familiar, and she realized that it was from the paintings she had looked at intensely for several weeks. The predominant plants, scattered across the ground in thick groupings, were similar to the ones her grandfather called "jibs," only smaller. They were cone-shaped, thick-walled stalks that had been bent into the shape of the letter "C" by the wind. They were a striking bright sky blue, more like the color of flowers than any foliage Christy had ever seen.

What looked like rounded puffballs with a fur coat were clustered thickly around the bases of the cone-shaped plants. Her grandfather moved slowly through the first few groupings of the strikingly blue plants before stopping and gesturing with his hand for the rest of them to halt. Danny bumped into Christy as they both stopped behind her grandfather.

Not sure what they were waiting for, Christy watched as her grandfather inched toward the closest cluster of plants. He was being careful not to step on any of the furry puffballs or the bases of any of the blue cones, as Christy quickly came to call them.

Slowly he eased himself down, squatting on his heels with his arms in front of him, the fingers of his left hand touching the spongy ground for support. He waited, motionless. Danny fidgeted briefly, and Jack motioned for complete stillness. Christy squeezed

Danny's shoulder in support, and they both waited, watching.

Suddenly Jack sprang into action. With lightning quickness, he reached with his right hand, grabbing one of the fur puffballs. The second he did, dozens of the puffballs nearby rose up a couple of inches, and without warning, a mist shot out from underneath them and covered the ground. Once that happened, the strong wind took the furry things and shot them forward. Some of them bumped into the cones and whipped over them, shooting forward in the air. The ones that didn't bump into any of the cones rocketed across the ground and either hit other puffballs, which then also sprayed mist and shot off pushed by the wind, or continued on till they were out of sight. Within seconds, none were left except the one that Jack had snatched. He was cradling it, trying to keep it from breaking free. It had sprayed Jack's pants legs and was squirming frantically.

Christy was fascinated. She realized this was the first live creature they'd seen, not a plant. Her grandfather was stroking its fur, trying to calm the animal down. It was the size of a squirrel, only with a more rounded body. It only took a few seconds of stroking for the creature to calm down and stop squirming. Jack stood up, putting the little thing into an empty canvas bag slung over his shoulder, and then motioned Christy and Danny to follow him.

They continued on through the bright blue cone plants, picking their way around them to avoid the stained ground from the mist sprayed by the furry creatures. Christy wasn't sure why they did that till her grandfather signed that the spots were oil and to be careful not to slip on any of it. With the strong wind, any misstep could have serious consequences.

Within a mile of where Jack had captured the little creature, the terrain changed again to more rolling hills. They began to climb up the gently sloping ground till they came to where it dipped down again. Just beyond the first crest of the continuing hills, they stopped, and Jack let them take in what took Christy's breath away.

Spread out in front of them was the first manmade structure that Christy and Danny had seen, except perhaps the portal and the tunnels. But what they were gazing at now was definitely manmade. It was a network of piping made from the bamboo that Jack had said they would see. Five-foot-high stakes driven into the spongy Earth were spaced about ten feet apart. Topping the stakes, and lashed securely by some type of plant strands, were the bamboo pipes, about six inches in diameter. As far as Christy could tell, all the bamboo was of that same uniform six-inch diameter. The pipes looked like nothing if not like the pictures Christy had seen of the Alaskan Pipeline, except they were bamboo and laid out in a crisscross pattern.

The whole network meandered into the distance and branched off in all directions as far as the eye could see. It was an impressive display. Jack walked up to the closest pipe setup. He pried off a cap made out of larger diameter bamboo and cut into a four-inch piece and fitted over the smaller diameter piping. The cap may have fit snuggly, or it may have been held securely in place by the strong wind.

Once the cap was off, the open piping began to vibrate visibly as the wind entered. Jack walked fifty feet down that straight section of piping, and at the first junction where it branched off into more than one direction, he pulled a flat circular piece of wood out of the piping. Then he felt the bamboo at the junction and nodded to himself, satisfied. Just by what she was seeing, Christy could tell that the piece of wood had acted like a block, and that by pulling it out, Jack had directed the wind into the direction he wanted. But as for why, Christy couldn't even guess.

Jack made his way back to the group with a big grin on his face. He sat down and motioned the two to watch him. He rummaged in his breast pocket for a small square of paper. Using a stub of a pencil, he scribbled something on the paper. Then he reached into the canvas bag slung over his shoulder and pulled out the creature he'd captured. Holding the thing in his lap, he used his fingers to explore for something. The creature squirmed a bit, but Jack held firm with one hand, and with the other, he stroked its fur till it calmed down. It looked like he was patting a fur-covered ball.

Once it calmed down, Jack continued his exploration of the little body. Cradling it with his knees against his stomach to help keep it from running away, he removed his restraining hand. With his now free hand, he plucked the small piece of paper he'd scribbled on from the hand gently stroking the creatures back. Then, very slowly, he slipped his hand with the paper under the belly of the creature. His fingers disappeared into its fur. When he removed his fingers, they were empty.

Jack stood up and, still cradling the furry thing in his arm, walked back to the bamboo he'd removed the cap from. Picking the creature out of his arm with one hand, he held it gently and placed it into the open end of the bamboo. As soon as he let it go, it disappeared into the bamboo. Jack peeked into the end and, apparently satisfied with what he saw, waited for a few more seconds before putting the cap on again.

Rejoining his three companions, he explained. "These little furry creatures I call bowling ball babies, they're harmless, relatively tame creatures who have a unique ability to roll themselves into a ball and secrete a slick oil-like substance and let the wind take them out of danger. That's why they are perfect for the pipe system."

Jack motioned them to follow, and they all continued their journey through the wind and noise, picking their way amongst the impressive network of bamboo piping. At one point, Danny almost walked in front of an end pipe that was tilted down toward the ground and was open with no cap. Jack stopped him abruptly and pulled him around it, out of its path. He signed to the two of them to stay clear of them and pointed out several more end pipes in the same downward configuration and without caps.

Christy was dying to ask what they'd just seen. She could see Danny giving her grandfather sly glances, so she knew that he was itching to ask too, but with the ear protectors on, and the fast pace they were keeping, neither had the opportunity to sign a question.

Three more miles and they left the rolling hills with the network of bamboo piping behind. Shortly after entering a stretch of terrain that vibrated and wobbled more dramatically than the slightly spongy ground they had encountered so far, they saw their first river of the journey up close. Little whitecaps danced and skipped sideways across the water in defiance of the natural flow downstream. It illustrated the power of the wind.

The river was an impressive width. The far shoreline was a good hundred yards away. Christy stood with her grandfather, taking in the scene. Danny was walking apart from them, slowly following the shoreline, occasionally stooping to examine some plant growth or other.

Without the ability for speech, they had all gotten into the habit of glancing constantly at their companions. Broad gestures worked best for quick communications. Christy was still very new at signing, so the almost complete abandonment of it during their hours traveling was a relief.

They followed the meandering river by walking along the shore for a few more miles. Part of the time, it brought them face into the wind as the river bent back on itself. Up to that point, they had always traveled with their backs to the wind or at least walking perpendicular through it. Christy had almost reached her limit of endurance, and the fighting against the wind wasn't helping. She wasn't sure why her grandfather was religiously following the path of the river and not taking the shorter, straighter way that also would avoid heading into the wind.

When Christy stumbled momentarily and came down on one knee, her grandfather signaled a halt. To Christy's surprise, he removed his ear protectors and motioned for the others to do the same.

When they were grouped around each other, Jack spoke and signed, "We've been out of the noise for about a mile or so, but I didn't want to stop till we had to." Then he looked at Christy and asked, "How are you holding up?"

"I'm all right," she said. "I could use a few minutes to rest, though."

Jack smiled at her and turned to Danny and signed, "You looked like you could use a break also."

Danny was about to shake his head no but looked at Christy and changed his mind. "Yes, I am a little tired," he signed and said out loud.

Christy looked at him and smiled her thanks.

Danny got Rob's attention by tapping him on the shoulder. Rob turned and faced the younger boy without any enthusiasm on his face.

Danny asked out loud and signed simultaneously, "How are you? Would you like to share some of my water?"

Ignoring Danny, Rob turned to Christy and asked halfheartedly, "He doesn't hear anything at all?"

Christy could tell that Danny had read Rob's lips, but he let Christy answer.

"That's right," she said, nodding. "Danny lost his hearing years ago." She hesitated for a minute then said, pointing to Danny and herself, "He's been teaching me sign language this summer."

Rob looked at the two of them with still mostly an indifferent stare, but he slowly nodded his understanding then reached out his hand. Danny grinned and gave Rob his water bottle.

Jack signaled for everyone's attention and said, "I know we backtracked a bit there, but if you stray too far from the river in this area, the ground becomes unstable. It's like walking on a water bed. It's much worse than the slightly spongy to wobbly footing along the shoreline of the river. I can't explain why the ground is like it is, but it seems that the top soil is floating on a lake. In some areas, it's more stable than others. Why it is more stable just at the shoreline of the river is also a mystery."

"What did you do with the little furry creature?" Christy asked. "And what were those bamboo pipes?"

Jack smiled again. "That was the delivery system I told you about. We'll see isolated pipelines running parallel with us and crossing our path from time to time. What we saw back there where I put the bowling ball baby, was like a mailbox or central clearing area. From there, if you use the right pipeline, you can communicate with any settlement around this world that has tied into the system "It's amazing to think that they have evolved like this in response to the strong wind. They also have almost imperceptible ears, probably in response to the sound. They are marsupials. I put a note into the pouch of the thing and sent it off to Clacker. Remember I said it was unwise to come unannounced? Well, that was our announcement. It doesn't hurt the creatures to use them in the pipes, and they get fed well wherever they come out. It's a rule of this world that most intelligent beings follow."

"Wow," Christy said just above a whisper.

Jack nodded. "There is an intricate carved map and symbol system and small painted dots of various colors right on the various endpoint pipes that indicate where each pipeline goes. Once you learn that, you can send off any message to anywhere in this world that's connected if you understand the switching of the blocks slid in at the junctions to redirect the wind in whatever direction you need. It took me years to learn it properly."

As Jack finished his explanation, he motioned for them to get up and follow him. A short walk farther and they came to another manmade structure that startled Christy and Danny. It was a sturdy bamboo bridge spanning the river. Jack never hesitated: he started across and glanced back to make sure the three youngsters were following.

Once on the other side, they headed down hill and into taller plant growths that could almost be called trees—but trees with branches that had looped over into the prevailing strong wind and anchored into the soft spongy ground. That the branches had been able to grow toward the relentless wind was a study in determination.

When Christy walked past the first group of them, she saw that the trees had some leathery leaves only on their leeward sides, protected from the winds. While she was taking in all the unusual characteristics of the odd plant growths, she at first failed to notice that they were coming into a small village built out of the bamboo. Once she did notice, she and Danny looked at each other in surprise. Finally ... people!

"Village," though, was too grand a term for what they were coming into. It was really only three small huts and one lean-to. The huts were all facing in one direction, their doorways away from the wind. Jack headed right over to one of the huts and stood outside the back wall. He knocked on the wall and stepped back, joining the others who just stood there, quietly not understanding what was going on. Jack kept just as quiet, not offering any explanations.

Within a few seconds, a tall nightmare walked around from the front of the hut and into view. Whatever the creature was, it gestured with its two arm-like appendages. Christy was surprised when

Danny signed and grinned at the thing. Jack smiled and signed at it also.

Christy was flabbergasted. Taking her cue from Danny and her grandfather, she stared in wonder. If she was confronting the thing without benefit of Danny's and Jack's reactions, she would have screamed and ran. Rob would have too by his reaction. He cowered behind Christy.

What had come around the corner was a creature unlike any Christy had ever seen or could ever imagine.

The creature's head was as shiny as a football helmet, what they could see of it, which wasn't much since it was covered with a soft fabric of some kind that showed the bullet-like shape of its head beneath. It had a segmented body, and both its legs and arms were in three segments. Unlike its head, its arms and legs were bare of any clothing or adornments, but they were covered with what looked like shortening, slathered on unevenly.

But over its segmented body was clothing of a sort that was very different from that covering its head. Tough-looking grayish leather hung suspended from what could be called its shoulders, hiding the top half of its trunk. Just below the grayish leather shirt, its body segmented, and around its lower trunk was an ornate belt holding up a dark green leather skirt. Clasped around its neck was a silver chain of sturdy thick links. Yarn-like material looped through the links and fastened a small piece of a much darker gray leather suspended over the shirt and covering the creature's chest segment. Small intricate designs executed in bright colors covered the small dark piece of leather in swirling patterns.

While they stood facing each other it signed "Hello" with its pincher-like hands.

CHAPTER 16

Jack stood, grinning, and signed furiously at the creature. Danny had a hard time understanding since it was signing only in the crudest sense. When Clacker responded with his own crude basic signing by using his pincher hands, Danny seemed almost completely mesmerized by the exchange.

Christy had no chance to understand and looked at Danny for guidance. When she saw him frowning and obviously struggling with the gestures, she just gave up trying and simply watched, waiting. Rob, for his part, also showed a fascination with the creature, and he stood staring at the whole scene with as much interest as Christy or Danny.

Finally Jack stopped signing and laughed out loud. He turned toward his three companions and said, "He told me I'd make good food for his nest young. I told him I'd turn him into chocolate-covered ants and stuff him into a box of Valentine chocolates."

Christy was about to comment when her grandfather continued: "I'm never quite sure if he's serious or not. Although, since I'm still here and he says the same thing every time we meet, I assume it's just a greeting."

Jack turned back toward their unusual host and signed some more. Christy noticed that his gestures were broad in scope, much less specific than actual signing. Jack bent down at the knees several times and twisted at the hips at various junctures in the ongoing communication. He clapped his hands together in various positions and used his individual fingers less than he would if he were using real sign language. He used his whole body much more also, turning his upper torso as he gestured, as well as the constant bending and twisting of his legs. He did a lot of mimicking of pinching gestures using his thumbs opposing his four fingers, which never separated into individual digits like would be typical of actual signing.

Christy was fascinated watching Jack, and when Clacker responded to a series of gestures with a string of his own animated movements, she understood the probable origins of her grandfather's twisting and bending, as well as his pincher-like hand movements. Watching the whole process made her laugh and think more of family games of charades than two people communicating through American Sign Language.

While Christy initially understood almost none of it, only watching with a curiousness borne of witnessing the strange process and somewhat frightening creature conversing silently with her grandfather, Danny seemed intent on more. He stared and occasionally mimicked a gesture or body movement, smiling as understanding came to him at various points.

Several times, her grandfather gestured, pointing in what seemed to Christy to be a reference to where they had just come from. When Jack pointed to her, his attitude as well as gestures seemed to deflate, and he frowned and looked sad. Christy figured that he was telling Clacker their story.

After a good ten minutes of gesturing between the two, Jack nodded and broke off the process, walking toward the three companions. He guided them over toward the lean-to structure, and the four of them huddled in it out of the worst of the wind.

Before Jack could explain anything, Danny began signing and filling in for Christy with some speech: "Clacker isn't coming with us, is he? But he knows where we need to go, I think."

"That's a sharp bit of understanding," Jack said. "I have to tell you, it took me a lot longer to get most of Clacker's gestures understood, and that came only after I began to understand his rudimentary sign language."

Danny nodded with a little smile in acknowledgement of Jack's praise.

"Danny is right," Jack said. "The gist of what Clacker said is that we need to go to the Orator. Clacker can't help us for two reasons. One, the Orator hates him, and two, Clacker's about to molt. Even though he's an adult and will never get any larger, due to his species evolutionary history, his kind still molt every couple of years.

"From what I can gather, since they became intelligent and their life expectancy increased to the equivalent of us, they have adapted to the longer lifespan by molting continually, which replenishes their bodies. If they hadn't adapted, their bodies would have worn out quickly with the much longer lifespan than their original ancestors, who were, from what I can gather, more like crayfish or lobsters than insects. Although, he looks more like an insect, doesn't he?"

Jack gave a quick look at Danny. "Danny? Are you following this?" Jack asked, no doubt realizing the complicated concepts he was talking about and trying to signing as he spoke.

Danny nodded enthusiastically.

"Good. The reason the molting interferes with Clacker's mobility is the same for a lobster. He is vulnerable in his soft-shell state, so to speak. He calls it the 'renewal state.' During it, he has to stay in his hut and barricade the door against predators. If he were to come with us and begin to molt, he would almost certainly die from some accident, or a predator would get him.

"Even if he weren't about to molt, if he came with us, the Orator would bullhorn him before he could get to within a quarter mile of his temple."

At that comment, Jack must have realized his three companions were bewildered.

Jack smiled. "Look," he began, "I'm going to have to explain a little more than I have up to this point. I haven't been secretive because I wanted to be. I did it so you could take in for yourselves the sights and wonders of this place without a lot of details that may have been beyond your comprehension till you actually saw some of this. Plus we were in a real hurry to get here, and the wind and noise limited conversation anyway."

Jack leaned back against the wall and motioned for the children to do the same. He helped them situate their packs and then began again: "You have seen very little of this world. Clacker has explained to me his impressions of these wind and noise zones. He insists that they are manmade, not natural, and that they are here for the express purpose of killing his species.

"He makes a good argument for it since his exoskeleton can't tolerate wind. It dries out his meager natural supply of body oils. That is why he covers himself from head to toe either with thick protective clothing or a horrible-smelling fat rendered out from a plant-eating creature that is fairly abundant here. The noise also is deadly to him, even more so than to us. Plus the portals are, or were, all underwater, which his species can't go into. So, despite the appearance, I guess he's not descended from a lobster," Jack said, grinning.

"He doesn't think—in fact, he's sure—that his species isn't native to this world, but he thinks the Ancient Ones are. The Orator is an Ancient One, as he calls them. They are humans, or at least humanoid. When you see one of them, you'll see what I mean. They are smaller than us, but they are what I'd call barrel-chested. They have very strong legs, probably to support their weight, which is considerable for their size.

"Their heads are roughly the same size in proportion to their bodies as ours, but more pointed in front, creating two flat sides almost like a deer or horse, except it's shaped more humanoid. Their two-sided face tapers to a nose and mouth that are about in the same place as ours. Their eyes are a little larger than ours, but their stereo vision must be less since the eyes are located well back near their ears on either side of their face. I have noticed that their eyes can see in the front by turning with very strong muscles toward the front of their heads. In normal situations, they stare out toward the sides, sort of like a horse. They only have three fingers—a thumb and two others—and their arms are short in proportion to the rest of their torsos.

"I haven't seen too many of the Ancient Ones, since they seldom venture into this area, but occasionally they come through and we communicate with actual sign language. By the way, one of the mysteries of this place is that everyone here—human from Earth, humanoids like the Ancient Ones, or Clacker's species—all have been communicating for dozens of years, according to Clacker, with American Sign Language. So far, I haven't been able to figure it out. I know too little of this situation. Some of the others humans here can speak the language of the Ancient Ones, but I have only picked up a few dozen words.

"Clacker's species and the Ancient Ones hate each other, although it seems that it's more one sided that the Ancient Ones hate Clacker's species than the other way around.

"In fact, the first time I met some of the Ancient Ones, they were coming into this area hunting members of Clacker's species and killing them when they found them, with a portable noise device like a bullhorn. I mentioned that's what the Orator would probably do to Clacker if he knew Clacker was coming to his temple. One blast of that horn and it kills members of Clacker's species almost instantly ... and even from a distance of two hundred feet or so. Any more than that and it only incapacitates, but still very painfully."

Christy and Danny looked at each other as Jack continued.

"The Orator actually is pretty nonviolent, for an Ancient One. I don't believe that he'd kill Clacker, but I can't be sure. Clacker certainly thinks he would. Anyway, it was the Orator who told me about at least one other portal and first told me about settlements of humans who speak French. He thinks that one portal—only a few days from here—may lead to France, since so many French-speaking humans are here."

Christy nodded. "Like you said in a couple of your letters to Grandma."

Jack looked regretful and replied, "Yes, I wish I'd tried to find that portal to get back home, but honestly, I thought that my portal would start working again. Stupid of me probably, but that's what I thought.

"Clacker says there are other species on this world also, and he is pretty certain that they are also not native to here. I haven't seen any, but Clacker says he has." Jack grinned then and said, "My one problem with Clacker is that he talks a good story. I'm never quite sure what to believe from him. His species is big on structure and orderly history. Of course, he doesn't know really where he came from, neither did any of his family nest, but they passed down stories of their history to him, which is where he gets most of his ideas about this place.

"According to Clacker and the histories passed down to him—and the Orator corroborates some of it too—this world held an advanced civilization, the ancestors of the Ancient Ones. It must have been a long time ago since there aren't any signs of it left that I've ever seen, except scarred markings on some of the cliff faces and tunnels, and a few scraps of metal that I mentioned before. No buildings, no other artifacts of any kind, have survived that I have found. The

Orator claims that there are some ruins of an ancient civilization scattered in isolated areas of this world. Clacker hasn't seen any signs of the ruins, nor have I, so I don't know whether to believe the Orator any more than I can believe Clacker in some of his stories. But regardless of what is fact or rumor, we know that portals exist because we've used one. That one of them might connect to France also seems likely since there are so many French-speaking humans here. Well, 'so many' only in contrast to other people who are here. So in that at least, I think we can believe the Orator.

"Whatever the situation or history of this world is, remember that I said I've seen signs of great, massive destruction. I think that possibly something really could have been here, some kind of advanced culture. Again, remember, we have the portals that I think can't be natural. Those suggest an advanced civilization of some type. The combination of some form of massive destruction, plus the passage of thousands of years at the very least, could have obliterated much if not all of a past culture here.

"How Clacker can say with certainty that the Ancient Ones are native to here is beyond me, but his stories, passed down from his elders through generations here, tell him that fact, and also tell of the animosity between his species and the Ancient Ones.

"So while I'm not ready to really believe everything he tells me as the gospel truth, I'm also not going to dismiss it out of hand, either."

While Jack was talking, he watched first Christy's eyes then Danny's. Christy was absorbed in the story, excited at hearing more about where they were. But Danny was clearly worried. Jack could sense it. It wasn't anything to do with his deafness and any lack of understanding of what Jack was saying and signing. Jack knew the boy was sharp, and so he asked him, "Danny, you understood a lot more of what Clacker said, didn't you?"

Danny hung his head at the question but nodded yes. He glanced at Christy but quickly looked down to avoid eye contact.

Christy looked first at her grandfather then at Danny, who was avoiding her eyes. "What? Tell me!" she demanded, panic and worry in her voice. "What did Clacker say?"

Jack patted Danny on the shoulder and gave it a reassuring squeeze before answering Christy: "It seems that most of the humans and even some of the Ancient Ones we may meet are going to either try to kill us, or take us and sell us as slaves. And we have a long way to travel through territory I'm unfamiliar with, since I usually stick close to my home. I did say that it's dangerous here, and Clacker thinks it's too dangerous for us to head over to the Orator now. I have been left alone because I live in one of the most dangerous areas, which is directly in the middle of one of the wind and noise zones. Now, after these few years, I have built up some recognition and acceptance from the longtime residents of this place, which also helps to keep me safe. But it means absolutely zip as far as influencing any decent civilized behavior out of anyone else beyond these few square miles. And you are likely to see more of this world than I'd hoped you'd see." Jack paused before continuing. "Danny was picking up on Clacker's fear for us."

"I thought you just said that you've been to see the Orator before and know him," Christy said, almost whining.

"Yes, but unfortunately Clacker says he's picked up stakes and moved from where he's been for years. Now it's a dangerous trip of a few days for us. But I see no other alternative. Only the Orator can give me any hope of finding one of those supposed other portals. And that's not the worst of it: Clacker doesn't know exactly where the Orator has gone. Only that he's crossed the swamp he used to live next to and headed off from there."

Now Christy looked as worried as Danny. Thankfully Rob seemed content to just sit and wait for the next thing to happen without having any understanding of what was being said.

"Listen," Jack said, "we may not meet anyone at all. This world is really sparsely populated. I've talked of French people, ancients, and others of Clacker's species, but really, the villages or settlements of people are few and far between. We're more likely to come across an isolated traveler or two than a whole village or settlement. I hope we'll be able to avoid seeing anyone actually, but that may not be possible."

Christy let out a sob, clearly not convinced by her grandfather's assessment of their chances of seeing anyone. Turning to face Danny and Rob, she said, "I'm sorry, guys! It's entirely my fault."

Jack gestured violently with a cutting-off motion. "No, young lady! If you want to play that card, the blame goes all the way back to me, not you. Then your grandmother, too, takes the blame for giving you all the information and paintings from this world. But the real person to blame is the thoughtless Peters twin who carelessly pushed Rob into the pond. When we get home, I'm going to kick that little brat's butt."

CHAPTER 17

Jack gathered the kids around him as they knelt down in the lean-to next to Clacker's hut. He took out his pad of paper and, turning to a new page, drew several lines and circles and then made a crude compass in the corner. He then spent a few minutes labeling things and drawing a few landmarks. He added a couple of mountain peaks and designated a couple of the squiggly lines as rivers.

Once he was satisfied with his efforts, he said, "I have actually seen some of what I've just drawn, but some is only what I've heard about from Clacker or the Orator, mostly from the Orator. We have a swamp to cross, which I've only seen, not crossed through. The

Orator's hut, or what used to be his hut, is right on the edge of the swamp. We should find a boat or maybe several left behind from when the Orator moved on. He kept a fleet of eight or ten dugout canoes and bartered for goods with travelers who needed to cross the swamp. He always got them back because there were always travelers coming to his side of the swamp, and they'd bring the boats left on the other side back here to get across. I imagine that travelers don't steal the boats because they're so heavy. They just leave them at the edge of the swamp when they cross, and then travelers going in the other direction have them available. Works out for everyone.

"Now, this is an eerie place we're headed for. If I interpret Clacker correctly, he calls it the Living Swamp, but I don't think we'll see real danger till we get on the other side of it and head toward the river beyond. I do know that nobody tries to cross the swamp at night, but that could be a superstitious thing."

When none of the children said anything, Jack nodded and began to rise.

"You kids stay here and I'll say good-bye to Clacker."

Jack scooted out of the lean-to but was gone for only a few seconds.

"Guess Clacker was ready to molt sooner than he thought. His door is barricaded shut already. There's nothing we can do here now." Jack stepped out and looked up at the reddish sun before ducking back in. "We'll stay here for the night and get an early start tomorrow, even though there's a couple hours of daylight left. We'd be hitting the other side of that swamp too late in the day today, if not in the dead of night, for my liking, so we'll tackle it tomorrow. Let's get settled for the rest of the day."

The kids, especially Christy, were grateful for her grandfather's decision, although none of them would admit it out loud. Once they were seated and unrolling their bedding for the night, Rob tore off his left sneaker and sock and began gingerly examining the heel of his bare foot.

Danny watched for a few seconds and then searched in the pack that Trevor had hastily given him.

"Ah, found it!" Danny exclaimed.

The others, except Rob, looked at him for an explanation. He held up a small sealed sandwich bag with Band-Aids in it. Then he opened the bag and rummaged for a large Band-Aid. Danny tried tapping Rob on the shoulder to get his attention, but Rob angrily batted his hand away without so much as turning to look to see who it was or why they wanted him.

Jack watched the exchange and stepped in. He stood up and, in one step in the cramped quarters, got to Rob. Reaching down, he grabbed Rob by the shoulders and lifted him up and promptly planted him on his feet.

Keeping hold of him, he said, "I've had enough, young man! You apologize to Danny, pronto!"

Even without his hearing, Rob clearly knew what Jack wanted of him. He jerked free of Jack's grip, turning away, but he did shout out, "I'm sorry!" Then he sat down again with his head between his knees.

Danny waited a few seconds then tried tapping Rob's shoulder again. This time Rob just ignored him for almost thirty seconds, but then he turned to stare at Danny. Holding up the Band-Aid, Danny pointed to Rob's bare heel, where they could plainly see a blister had formed and broken sometime during the last two days of walking.

Rob stared first at Danny, then at the Band-Aid in his hand. Danny expected something next, but Rob just sat there staring. Danny shrugged and gave up, placing the Band-Aid next to Rob's foot, and then turned away to continue setting up his bedroll for the night.

While they were all busy, Rob must have grabbed the Band-Aid because shortly thereafter, Christy looked over and saw the empty Band-Aid wrapper and smiled to herself.

The next day was the hardest of the three days walking so far. The wind continued, but they'd gotten used to it and compensated by leaning into it as they walked perpendicular to its force. The real problem was the footing underneath. It continued to be almost like walking on a waterbed that was under-filled. The truly astonishing thing was that they didn't see the whole ground quivering before and behind them. It seemed to be only their immediate steps that caused a quivering and buckling underfoot that immediately stopped once they were past and didn't set up a quivering ahead of them. Until they actually stepped on a spot, it all looked solid.

This was unlike the earlier terrain that quivered and undulated in wavy swells long before and after they stepped on it. Jack at one point called a halt, and they stood still. He cautioned them silently to keep still. When they did, the ground immediately stopped quivering underfoot.

Danny signed then: "It's almost as if it doesn't like us walking on it."

What they were walking on, what was causing their difficult footing, was some kind of moss. As far the eye could see, moss seemed to have displaced any grasses or other low-to-the-ground plants. It looked like a carpet that their feet would sink into for only a half inch or so, and then as they passed, the moss would spring back, erasing their prints almost as soon as it stopped quivering. When they looked behind, it was as if they'd not even been through where they'd just travelled.

Most of the moss was a light tan color, but some sections—sometimes patches as large as a few square yards—were tipped with a bright orange and occasionally had an even smaller tip of bright indigo. But those patches were few and far between and startlingly beautiful in contrast to the drab tan of the majority of their footing.

The moss continued to bedevil them and wear them down all morning. By midday, they had taken several needed breaks, and still they were dragging.

Christy's sense of wonder came and went in inverse proportion to her level of fatigue. Rob trudged on with his head down as much as possible, only lifting it up as was necessary to traverse the difficult terrain. Christy could see that Danny was completely fascinated. He was constantly turning side to side and shaking his head. She even saw him open his mouth in surprise as new vistas opened up before them, and around each turn, some new odd-looking plant waved in the stiff wind, or, having adapted over thousands of years, stoically stood its ground against the wind. Occasionally they saw some familiar-looking tree, stunted by the wind. And behind a few outcroppings of huge boulders, some the size of two-story houses, they would see some familiar plants taking advantage of the protection and growing profusely. They even stopped and picked some blackberries, which were a welcome treat after their arduous hike. In these protected areas, the moss disappeared, replaced by a riotous profusion of familiar Earth weeds and shrubs as well as alien plants by the dozens. And the footing was solid.

By the time they reached their destination, they were all ready for a rest. Fortunately for the group, the strength-sapping moss underfoot had gradually disappeared to be replaced by more familiar types of vegetation, including even some grasses. So while they were all bone weary, they cautiously approached the former home of the Orator with a lighter step.

The abandoned hut was tucked behind another of the boulder outcrops they'd seen several of on their journey. A few trees of odd shapes and alien origin were growing up all around the boulder and behind the hut. Just past the hut and stretching off into the distance, they could see the swamp. It was as eerie as Jack had warned them it would be. The water visible was dark and in spots brownish as the sun reflected off the dead vegetation inside the constant waves kicked up by the wind.

Sticking out of the water at regular intervals were the dead remains of what must have been some sort of local tree or large vegetation that served for trees in the world they were in. The stumps, although they didn't look like typical Earth stumps found in swamps, were shaped like shark fins and at most were sticking out above the water three or four feet. They were all aligned in the same direction with their narrow edges facing into the wind. They were a dark gray color, and what gave away the fact they were the remains of a forest, flooded long ago, was their obvious decaying-vegetation look, complete with signs of fungus or something clinging to them in irregular patches.

Ringing the whole swamp, as far as the eye could see, was what looked like typical Earth vegetation associated with swamps. Reeds of some kind and shrubs and clinging vines hid the shoreline except where things had been trampled or cut out for access to the water, like the spot they were entering. But because of the wind, the Earthlike plants had evolved to withstand it by developing thick stalks similar to the bamboo that had survived and proliferated.

Jack held up his hand, signaling a stop, and cautioned with a finger to his lips for them to be quiet. He signed that he'd take a look around and for them to stay put. He got Rob's attention and made sure that the difficult boy understood what he wanted before slowly walking off and disappearing behind the huge boulder.

When he came back around from behind the boulder, he had a pistol in each hand. He smiled and gave the all-clear signal. The three kids all looked with wide eyes at the guns. Jack smiled again.

"Sorry," he said, "I should have showed these to you before now. I told you this place can be dangerous, and I wasn't going to take you guys into danger without some protection."

Slipping the guns under his loose tunic, Jack motioned them all forward. "Let's go right down toward the boats; I only peeked into the hut to make sure nobody was there."

They followed Jack behind the boulder and past the hut down a short path, stopping just short of a weedy shoreline that held depressions of many boats, but nothing that floated was in sight. The section of shoreline cleared for the boats was only twenty or so yards wide, but it was empty.

Jack swore under his breath. "Now what?" he asked out loud, his disappointment showing. He grunted and said, "Oh well, let's rest against the hut out of the wind for a while and see what we can come up with."

The break from walking was very welcome, but Jack's disappointment was rubbing off on Christy and Danny. Rob seemed just tired, but since he wasn't really a part of any of the conversations, only getting the bare minimum of any meaning in the sign language or the body language, he couldn't fully comprehend their situation.

Danny had slid down, exhausted, right next to Rob and Christy. As Danny was about to close his eyes, he felt a tap on his shoulder. Turning slightly, he nodded at Rob, waiting. Rob looked uncomfortable, but he handed Danny a piece of notebook paper. Christy leaned over Danny's shoulder and read it at the same time. It said: *"I'm sorry, Danny. Do you think you could help me learn some sign language so I can understand all of you better?"*

Danny smiled and nodded. No sign language was needed for that answer.

Before either of them could say or do anything more, Jack began speaking and signing: "I don't see any other way across the swamp. There must have been a large party that came here and needed to use all the boats to get through the swamp to the other side. We may be forced to sit here waiting for some of the boats to come back as travelers need to get to this side."

"When will that be?" Christy asked.

"Your guess is as good as mine, Christy. Could be minutes, could be months, no telling at all. But, for now, we need to rest since we can't do anything else. Christy, you and Danny get some rest. Rob and I will take first watch for boats coming in. If any do, we need to hide till the party has left the boats behind and gone on their way. From here on out, we have to assume anyone we see is an enemy."

Both Christy and Danny nodded their okay and settled down against their bedrolls for a rest. Within minutes, Danny was asleep. Rob was nodding off too, and Christy watched, half asleep herself, as Jack searched through his pack and brought out a small but powerful pair of binoculars. He nudged Rob back awake and gestured with the binoculars out over the water. Rob got the idea, and taking the binoculars, he first looked through them quickly and smiled. He then brought them down from his eyes and turned them over in his hands, admiring them before settling down with his elbows propped on his pack and the binoculars pointing out over the water.

Christy and Jack smiled at each other. Rob had agreed to do something without protesting and without his usual sour face.

The next thing Christy remembered was her grandfather shaking her and Danny awake. She noticed that Rob was sound asleep, the binoculars resting in his lap. Quick signing brought the two up to speed, and Jack took the binoculars from the sleeping boy and handed them to Christy. He signed, telling them to wake him in about an hour's time unless they saw something coming across the swamp.

Danny was left to quietly explore their area as Christy took the first watch with the binoculars. Scanning the water's edge, Danny saw something small jump at the edge of the swamp in amongst the muddied-up tracks of what must have been dozens of impressions of the boats dragged back and forth over time, Danny walked down toward the edge hoping to get a glimpse of what it was.

As he was beginning to stare at the water, a pebble came from behind him, hitting him in the back.

Annoyed momentarily, Danny turned and signed, "What?"

"Can't see, move out of my way, please," Christy signed back.

Danny acknowledged her with a thumbs-up and stepped to the side as he intently scanned the water's edge looking for any signs of whatever it was that had jumped. Not seeing anything in the dark, almost deep coffee colored water, he turned his focus onto scanning the shoreline at his feet. Soon his training with Trevor about how to follow and interpret tracks and other signs and impressions in the ground had him intrigued. What he saw was at first a meaningless jumble of crisscrossing patterns and partial footprints. But after making a couple of assumptions based on what Jack had said this area was used for, he began to see some sense to the patterns and footprints.

Stepping around a few deep impressions in the mud, so as not to ruin the evidence, he followed other fainter impressions in the ground. He stepped slowly, scanning as he went off to the side a bit then back toward Christy and his sleeping companions, where the impressions all but disappeared. Stopping just next to Christy, who was still intent on scanning the swamp with the binoculars, Danny took a minute to formulate a working hypothesis. Then he tapped Christy on the shoulder, and once she looked up, he began signing.

"Didn't your grandfather want to get across as soon as we could? Before it got too dark?"

"Yes," Christy signed but then shook her head in exasperation and continued. "But we don't have any boats."

Danny smiled, his excitement getting the best of him. "I think we might," he signed.

He then began to gently shake Jack. Christy started to object, but her grandfather was already waking up.

"What?" Jack woke with a startle and looked at his watch. "Is something wrong, Danny? It's only been twenty minutes."

"Those boats haven't gone. I think they're on this side somewhere close." Danny could barely contain himself as his fingers flew with what he thought.

"Whoa, Danny! Slow down! I can't keep up with your hands," Jack said with a chuckle.

Danny pulled at Jack's arm and motioned for Christy to follow too. He brought them over to the water's edge and stood back from the deep impressions and footprints.

He began to explain with signing and talking, hoping they'd both keep up with him: "See those footprints? Most of them are heading this way, not out toward the swamp. It looks like a group of people took the boats past the hut here, probably carrying them on their shoulders. Where the ground is softer, you can follow the prints from the water's edge to past where we've been sitting. Those prints are too deep to be made by people just walking. They must have been carrying something, probably the boats."

Danny stood back, allowing Jack to examine the prints and impressions near the water, and he watched as Jack slowly followed the prints up close to the hut where things all disappeared.

Jack slowly turned once he got to where the prints disappeared. He was smiling slightly but still puzzled by what he saw. "Okay," he acknowledged. "It sure does look like that's what happened here. But why? Why take the boats inland here? Danny, you said you thought the boats must be close. Why?"

"It's the only thing that makes sense," Danny began, again speaking and signing. "If this is where people use the boats—either here, or if you're on the other side of the swamp, you use boats to get to this side—then taking the boats away doesn't make any sense. But what if you're a large group and you'd need, let's say, all the boats usually found here, but you're not going across right now and you're afraid that when you want to cross, some or all of the boats might not be here?"

Jack was grinning from ear to ear and then let out with his big belly laugh. He finished what Danny had started explaining: "You'd hide the boats ... to make certain you had them when you needed them!"

Jack took three or four large strides back to where Danny was standing with Christy and lifted the boy off his feet and swung him around before planting him back on the ground and giving him a big hug.

"Danny, you are an Eagle Scout in my book, young man. That was some piece of work there!"

Jack let the boy go, and Danny stood momentarily stunned by the older man's praise. Christy, who was grinning too, gave him an affectionate pat on the shoulder.

Jack brought them back to reality quickly: "Let's get Rob up right now! We need to find those boats real fast. This theoretical travelling party could be returning for those boats anytime. We would have been in serious trouble waiting here with our focus on the swamp and not behind us. If we find those boats, then this theoretical large party becomes all too real, and real dangerous!"

Christy shook Rob awake and scribbled a few sentences on the notepad she had borrowed from her grandfather. The boy was grumpy, but the word "dangerous" at least got him going without too much grumbling.

Once they had their packs on and were all standing in a group, Jack spoke and signed, "Danny and I will walk in front looking for prints or some other indications where the party might have taken the boats. Hopefully they're close. I saw the boats several times when I was here talking to the Orator. Those boats are big and heavy. It takes two full grown men to carry one. They can't be far."

And they weren't far at all. Danny, again using his keen observation, spotted several footprints less than a hundred yards farther down the shoreline. From there, it was easy to see the trampled bushes and reeds and the cut vegetation that had been hastily used to cover the nine boats they found. It was easy, but only because they were looking for it. Someone just passing wouldn't have noticed there was anything sitting there along the shore. The strong wind did help them some to locate the boats, since whoever had tried to camouflaged them hadn't secured the cut foliage all that well and some of it had shifted or blown away completely, exposing better views of the boats. All the boats had their paddles neatly tucked inside them, with two per boat.

None of them had ever seen a real dugout canoe before. Each was made from a ten-foot section of tree trunk, and painstakingly hollowed out by using burning coals.

They picked two boats that had been stored closest to the water and slid them right in. The mud and trampled vegetation under them acted like grease, and even Danny and Christy together were able to slide one into the water.

Before they climbed in, Jack gathered them around him and spoke: "Christy, you and Danny will get into the second boat. I'll take Rob with me in the lead boat. I'm going to tie the two boats together. With the wind at our backs, I think paddling will be easy, but I don't want to get too far apart."

He then took two hunting knives and the binoculars from under his tunic. Removing one of the knives from its sheath, he said, "Here, Christy, you take this; I'll keep the other one. This is in case something happens and one of us has to cut the rope joining the boats. If I think my boat's in danger, I may want to cut your boat free to give you a chance to get away from the danger. If for some reason, I can't cut you free, but to keep your boat safe, that needs to be done, then you'll have to do it. Understand?"

Christy nodded and Jack continued. "I don't expect any trouble since people of all sorts travel this swamp on a fairly regular basis. Just in case we may be followed—let's say because whoever hid these boats comes back and sees us on the water—I want Danny to take the binoculars and occasionally use them to look back behind us."

After giving Danny the binoculars, Jack used the butt end of his hunting knife to drive two spikes, hastily pried from the now abandoned hut, into the boats. One he nailed to the front of Christy and Danny's boat; the other he nailed to the back of his and Rob's boat. After tying the two boats together with a long length of nylon rope he produced out of his backpack, Jack gave each of his companions a quick hug and said, "Let's go! It's a large swamp and we want to get to the other side ASAP."

The swamp was eerie and beautiful all at the same time. It was Christy's first time in a swamp. She knew that Trevor, through his scout troop, often canoed various swamps in Maine and New Hampshire. She was pretty sure he'd never seen one like this, though.

The stumps protruding out of the water lost some of their appearance of shark fins on closer examination as the two boats were simultaneously pushed by the wind and paddled quickly past. The moss or fungus on the decaying wood was a florescent yellow, and crawling all over it were what looked like silver or steel balls the size of marbles. The sun reflected off the curious insects just like it would off metal, but clearly—since whatever they were, they were moving in irregular patterns—they were alive. Danny became curious and at one point tried prodding one of the crawling marbles, and it startled him and Christy by unfolding into what looked remarkably like a large iridescent silver butterfly. Once it unfolded, it launched itself or was forcefully picked up by the wind high into the air, catching the strong current. With its wings rigid, it sailed off at the speed of the wind like a stringless kite.

Even though the wind was a big help, it also hindered them. The waves that perpetually moved along with them also rocked them from side to side precariously. It took quite some time before they got the hang of constantly shifting their balance to compensate for the rocking action. The passage through the water in the boats might generally have been safe, but nobody wanted to chance what might be lurking in the water should one of the boats tip over.

Since the wind was doing a nice job of propelling them forward even as it threatened to dump them out of the boats, Jack was content to only occasionally put his paddle into the water and take a lazy stroke or two. He used his paddle mostly to push off of and guide them around the stumps that were in their path. After half an hour of repeatedly avoiding collisions with the stumps, he noticed a stretch of water well to their left that was a wide stump-less path that seemed to go straight on to the other side of the swamp. Motioning his intentions of changing their course, he started paddling in earnest and pushing off as needed to get to the more open water. Christy and Danny picked up on it right away and started paddling and pushing off.

It took them almost half an hour to reach the open water. Once in the wider channel with almost no visible stumps, they laid down their paddles and let the wind and waves take them.

After fifteen minutes or so of relaxing with the wind doing all the work in the wider channel, Danny took out the binoculars to scan behind them as Jack had asked him to periodically do.

Planning to make just a cursory pass over the distant shoreline and intervening water they had left behind, Danny scanned through the binoculars looking to see if he could find the Orator's abandoned hut. But something in the water caught his eye. Steadying his view as best he could, he tried to focus. But even with the binoculars, whatever it might be, it was too far off to see clearly. Yet Danny was pretty certain what he was looking at. He could see half a dozen or so specks swelling up and down with the waves, along with the tiny black outlines of what must be paddles determinedly stroking in unison.

They were being pursued.

CHAPTER 18

"**C**hristy!" Danny shouted, forgoing any signing as he turned to the front of the boat toward her.

"What?" Christy asked, turning so Danny could read her lips.

"Someone's coming after us!"

Without even replying to him, Christy turned around again and gave a tug on the rope connecting the two boats.

"What is it?" yelled her grandfather. But his voice was beaten back at him by the wind.

Christy couldn't hear what her grandfather said, so she signed, "What?"

Not even waiting for her grandfather to repeat himself with sign, she shouted, panic in her voice: "They're after us!"

Christy's voice traveled without any difficulty to her grandfather since the wind pushed it forward instead of hindering it. Jack nodded he had heard.

"How far back?" he asked, signing, realizing his voice hadn't carried to the second boat against the wind.

Christy conveyed the question with sign and Danny shouted toward the front boat: "Way back, but they're paddling real fast!"

"Paddle as fast as you can," Jack signed. "If we make it to the other side, we grab our packs and run. Understood?"

Christy waved her answer and then told Danny with sign and quickly spoken words. But he was already paddling furiously. By the lurching forward of their boat, Christy could tell that her grandfather was also paddling harder. Christy took up her paddle and started to keep time with the other paddlers. As she settled into her rhythm, she saw Rob up ahead in the rear of her grandfather's boat also begin to paddle for his life.

They had been paddling fast for ten minutes when the near shore came into view, but it was still a long way off. The sight of their destination gave them renewed strength, and they continued as quickly as possible. Danny chanced a glance behind and was momentarily crestfallen. He could see the boats clearly without the binoculars. They were gaining rapidly although still far behind.

Christy saw her grandfather shouting but heard nothing. When he almost immediately resumed his paddling, she shrugged and kept on paddling. The shore in front of them seemed to never get any closer, and each time Christy glanced behind, the pursuers were closer, their menacing presence looming larger with each coordinated and obviously powerful stroke of their paddles.

The last time Christy looked back, she could almost see the actual faces of the pursuers in the lead canoe. They were now so close that she could tell they were Ancients, based on how her grandfather had described them.

Soon her grandfather's canoe was within a hundred yards of the shore, and another quick glance behind by Christy showed that the pursuers were still far enough behind that there was a good chance that they'd get their two canoes onto shore before being overtaken. But now the real question was whether or not they could put enough distance between themselves and their pursuers on foot to escape completely. Or would their pursuers be able to overtake them on land? Who would win that race?

A few minutes later, Jack and Rob's boat slid into the shore and jarred to a stop. Jack jumped out and pulled on the towing rope to pull the other boat in almost instantly. He helped the kids out, and they all grabbed their packs and scooted up a small embankment.

"Run!" Jack yelled. "Follow me! We can't stop for anything."

They followed Jack, and he barely had to slow down for them. But despite their conditioning, ten minutes after starting their escape, they were all ready to collapse. Jack waved a halt behind a small stand of bamboo that gave them some protection if their pursuers came upon them. Jack took out one of his pistols.

"Okay," he said, "I've never been here before, but I've had numerous descriptions of where we need to go next to find the new home of the Orator. That's our best bet if we can't find a place to hole up, which I doubt we can do. If I knew these pursuers were armed and how heavily, I might try to scare them off with my pistols. But I don't think we can take that chance unless we have no choice."

Danny nodded he understood, but Rob was almost in tears. He'd seen the pursuers, but after that, he just had to follow everyone else's lead. Christy began scribbling a few sentences for him. Her grandfather started to protest but she shook her head at him.

"Grandpa, Rob has to know what's going on or he could get us killed. Plus we've made him scared and he doesn't know why."

"Sorry, honey, you're right. But hurry!"

Christy wrote quickly and handed the scrap of paper to Rob, who read it and nodded.

"Okay, let's get out of here. Follow me!" Jack said.

There was a well-travelled and beaten-down path, and they followed that farther away from the swamp at a slower pace than their initial flight. Unfortunately the ground soon turned into the same frustrating and strength-sapping moss carpeting that they'd dealt with on the other side of the swamp. Fortunately for them, though, the terrain was more rolling than they'd encountered in a while. It made for more difficult walking but also meant that they wouldn't be visible to anyone looking for them from long distances. Also, some taller vegetation would help hide them.

The plants weren't actually trees, but rather several different types of tall plants growing in clusters all along the worn path and serving the same purpose as if the group had entered a forest of small pine trees. Each type of plant had obviously adapted well to the wind. Most types seemed to be bare of any visible foliage. Only if examined closely would it have been evident that what once was foliage thousands of years ago, had through constant wind stress, and generations, evolved elegantly into continuations of the plant stalks or trunks and branches. The only way to tell where the stalks or branches ended, and the foliage began, was by the sometimes dramatically different color of the foliage in contrast to the stalks and by the nonstop fluttering and flapping.

They had been pushing ahead at almost a run for over twenty minutes when they reached a rise in the terrain that gave them a view behind of the swamp they were so eager to get as far away from as possible.

Jack signaled another halt. Taking the binoculars from Danny, he trained them on the swamp. His frown told the rest of the group all they needed to know.

"We can't hope to outrun them," he said. "They're still several rolling hills behind us. They must have stopped to secure the boats before following. But if they're determined, we don't have a chance. We need to think of some—"

Jack stopped in mid-sentence and tilted his head slightly so his right ear was directly into the wind. He quickly pulled out the hastily drawn map he'd done and looked at it for a second. Then he turned all around, as if looking for something or getting his bearings.

Pointing off the path through a slight gap in a large stand of the strange-looking treelike plants, he said, "Quickly! Take out your ear protectors, now!

Once they all had their ears protected, Jack signed to them: "Less than a mile, straight through this clump of trees, is another of those sound areas that are deadly. If we can get there, they—whoever they are—probably won't dare to follow. Let's hope when they realize that we've headed directly into the sound, they'll give up, turn around, and be content with getting their boats back."

With a nod and a gesture to move forward, Jack led them on into the increasing sound. Even the relatively short distance of less than a mile was a long stretch for all of them since they had spent time paddling for their lives and then pushing forward on foot at almost a run just to get to where they were. But Jack set a brisk pace and his young charges had to keep up.

They walked for almost fifteen minutes before Jack, signaled a halt.

He signed, "If what I, and others I've talked to over the years, think is true, there should be a cave or protected area around here not too far. It may have held a portal at one time. Now I'm just looking for a place to hide and get out of the wind and sound—unless we get lucky and it's still a working portal. If not, since it's getting toward night, we can maybe rest before we continue on with searching for the Orator."

The terrain had continued to be rolling, and the footing relentlessly sapped their strength, but looming up ahead, they soon saw a large bare boulder outcropping. Recognizing what it probably was, they walked as rapidly as the ground would allow toward the hoped-for sanctuary.

As they got closer to the outcropping, they saw that on the protected side, it harbored a profusion of more Earthlike plants. Gaining the protection of the outcropping, the group searched and found an opening in the rock face that turned out to be the entrance to another of the eerie, lighted tunnels.

They moved deeper into the tunnel for several minutes. Then, since they didn't encounter any widening of the walls or any other signs that a portal was ahead, they stopped. There was a bend in the tunnel just ahead, but they chose to stop right there and not go beyond it. Sliding down to the floor, all four of them relieved themselves of their packs. Jack pulled his ear protection away from one ear, testing. Apparently satisfied, he took his headset off completely. The others followed suit.

Turning so that Danny could see his lips , Jack spoke: "We still could be in grave danger if whoever was after us follows. But at least with that horrid moss, or whatever it is, there aren't any footprints for them to track us by."

The walls reverberated with and amplified Jack's voice. As the echoes of Jack's voice died down, they heard footsteps beyond the bend in the tunnel, and then a powerful yet not quite human-sounding voice spoke: "You are safe from those who were pursuing you, Jack. They went back to their boats."

Stepping into view, a figure, although human–looking, clearly was not. Its chest was broad with an elongated upper body and its legs short in comparison to a human's. Its hands only had three fingers. Its face was what was really startling. It looked as much like a horse's face as a human's. The eyes were large and black and set on the side. Adding to the horse-like effect was the elongated narrow face ending with a pointed mouth and nostrils.

The figure walked up to the seated group and stood over them. The expression on his face was unreadable by the three youngsters, who stared in fascination at the being.

Jack looked up and smiled, then said, "Your English has improved. I'm impressed." Then, addressing his three companions, he said, "Kids, meet the Orator!"

CHAPTER 19

K im Upton was waiting for her husband when he walked through the door. She hadn't been a part of the group that had gathered to see if Trevor had been telling the truth. Bob looked at his wife and knew she'd just spoken with someone who had been at the pond with him a few minutes before.

"Connie called me," she said.

Bob cut her off with an angry, frustrated gesture. "There was nothing there at all! This isn't going on any longer. I'm going to see to that. I'm going to report the lot of them!"

"Connie says something did happen. It was exactly what they were expecting, was what Trevor and she had seen before, or what Lillian and Jack Renfrew described in their letters. Why are you not telling me the truth?"

"Something was there because they wanted to see something!" Bob said.

"Connie says you saw it too!" Kim snapped.

"I don't know what I saw, and neither do any of the others who were there!" Bob stood facing his wife with his hands on his hips, determined to ignore her defense of the others. He let out a short breath, then softened his tone slightly as he said, "I just don't know if I should call Chief Peters first or go directly to the FBI." Just as fast, his expression became bitter again. "I'd ask you about whom I should call, but I know what you think. You've been taken in by the others and listen to them against all reason!"

"It's you, Bob, who are going against all reason!" Kim said.

"Me?" He laughed. "Are you joking?"

"No, I'm not joking. You can't have things both ways, Bob. On the one hand you want to be the first to profit from this world when people find out about it, and yet you belittle everyone who believes in it."

Kim stood facing Bob and mirrored his stance by putting her hands on her hips. Then she ratcheted up her attack before he could interrupt: "So where do you stand, Bob? What do you believe? Because I believe that there's enough evidence to show that this world really does exist. And if it doesn't, where does that leave Rob?"

Kim teared up and almost gave into her sorrow for their missing son. But she took a deep breath and continued. "And you want to talk reason? What's reasonable about calling the FBI? You know full well that if the FBI came into this that the pond would become off-limits to everyone but a team of researchers who would study and study for days, months, even years without doing anything. Or they would send a team of researchers through that portal, and we could forget about our missing children."

Bob was visibly upset with Kim, but her verbal attack made him think for a second. Wavering only slightly, he said, "Okay, I'll talk to Chief Peters instead. He doesn't have any kids of his missing, and maybe he'll tell me what to do."

"Do that, Bob, if it will make you feel better. Maybe Trevor and the Peters twins are lying about what happened. Maybe Rob, Christy, and Danny really have all run away. If there's no portal, if that other world doesn't exist, then they all must have run away. Because to think that three children would all have drowned fifteen or twenty feet from shore in that pond in one week is beyond belief. We have an in-ground pool, Bob! Rob is a virtual fish. He's been swimming his entire life. I don't know if Danny can swim, but Christy came over here when we had that pool party for Rob's sixth birthday and all the neighborhood kids came. She could definitely swim well, and she had to be only seven then."

Bob knew that to continue his point of view was fruitless. He turned and stomped out the door, saying as he went, "I'll be at the Peterses' house if you need to find me."

Bob said he'd be at the Peterses' house, but there was nobody home when he got there. He left and drove around town, periodically driving past the Peterses' home till at last he saw their car in the driveway.

When Bob knocked on the front door, Police Chief Wendell Peters opened it. He didn't seem too surprised to see Bob.

"Come on in, Bob," Wendell said, stepping aside to let Bob in the door. "I figured someone would either call or show up, seeing as I got a couple of messages earlier from Connie Walker and Katie Lake saying you all were going down to the pond to try and see what that thunderstorm would produce."

Bob didn't immediately respond, so Wendell asked, "Well, what happened?"

Bob didn't quite know where to start, how to approach what he wanted to say, since he was unsure of what Wendell's reaction would be, but he began anyway: "I want to know what I should do ... what we should do. I'm not sure what happened this afternoon when the storm came overhead. The others all think that the circle of light that appeared was what we were looking for."

"And you saw the light too?" Wendell asked.

"I ... I did, but I acted like I didn't believe it," Bob said.

"Why?" Wendell asked. "Was it anything you'd ever seen before?"

"No, it was the strangest thing I've ever seen, but I've never seen lightning hit water so close to me before, so who really knows?" Bob said.

Before Wendell could ask any more questions, Bob said, "We have to call someone. The FBI or something. If they've all run away, we're wasting—have wasted over a week now. And if they did jump into the pond, don't you think we need to find them? Send divers or something in there to look for the bod—" Bob halted, unable to bring himself to finish his sentence.

Wendell was shaking his head in sympathy. "Bob," he began gently, "if they're in there, we will search for them, I promise you that. And as to wasting a week, don't think for a minute that just because I haven't released any info to the press, I'm not actively searching for them. I have inquiries out all over New England and even beyond."

Bob nodded in gratitude, and then Wendell continued. "Listen, Bob, because I admit my kids, especially Cory, can be liars—and as much as I hate to admit it, I don't know if I can believe the story they're telling about this thing—I'm leaning toward bringing in a diver, just in case. Hopefully that won't turn up anything, but then it will at least have ruled out that possibility."

Bob nodded. "Good, that covers the bases, but after what I just saw today, there ... there may really be another world. And they're all three there. I ... I don't know. Do you agree with the others that we should not call in the FBI or someone else who may be able to mount a rescue? Do you believe that any type of government authorities we bring in would only ruin our chances of finding the kids? Do you think we should try to find them there ourselves, like the rest of the group of us do?"

"Whoa! Bob, slow down the questions. I don't know what I believe, but I can't see how bringing in some higher authorities would hurt anything, assuming there really is something to this portal thing."

Just then, Abigail Peters stormed into the room. She had obviously been eavesdropping because she started by saying, "What do you mean that you think the FBI or some other government authority couldn't hurt? Are you not thinking clearly? Of course it would hurt! Wendell, don't be stupid or naive!"

Abigail then turned toward Bob and addressed him directly: "Bob, do you think for a minute that anyone would give a hoot about your kid if there was a portal to a strange world in that pond? I thought we'd gone over this when the kids went missing! And as for sending down a diver ... none of those kids are in that pond, I'm certain of it. I've been watching that pond for years, and I saw Jack Renfrew jump in and never come out—never! I don't care what anyone says about him probably sneaking out while I wasn't looking. And remember, a diver did go and search extensively after Jack Renfrew disappeared. That diver found nothing.

"So," she continued, "don't go getting the FBI involved, especially if there's a chance to get your kid, and the others, back. I believe my boys' accounts of what happened the night your boy disappeared, even if Wendell doesn't. I know my boys can be liars, but they're telling the truth here ..." Then she added with a frown, "... although they are hiding something, I think."

Abigail sighed and looked at her husband. "I don't want to hear another thing about the FBI or any divers," she said, then promptly left the room.

Wendell and Bob watched her go. Bob leaned in close to Wendell and whispered, "I don't care what she says. I'm this close to calling the FBI." And he held up his hands about an inch apart from each other.

Wendell then whispered back, "What if it really is a portal?"

Bob thought for a second. "Well, if they haven't run away and they haven't drowned, and the detective and the rest of them don't want to take their own action, I'm going to make sure I'm there if and when it opens up again. I want to see what's under that pond even if we have to drain it. And I'm not going to just stand there on the dock and watch. If the doorway—or whatever it is—becomes exposed when it's drained, I'm going to jump in. I'll see this place for myself."

CHAPTER 20

The Orator bowed slightly at the waist in response to the introduction, then addressed Jack's observation: "I have had practice—much practice over many cycles. Many of your species, and my own, have visited me on a regular basis. And, of course, I was next to a well-traveled route through the swamp. Even those of your world you call Frenchmen have wanted to communicate in English. And it has been several cycles since we have seen each other. Am I using verb tenses correctly?"

Jack smiled and replied, "Yes, you are. 'Have had,' 'have wanted,' 'have seen,' … very good use."

The Orator nodded. "I am content, then. Compared to most, it is a terrible language to learn. The gesture language you call sign language, which most everyone here on my world has adopted over the last fifty cycles, is much more direct and…" Struggling to find a word, he finally finished the sentence: "…elegant." Then he asked, "Was that an appropriate usage of the word?"

Jack nodded. "Yes, it was the most appropriate word. I would have used it myself."

The Orator mirrored Jack's head movement, clearly pleased with the response. Then he directed his gaze at the three young humans. "Children! I believe that is what you call your immature ones. Are any of them of your descent?"

"Yes. Christy, the female, is my granddaughter—my child's child. The two males—Danny the younger one, and Rob—are friends of Christy's."

The Orator nodded in understanding. Danny took the opportunity to sign a greeting while saying his name and prompted Rob with a nudge. Rob shied away from it instinctively but gave the simple ASL sign for hello.

"I'm very glad to meet you," Christy said. "My grandfather has told us about you." Then she blurted out, "I hope you can help us get back home, please!

The Orator opened his mouth and out came a loud hissing sound that was just like static from a radio. Christy gave a small cry of surprise, and her grandfather put a hand on her arm.

"Honey, don't be alarmed. I believe that is how he laughs. The Ancient Ones don't seem to vocalize laughter the way we do. If you notice, his normal speech comes out sounding deep and raspy all at the same time—and with an echoing quality to it. Clearly their vocal chords are much different than ours."

The Orator waited for Jack's explanation to end before he added, "But they are enough alike that I am able to mimic your speech." Then the Orator directed his words to Christy: "I did not mean to startle you. I was simply struck by how so like our young you are. They, too, get right to the point without the ... I think the phrase is 'beating around the bush' ... that adults of all species like to call ... in your language, the term would be ... social graces."

The Orator promptly seated himself opposite the little group and continued. "You are tired, so we will stay here for now. No beating around the bush, though. I knew of your coming. Jack, your friend the Cleaner—the one you call Clacker—sent me a message through the system. He didn't know if it would get to me, but it did. It is good that he did not try to tell me in person. I might have never let him get close and wouldn't have known you were coming. Knowing Clacker had sent you through the swamp to search for me, I reasoned that you would take shelter in this, the closest protection zone on your map. I did not suspect you would face danger crossing the swamp."

"But we did!" Christy said.

The Orator nodded and raised a hand. "Yes, I know. Those who followed you were of my race, but I hold no power over them, so it was good that you were far enough ahead to get to the zone before they caught up with you. I watched you enter the zone from up above us. The wind is even more fierce on top, but it was the only vantage point I could use to watch for you. And, of course, the sound is always present in these areas."

"Wait," Jack said. "We haven't seen any of the system tubes for days now. How did you get a message through one?"

"They were but two thousand paces from you the whole of your journey from Clacker's hut. But you would not have seen them with the rising and falling of the ground between. I travel each dawn to check on them. Occasionally I have a message. That you did not know they were near did not matter. They would have been of no use to you in any case. You took the most direct path here."

"Sir?" Christy said.

The Orator focused on her. "Ah, the term 'sir' is a honorific, if I heard you correctly. If so, polite Christy, what do you wish to say?"

"Would it be all right for me to write some of what you are saying so that Rob and Danny, if he can't read your lips, can follow along?" she asked.

The Orator seemed startled, then asked, "Cannot the two young males understand me?"

Jack answered for them: "Danny and Rob both cannot hear. Danny's hearing loss is irreversible, and he can read lips and sign. Rob's hearing was damaged when he came through the portal. He's had a few encouraging signs that it's getting better, but he can't read lips or sign yet. I think he's hoping he won't have to do either."

Danny leaned forward and spoke and signed, "I have followed some of what you said. But your mouth is very different than ours, and it's difficult for me."

The Orator nodded and said, "Of course you can write my words for them, Christy. And I am sorry for my oversight. I did not realize when Danny spoke as well as signed that he could not hear me. Perhaps I should have realized it. I will sign as well so that Danny does not have to read your notes as I speak." He then waited.

Christy took out a pen and the pad of paper she had been carrying all along and got ready. She motioned for Rob to come close to watch her as she wrote.

Christy signaled she was ready, and the Orator continued. "I have come into more information about the possible working portal that I have spoken to you about in the past, Jack. I now am certain of where it lies. When I learned that you were on a journey to find me, I sketched as detailed a map of it as I could. You must understand that even though rumors of its working persist, I have never met any being who actually said that they came to my world through it. The French people I've spoken with, and mentioned to you many cycles before, have grown up in this world and are only telling me what has been passed down to them through stories from their elders who heard tales from their ancestors.

"And I believe that you have told me you met one or more of this community at one time and were told the same stories of a working portal. It was not even from those of the French community that I learned exactly where the portal is. Those of the community either don't even know, or for some reason the information about where the portal lies is taboo for them to talk about. That in itself should make you very cautious in your approach to the portal. I can show you the map and explain some things about the area, but you are going to have to find the way across."

"The way across?" Jack asked. "Across what?"

The Orator hesitated momentarily, then said, "The portal lies on an island separated from the mainland by a dangerous strait. I believe that is what you would call the body of water between the island and the mainland. This strait has fierce currents that run counter to the never-ending wind and are made worse by it. I included in my sketch the direction of the wind and the currents. It may aid you in some fashion. No boat can make it across, I have been told. The mainland shore overlooking the strait and out across it to the island is, for many days journey in each direction, a range of sheer high cliffs that the waters crash against unmercifully. There must be a way across. But what that is, I do not know."

"Then this is the portal I've heard of off and on over the years. How do you know of this?" Jack asked.

"Who, if not the French community, gave you this information?"

If she could interpret the Orator's expression correctly, it was that of sadness at what he was about to say.

"I am reluctant to speak this because it only will create more fear in you. But you must be told so that you can be as cautious as possible. I would wish that you did not have children with you, Jack. You humans are like my species: you try to protect your young at all costs. I see no way you can shield them from this danger if you wish to get to your own world again."

The Orator hesitated again, then said, "It was one of the Cleaners. It was a male of the species. One day, more than a cycle ago, he stumbled into my protected area. He was near death from malnutrition and abuse from those he called his enslavers. As you know, Jack, I am able to understand the language of the Cleaners fairly well. Know thy enemy, I guess. He communicated to me that he had been a slave for half a cycle to a village of my species who guard the way across the strait. The only reason he was kept alive, according to his account, is that he was to be a sacrifice as part of some ritual that he did not understand. I had never heard of this village or of this custom of sacrifice. But I believed him. He was in terrible condition.

"He escaped with the help of a member of the village who sympathized with his plight and did not approve of the ritual of sacrifice. If he had come into my home as a healthy Cleaner, I would have killed him if I could. But no matter my hatred, I could not abandon someone as in need as he was. As I helped nurse him to recovery over the span of many sunrises and sunsets, he described the area of his captivity and the view of the island in such detail that I was able to make the map I will give to you."

The Orator cleared his throat, at least that's what is almost sounded like to the four listening. Then he continued.

"We will stay here while you rest. Sunset is almost here. At sunrise, you can go on your journey. If you do not avoid the villagers somehow, I fear for your safety. Past the village right next to the cliff's edge overlooking the island, there is an open area built up with what my patient described as religious monuments. He had been taken there several times and forced to clean and repair wooden structures. He later realized that the area was the place of sacrifice. It is maybe, by your method of counting, several thousand paces beyond the village. That is where you can study the island and hope to devise a way to get across.

"One thing you will not have to contend with is the sound. My patient told me that even though the wind is as fierce as everywhere else, the sound is silent. It may be one of the reasons some of my species have chosen to live there, as well as because of their duties to guard the strait."

Unnoticed by the others, Christy had begun to sob silently. Finally Danny saw and tapped her on the shoulder. She looked up.

"It's my fault we're here," Christy said, "and I promised Trevor back home that I'd bring Rob back. And I've messed up even further by dragging you into this too, Danny! And now it sounds like we could be hurt or worse—all because of me!"

Danny shook his head and signed slowly: "I chose to come here. It's not your fault I'm here. Trevor asked me to protect you. He was right to. You can't blame him, either."

Christy took little comfort from Danny's words but smiled at him anyway. Danny, sensing she wanted to be left alone, sat down next to Rob and, through gestures, asked if Rob wanted to learn more signing. Rob nodded yes, and the two of them faced each other and began.

Jack watched it all and smiled, signing with the Orator and explaining what had just taken place. The Orator nodded understanding, and then the two of them silently conversed, their hands flying, sometimes using sign language and other times reverting to a modified sign language that had evolved for convenience of the Ancients who had adopted it.

Before too long, the arduous day took its complete toll, and all of them but the Orator settled down for the night. The Orator sat quietly next to the sleeping forms for a while then silently left them to their rest.

The next day, the group said good-bye, thanking the Orator. He had resupplied them with some fresh water and dried meat and fruit for their trip to the coast. Shortly after getting underway, they had to turn more northerly, which put them going almost directly into the wind, not perpendicular to it. The added difficulty forced them to stop more often to rest than they wanted to. By midday of the second day out from the Orator's cave, they came out of the zone and could take off their ear protection and once again converse out loud.

The terrain thankfully was more solid than they had encountered almost since they'd left Jack's cave. With the wind directly in their faces, they soon began to smell water.

Jack sniffed deeply while they were taking a short break. "Ah! It's been too many years since I've smelled that smell. The water up ahead definitely is saltwater. Smells just like the ocean to me." Then, motioning them forward, he said, "This is where we really begin to be cautious. We must be getting close to the cliffs and the village."

Looking at the map the Orator gave them, he said, "Soon I think we should veer off slightly to our left and come out to the cliffs just about a day's travel south of what should be the village. I don't think there's any point in trying to go to the village first. Let's go see this site or shrine or whatever it is, and the island beyond it."

Within half an hour of veering off to avoid the village, they came within sound of the water. Finding a patch of growth that could hide them, Jack motioned them all to sit down. Then, after cautioning them to silence by a finger to his lips, he used sign language to communicate: "I want you all to stay here while I go farther on and see what's up ahead."

He took out one of his pistols, and with another cautioning finger to his lips, he was off.

Christy quickly wrote a few words to get Rob up to speed on what they were doing in case he hadn't caught the gist of it by her grandfather's expressions and gestures. Rob nodded. Danny passed around a canteen of water, and the three of them shared a drink. Then Rob tapped Danny's shoulder and, using the notebook, asked if Danny would teach him some signs. Danny spent the rest of the time waiting for Jack by giving Rob some signs to practice and writing down on the notebook what they meant.

Jack was gone for just over an hour. When he returned, he risked speaking while he was signing: "The site that appears to be some sort of shrine or monument is within a few minutes' walk from here. I watched it for any signs of activity, and for the forty or so minutes I was there, there wasn't any movement that I could see. No guards, etc. There are several small buildings made of wood. Most likely, those were the buildings that the captured Cleaner had to repair. I can't be sure that nobody was inside. It does appear that there is some sort of altar that has some dark stains all over it. Probably a sacrificial altar. But there's so much more to the site, including, I hope, our way to the island."

Christy and Danny jumped a bit at the last statement, but Jack waved aside any questions for the moment and continued.

"We'll take up a position hidden from anyone who might be at the site and see as much as we can. I have the binoculars, and we'll take a close look at the island to gather as much information as we can about it too. Remember, once we get to our spying vantage point, we only use signing till nightfall, when we can see if any fires come up in the buildings. There are several windows on each building with tied-down oilcloth covering them, but we should see some light coming through if there's anyone in them."

"You saw a way across to the island?" Christy asked.

Her grandfather hesitated and frowned before replying. "I hope so, but wait till you see what I saw. Then maybe we should come back here so we can discuss it a little more easily before going back to watch for signs of anyone guarding the place. Let's leave our packs hidden here, and I'll lead you there. Again," he cautioned, "no talking! Follow me."

Christy scribbled a quick two words on a page of her notebook—*"No talking"*—and showed the page to Rob as they followed her grandfather.

It only took a few minutes. Jack led them up a small rise in the land, and they came to the impressive cliffs that constituted the entire shoreline for miles in each direction. Just offshore was the equally impressive island. They hid amongst some five-foot-tall plants whose adaptation to the wind had been to group themselves close together and intertwine their branches for mutual support. Since the foliage of the plants was now just thin leather-like ribs running the lengths of the branches, the group was able to position themselves behind the plants and still have a view of the site in the clearing below as well as still be able to see the island and the strait between the island and the cliffs.

The clearing was roughly a circle a hundred yards in diameter. One part of its circular perimeter came right to the cliff's edge. Evident to all of them was the fact that there was either continual maintenance of the area or a considerable amount of foot traffic to keep the clearing from becoming overgrown with the persistent moss like ground cover.

Almost directly in the center of the clearing, and dominating the view with its impressive stature, sat a massive rectangular stone. It was at least twenty feet long, almost half that wide, five feet high, and made of a single block of what looked like polished granite. The stone was laid down with its short side pointing toward the cliff's edge a mere sixty or seventy yards away. While they all were focused on the massive stone, Jack tapped each of them on their shoulders and pointed to another smaller, less impressive stone, set off toward the edge of the clearing.

This one—with it ominously dark stains and measuring about eight feet long, four feet wide, and four feet high—was clearly the stone used for sacrifices. Turning back to the larger stone, they saw resting on top of that massive block of granite, was an open rectangular framework structure with wheels that enclosed what looked to be some sort of seating. On top of the framework, and collapsed against its sides and partially obscuring the seating underneath, was something made of what looked like silver cloth. The really astonishing thing about the framework was that it was made of metal piping. It was the first metal they'd seen since coming to this world other than the small nails they'd used on the dugouts.

The piping gleamed in the sunlight, and it clearly was well maintained and looked impressive with the sunlight reflecting off of it. The whole structure was tied down with ropes staked into the ground at intervals around the block of granite it rested on.

Off toward the edge of the clearing nearest the cliffs was what could only be described as a ramp on wheels. Unlike the framework on top of the granite block, the ramp was made of wood and lashed together with ropes. The wheels were crude, thick wooden disks that could have been, and probably were, sawed from a good sized tree trunk. The ramp itself was as long as the large block of granite and just as wide as the width of the block.

From their vantage point, they could see a walkway paved with slate or some other kind of smooth stones leading away from the massive block of granite straight to the cliff's edge. The path or walkway was at least as wide as the twenty-foot length of the stone. The walkway sloped dramatically downward. To enhance the angle of the slope, the path had been dug into the clearing ground so that by the time it reached the cliff's edge, it had to be at least fifteen feet lower than the surrounding clearing's edge. It looked like a huge twenty-foot-wide ramp angling down from the stone block straight to the cliff's edge.

Nearer to where they hid stood two small buildings, and off near the cliff's edge, just next to the wooden ramp, sat another small building. None of them looked particularly like dwellings. They looked more like small maintenance huts. But they each could have held a person or two inside.

They studied all the features of the clearing and then turned their attention to the island and the imposing water in between. The strait was less than an eighth of a mile wide, but the water flowing between the sheer cliffs and the shoreline of the island roiled with the narrow passage and constant wind. There didn't seem to be any way to cross safely. The island itself was only about a mile or so long and couldn't have been more than half a mile wide at its widest point.

Jack pointed to the near shoreline's northernmost point visible to them. At that spot along the small strip of beach stood a manmade structure. It looked to be all posts and beams, nothing with finished walls or even a roof. But there was something resting inside that framework, completely encased by it. Jack passed the binoculars for everyone to get a closer look.

After they'd each taken a turn looking, Jack began to point out other features of the island. The most obvious and impressive one was the hill rising up from the center a hundred feet or more and looming over the surrounding island. On the side directly facing them, the hill had been cut straight down from the top to the surrounding land at its base, creating a flat surface on the side of the hill. Generating even more excitement was the fact that, at the base of that flat surface, there was a door. The door was dwarfed by the hillside but had to be at least eight or ten feet high and almost as wide. Even using the excellent binoculars they possessed, it was difficult to tell, but it looked like the door was made of wood and covered with intricate carvings. At the top of the hill, an almost perfectly round hole led down into the hill itself. They saw flashes of light coming from the hole in the hill.

Since the island was devoid of any plant life taller than a full grown man, its many features were readily noticeable. Between the hillside with the door and the shoreline was a flat area the size and shape of a football field, which was almost white with a pinkish hue. It stood out in contrast to the tan and green of the vegetation surrounding it.

Each of them was given a turn with the binoculars as Jack silently showed them various interesting things on the island.

When he was about to signal that they retreat to their hiding spot a few minutes away, Danny reached for the binoculars again. Jack shook him off, but Danny insisted and Jack relented.

They waited patiently while Danny first scanned the island then trained the binoculars on the clearing and finally again on the island. Smiling, he handed the binoculars back to Jack and indicated he was ready to go.

They moved as silently and as quickly back to their hidden packs as they had come. Once they were all seated in a circle, Jack began.

Using sign and speaking, he said, "Do you all agree that there was a boat inside that framework on the beach on the island?"

Danny and Christy nodded agreement. Rob was struggling to understand and clearly not happy. Christy felt for him but didn't take out her pad of paper. She figured she'd catch him up once the conversation reached a stopping point.

Jack pressed on: "That means that a boat clearly can cross the strait. There must be one or more on this side, probably in the village of those Ancients. I think we will have to risk sneaking up on the village to look for one."

Danny started violently shaking his head.

"What is it, Danny?" Jack asked, surprised by the reaction.

Danny took a deep breath, clearly excited. He spoke and signed: "They don't use a boat. At least not from here to the island. They fly!"

CHAPTER 21

It was the day after they'd all seen the phenomenon at the pond. The swirling yellow mist with the blue sky and clouds seemingly right in the pond had convinced them all, Connie figured—all except maybe Bob Upton, who had stormed off. But then his son Rob was missing, and he didn't have the personal experience with it that she had. She was calmer about Christy because of it. That she'd briefly and by accident, been to the Empty World as a young teenager, she'd kept quiet about so far but she knew that if she told that story, it might come in handy. Not that she wasn't still worried about if they'd ever find a way to get them back, because she was, but knowing what she did, helped, at least a little.

And even though the Internet search was going okay, they still had no concrete plan of what to do next.

Connie and her husband, Doug, weren't very good with computers, she knew. That left the Internet searching to Trevor, Katie, and Detective Lockhart. Maybe she could convince Ginny Wentworth to change her mind and help. At least it would be one more person looking.

Connie asked Trevor to come with her to Ginny's, and she and Trevor were sitting with Cathy Wentworth in her living room, waiting for Ginny to come downstairs.

"I appreciate you coming to talk to Ginny, Trevor," Cathy said. "But where's Christy? I guess I don't understand why you, Connie, need to explain anything to Ginny."

"It's not just to talk to Ginny," Connie said. "We need to talk to you, too. Christy ... is missing, as well as the boy, Danny Lake, who lives in my old house. You probably also heard that Rob Upton has run away. That's not quite true."

Cathy was about to say something, but Ginny came bounding down the stairs and turned into the living room.

"What did you want, Mom? I was—"

She saw Trevor and Mrs. Walker and stopped in mid-sentence, staring at them. Then she turned and fixed her stare on her mom for an answer.

"Connie and Trevor have come to talk to both of us, I guess. So join us, if you will, honey."

Ginny frowned slightly then looked around the room. The cat was sleeping on the chair, and her mom and Mrs. Walker were on the couch, so since she didn't want to squeeze between them, she sat on the love seat next to Trevor, who smiled at her. She didn't return his smile, turning instead to stare again at her mom, who only shrugged and looked to Connie.

Taking that as an opening, Connie began. "Ginny, I know Trevor came over a few days ago to speak with you. He told you something and showed you a bunch of letters and photos." Connie pulled out the packet from her bag and put the whole packet on the coffee table in front of them. "I'm going to go over what Trevor told you again so your mom can hear, and we'll show you both the information and photos we have with us. Please just listen while I talk."

Half an hour later, Cathy was poring over the photos and shaking her head in amazement. Ginny hadn't responded to any of Connie's story, nor had she reached for any of the photos. She'd seen them already. Instead she kept her arms folded across her chest the whole time Connie was explaining things.

When Connie saw that Ginny still looked defiant, she addressed the girl directly: "Ginny, Cory is the one telling you stories, not Trevor. Actually Trevor has protected Cory by not telling Rob's parents, or the Peterses, that he pushed Rob in. Cory was supposed to call you to tell you the truth, because he's finally admitted that he's seen the lightning strike the pond and told us what he saw of the portal opening. And he described it well."

Connie had deliberately kept one detail from Ginny and her mom and now was the spot to tell it: "Cory described it well," she repeated, then said, "Because I've seen the same thing. In fact, many years ago, I went through that portal and saw the world in those photos."

Ginny's mouth dropped open. "How can that be?" she asked, reaching for some of the photos her mom had laid out on the coffee table to look at.

She'd seen them before, but really hadn't looked at them, not believing Trevor's story when he'd tried to show them to her. Now she looked at them with acceptance of what they really were. She hunted for a minute and found the letter addressed to Christy from her grandmother. She took time to read it while the others let her and kept silent.

When she put it down, there were tears in her eyes. She turned to Trevor, the last year's coolness between them gone completely, and asked, "Trev, couldn't you stop Christy? You were there."

Trevor snorted. "Stop Christy? You're joking right?" Then he added quietly, "I wish I had."

Ginny was now crying. "I'm sorry, Trev. I really miss you and Christy, even though I haven't shown it."

Cathy came over and enveloped her daughter in a hug as the girl continued to sob for a few minutes. When her sobbing stopped, Cathy asked Connie a series of questions about where everyone was with rescuing the kids.

After answering, Connie said, "The rescue effort is why we're here. Trevor, Katie Lake, and the detective could use Ginny's help searching—especially if she's kept up with her French."

Ginny nodded. "Yes, I have. I'm all the way through the intermediate course and into the advanced course of the program that I got for Christmas two years ago. In school last year, I was too far along for the French class I was in and there wasn't a more advanced one, so I helped tutor the other students."

"Then it's settled!" Connie stated.

Kim Upton walked toward her kitchen. It was early in the morning, and just like every morning for a week now, she was tired from lack of sleep. She had tossed and turned and finally cried herself to a fitful sleep again with nightmares of Rob and what might be happening to him.

As she was approaching the kitchen, she heard her husband in the kitchen talking on the phone. He was loud, which although was very much like him, this time, his tone was different. She hesitated and stopped short of entering and listened in.

"Yeah, that's what I said!" Bob growled. "No, you don't need any other permission but mine. I'm the police chief here. I'll see you there in three days. Yes … that's right. You can drain it right down into the stream that it empties into. I'm sure it won't cause any flooding downstream. There can't be that much water in that pond."

Kim was shocked. She'd just heard her husband impersonate Chief Peters to schedule a draining of the pond!

CHAPTER 22

Danny was signing so fast that neither Christy nor her grandfather could understand him. And his speech was too garbled in his excitement for them to even understand that. Jack grabbed the boy's wrists to stop his flying hands.

"Whoa! Slow down, Danny. Start from the beginning. What do you mean that they fly, not take a boat?"

Danny stopped, took a deep breath, and began again. He paced his speaking to his signing so his words wouldn't be garbled. "Don't you see? That thing on the large block in the center of the cleared circle is a glider. Its wings are folded or collapsed. That's what the bunched-up silver stuff is: the wings.

"With that wooden ramp wheeled up to the edge of the block facing the cliff edge, it looks like you could just push that glider off down the wooden ramp onto the paved path and it would continue right off the edge. The wind would probably keep it easily airborne, and it could sail to the island. That large cleared area on the island has to be the landing target for the glider. The boat in that structure on the island looks big enough to carry the glider back to here. If we peek over the edge of the cliff, I bet we see a small clearing at the base of the cliff where that boat lands. There must be a pathway back up to here atop the cliff, so they can bring the glider back up. How the boat gets back to that beach on the island, I haven't figured out yet."

Jack was listening to Danny's interpretation of what they'd seen in the clearing. When Danny stopped to see the reactions to his thoughts, Jack slapped him on the back.

"My word, Danny, you must be right. I wasn't thinking along those lines, but it makes perfect sense. That seating suspended under the collapsed wings looks like it could hold all four of us. Now the question is, does it still fly?"

Christy piped in with her thoughts once she saw the truth of what Danny had said: "Why wouldn't it? Look how clean it's kept and how whoever guards that spot has kept the area around it so trimmed. It must still work!"

Rob tugged at Christy's sleeve and signed, "What's going on?"

Christy signed, "Sorry," knowing it was one of the signs that Danny had already taught Rob. Then she took out the scribbled-on small notebook and began writing.

While Christy caught Rob up with her notebook, her grandfather laid out a plan: "We head back to observe the clearing till after dark. I could go alone but the more eyes the better, as Danny clearly illustrated just now since I didn't interpret what we were looking at the same way he did. If we don't see any signs of anyone, we'll come back here and get some sleep. Tomorrow early, we see if that really is a glider and if we can unfold its wings. If so, we decide if we think we can handle flying it across the strait to the island. I bet inside that door in the side of the hill, we'll find the portal back to Earth.

"Other than the obviously manmade smoothing of the hillside to put that door in, that hill looks remarkably like where the portal is that I used for so many years, right down to the hole in the top. I bet there's a pool of water inside that hill on the other side of that door, and if you look straight up from it, you'll see the sky through that hole. And those flashes of lights we saw coming from the hole—probably a storm on Earth. That's just what happens at the portal I used to use to get home. Now I wonder, though, where the portal from Earth to here comes out. If it's like the other again, on Earth it's all connected to one spot like our pond at home, but here it is two separate spots, one for coming here and one for going to Earth. The 'coming back from Earth' spot has to be somewhere on that island close. Or it could be in the village on the mainland here. That would make more sense. Not that we'll need that."

Christy, who had caught Rob up with their plans and listened to her grandfather at the same time, asked, "Should we try to find the village that the Orator says is here close by?"

Her grandfather thought for a minute. "I think not. We'll do our reconnaissance of the clearing, and if we see any signs of the villagers, then maybe we will change our plans and find out where they're coming from before we do anything."

Christy nodded.

"Then let's go!" Jack said, getting up from the crouch he'd been in while laying out their plan.

The group filed out of their protected hiding spot. Within minutes, they were again overlooking the clearing. They settled down to observe and wait for dark. To pass the time while they waited, Rob got Danny to show him some more signs. Rob practiced diligently and even smiled most of the time. Her grandfather occasionally glanced at the two boys and smiled to himself as Danny patiently taught the older boy.

They waited for an hour after darkness fell, but they saw no lights come on in the huts and no signs of anyone at all. Still being silent, Jack led them back to their packs where they settled down for the night to get some sleep for what they all hoped would be their last night in the Empty World.

The next morning, they gathered all their belongings and assembled again overlooking the clearing. Jack had them wait for almost an hour and observe again just to be safe. While they waited, Rob asked Danny for more signs to learn. Danny was patient with Rob, and after the time practicing the day before they'd had—and Rob's now almost obsessive desire to learn—the impromptu session went well. Rob signed his first real sentence and responded to Danny by signing. Christy and her grandfather, who were watching, both gave a thumbs-up, and Danny and Rob grinned from ear to ear.

When there was still no sign of anyone in the area, Jack risked speaking and signing: "Let's still be cautious. I'll go down there and take a closer look at the glider."

Jack hesitated, though, unsure of whether he should do something. Then coming to a decision, he took out one of his pistols.

"Christy, I think you should take this while I go down there. I'm sure you won't need it, but just in case."

Christy's mouth opened wide for a second, then she said, "I couldn't even begin to know how to use that. I'd be afraid."

Rob couldn't hear what was going on, but he could tell by Christy's face what she was saying. Rob held out his hand and spoke confidently: "I'll hold it. I've practiced with pistols at the shooting range with Cory and Brad and their dad."

Jack was unsure for a moment, but then reluctantly nodding approval, he handed the pistol to Rob. Promptly checking that the safety was on, Rob opened the chamber to check the ammunition and peeked down the gun barrel, and then gave an approving nod. Jack returned the gesture. Those simple safety checks by Rob had validated his decision.

Jack got up and crept down from their vantage point. The rest of them watched as he walked straight into the clearing, going directly to the large block of stone with the metal framework and what they hoped were glider wings folded on top. The top of the metal framework was out of his reach, so he climbed up onto the block and first checked out the seating within the framework. They watched as he poked his hands into the metallic material and felt around a bit. He seemed to examine areas of the framework as he lifted some of the folded material to free up what had been covered.

Then Jack jumped down and headed over to first one, then another, and then the last of the huts, peering into each of them through the windows by slightly lifting the coverings that had been lashed over them. Once he'd done that, he headed back up to join his three companions, who were patiently waiting and watching his inspections.

When he was back with the group, Jack said, "That definitely looks like a glider. Unfortunately the tubing for the wings isn't collapsed inside that framework. I saw what is probably the wing tubing stacked inside that third hut, over by the wooden ramp. I also noticed—on the main framework partially hidden by the wings—the joints where the wing tubing joins up. So we'll have to figure out how to assemble it. The wing fabric is just as we thought: some type of metallic cloth. What I could examine of it is in good shape. I didn't want to cut any of it free from the rope that's been used to tie it down and secure it to the frame. I was afraid it would flap too much in the wind.

"We should get started right away. Let's move the ramp into place first, so that it's there waiting when the glider is ready. It looks heavy, so hopefully those crude-looking wheels will work well enough that with all of us working together, we can push it into position."

Jack then waited to say more as Christy wrote in her notebook for Rob. When she was just about to hand it to Rob, Jack took it and the pen from her and he added some sentences. He handed it to Rob and waited. Rob read and then nodded approval.

Jack explained to Christy and Danny what he'd done: "I told Rob we need a lookout no matter how safe it's been so far. I want him to be our lookout, and so I asked him to keep hold of the pistol for now. He'll keep watch while we try to assemble the glider wings. Okay, we better get going and see if we can push that ramp into place."

The ramp was heavy, but the wheels were surprisingly efficient. Even at that, it took them quite a while and two rest breaks before they had the ramp in place. Then Jack positioned Rob on the end of the stone block as the lookout. He led Christy and Danny to the hut with the tubing, and they pried the wooden doorway open and gathered up the lightweight tubes. They were lighter even than aluminum. Jack risked a test and tried to bend one but couldn't.

Back at the glider framework, they cut just a few of the lengths of rope securing the wing fabric down so that they could access the joints where they hoped to connect the wing tubing to the frame. Then they spread out the wing tubing on the ground and began the process of identifying and separating the pieces into two distinct wing sections. Again, Danny's talent for visualizing a concept and applying it to the facts—in this case, the pieces of tubing—helped them tremendously, and they soon had two identical but mirrored sections laid out on the ground.

Jack was smiling at the results of their efforts, and Christy gratefully hugged Danny, who was already kneeling down and looking more closely at one of the ends of a piece of tubing. They hadn't tried yet to actually join any of the pieces to each other or to the wheeled frame. Danny stood up with the piece of tubing and touched the end he was so curious about. It felt different and was a different color of silver than the metal that constituted the lengths of tubing. Each piece of tubing was tipped on both ends with the same oddly different-looking and -feeling metal.

Danny took the tubing and walked over to the large stone slab. He looked up at the framework sitting on the slab and motioned for Jack to help him up onto the stone. Once up and grasping onto the framework for support, Danny searched the top edge by moving some of the fabric out of the way. When he found the joint spot he was looking for, he brought up the tubing in his hand. Gauging an angle approximately at ninety degrees that he felt might be right, he tentatively tried touching one end of the tubing in his hand to the tube framework at the joint. Immediately the tube in his hand jerked slightly and the angle changed so that Danny had to move his head back quickly.

The tubing in his hand had bonded seamlessly with the framework at the joint spot. When he took his hand away, the piece of tubing looked as rigid and permanent on the framework as if it had always been there. Not only had the wing tubing piece bonded with the framework, but it also adjusted itself to the correct angle.

Jack reached up and helped Danny down. They all, except Rob, had seen what happened.

With Danny's gift for visualization and the self-bonding ends and joints of the alien metal, they very quickly were able to assemble the bare framework of the wings into place. It also was quickly apparent that they couldn't make a mistake even if they had wanted to, because if they used a wrong piece, or tried to join a piece to the wrong spot, the bond just didn't happen. So even in the few instances where Danny's skill wasn't enough, trial and error got the job done.

Resting against the stone slab, they took a break. Rob joined them, and Jack began to explain their next steps. After days of doing it, it was now second nature, and he signed and spoke without thinking: "We now have to cut the fabric free and stretch it out over the wing frames. Let's hope that the fabric will attach to the framework as easily as the framework came together. We better get our packs into the seating area and secure them. There is more than enough space for us and our packs. By the wingspan this has, I'd say it should take all four of us easily.

"A couple things, though. The first is that with the fierce wind, we should get ready, stretch the wings, and at the last moment, cut the remaining securing ropes on either side that are holding down the glider to the stone slab—and then go. If the glider is going to fly, let's hope it is after it rides down the ramp, onto the path, and off the cliff edge, not by blowing backward the second we cut it free." Jack shook his head and paused, running his fingers through his hair. He was clearly thinking of the huge task ahead.

"Also, I guess that none of us have ever used a glider before, certainly not one built for what looks like six or seven people. Hopefully we can steer it if necessary. And the seats have seatbelts. We should use them. But if something goes wrong, try to undo them so that at least you'll have a chance, although slight, of surviving the strait. This will be the most dangerous thing we've tackled yet. If there was any other way, I wouldn't even entertain doing this. So ... we might just as well get to it."

It took only a few minutes to cut the ropes securing the fabric, which left only the ropes holding the whole thing down to the stone slab. It was easy to stretch the wings despite the wind because, just like the tubing, the second the wings were stretched to their final position, they molded onto the framework securely. The wind rippled the wings only slightly, and the whole frame didn't seem to be straining at all. After tying down their packs with the ropes that had secured the fabric, Jack helped them each into a seat. He had Rob sit on the far left. He gave the boy one of his sharp knives and showed him where to cut the rope when instructed. Then he had Christy sit next to Rob and Danny next to her. He had several packs in the next seats. He hoped that his weight on the far right would be balanced by the three children grouped closer to the left side.

When the three were settled securely, Jack knelt down in front of them. He had tears in his eyes. "In case something happens to us as the glider takes off or it doesn't make the island, I want to tell you three that I am as proud of you as I could ever be of anyone." He started to say more but choked up and instead gave each of them a big hug before getting up.

Jack walked to the back of the glider and cut the ropes securing the rear on both the right and the left sides. All they had left to do was cut the front ropes once Jack took his seat. After checking again that everyone was strapped in tight, he started to settle into his own seat.

Just as he finished buckling his seatbelt, an angry cry from behind carried on the wind. Christy and her grandfather turned in their seats and saw four people, clearly Ancients, just starting to surround the glider. In the time it took for Jack to get settled, the Ancients had crossed the clearing unnoticed.

Jack had no time to think, only react. With the knife already in his hand, he just had to make a quick slash to sever his seatbelt and then he jumped up, yelling as he did: "This is it, guys! I'll hold them off."

Only Christy could hear him and she screamed, "No, Grandpa!"

But two of the Ancients were already pulling at the front ropes.

Jack looked at her for a second. "I'm sorry, honey."

He turned toward the rear of the glider and saw the other two Ancients struggling to climb onto the slab, their small stature hindering them. Jack was torn, frustrated with the multidirectional attack on them.

Rob, seeing Jack's stance and Christy's horror-stricken face, quickly unbuckled and jumped up, brandishing the knife he'd been given. He stood next to Jack and pointed at the two remaining ropes with his knife. Having no choice, Jack nodded, and while reaching into his belt for the other pistol, he headed toward the back of the glider to meet the two Ancients struggling to climb the slab.

The Ancients grabbing the ropes seemed intent on only holding on, their plan apparently being to let the two climbing up the back get to the fleeing figures. Rob watched Jack fumbling to get to the rear of the glider only for a split second. Then he leaned toward the right side and, grabbing the rope, sawed through it quickly. Immediately a cry of frustration came from the Ancient holding the rope on the left, and Rob knew he had to get to it fast or they'd never make it off the slab.

Hearing the frustrated cry of the Ancient up front, Jack turned and saw Rob use lightning speed to cross to the left and take hold of the rope, then, using quick, desperate cuts, he sawed through the remaining rope. Jack was two steps from the rear of the glider, and one of the Ancients in the rear was just beginning to stand up on the slab. Jack ignored him, and with his next steps, he got behind the glider just as Rob was scrambling to take his seat again.

With his back toward the approaching Ancient, Jack grabbed hold of the glider and pushed as hard as he could. The glider fought him only slightly in the strong wind, and Jack pushed it the few feet to the ramp and gravity took over. The glider picked up momentum going downhill and rolled with increasing speed down the path and then off the edge of the cliff—and out of sight as the two Ancients on either side gestured and watched in frustration, loose ropes dangling in their hands.

Jack watched the glider disappear. Breathing a sigh of relief and clutching his pistol, he whirled to face the first of his adversaries, who were just a few yards away.

Christy had no time to think about her grandfather. The glider cleared the cliff, and then after a momentary scare as it initially fell almost straight down, it picked up loft and glided into the wind toward the island. Their weight distribution didn't seem to be an issue, but the wind buffeted them, so despite the seatbelts, the three of them held on for dear life. In less than a minute, they were across the strait and sailing over the island.

Seconds after clearing the strait, Danny pointed down at the spot they had seen through the binoculars and guessed to be a landing area. It indeed looked like it was for landing the glider. But based on their height, they were going to overshoot it if they didn't do something. Rob waved his hands for attention and pointed to the wings overhead. They hadn't noticed before, but they saw a bar just below the top cross tube as part of the framework surrounding the seating. Rob reached up and grabbed it, motioning the others to do the same. Then he tried pulling down and toward himself. Nothing happened at first, but when the other two caught on, they all pulled and the glider lost altitude. The bar was clearly the mechanism by which the glider was steered, and by keeping a steady pressure on the bar together, they guided the glider toward the ground. It hit the runway rather awkwardly, but the glider seemed to be designed to compensate for that, as it righted itself and rolled to a stop with the added help of the strong headwind. They had survived the crossing and caught the last few yards of the landing area.

The strong wind was in danger of pushing them backward, so they unbuckled and grabbed their packs. As soon as they jumped clear of the glider, the wind took it, spinning it around and blowing it, tumbling end over end, across the flat landing area and off into taller vegetation where it settled uneasily to a stop. The three kids could see the wind continuing to push at the now crumpled glider.

Out in the open and exposed to any eyes from the cliff across the strait that they'd just crossed, they hurried toward the hill ahead with the doorway. The smooth landing area they were crossing was made up of crushed seashells pulverized to a fine powder. The millions of crushed shells gave the landing area the pinkish hue they'd seen from the cliff with the binoculars. The wind pushed at their backs, and since they were now so accustomed to its force, they used it to their advantage.

Within a few minutes, they were at the doorway. It was as impressive as they imagined it to be from their glimpses of it through the binoculars. But they were too emotionally drained to appreciate it. They collapsed down in front of it, and Christy cried with her head between her knees. Danny and Rob were both also tearing up. They'd come so far together only to have their guide and protector captured—or worse.

After several minutes, Christy broke the silence, asking, almost imploring for a positive answer: "Do you ... Do you think he's still alive?"

But both Danny and Rob had their heads down, and couldn't hear her or see her lips, so they didn't even know she'd asked a question.

She didn't ask again. Finally she stood up, facing her two companions, and tapped them both on the shoulder. She signed and spoke, tears still streaming down her cheeks: "I have to go back. Will you help me use that boat up past the landing area?"

Danny spoke without signing after wiping his own eyes: "No, we can't go back. Jack wanted us to get here. We have to get through that door and get home. And if anyone is up there on the cliff still, they can see us here just as easily as they could see us on the landing strip. They may try to stop us."

Rob knew what was going on even without hearing or having Christy or Danny write it for him. He saw the pain in Christy's eyes when Danny responded to her.

Taking a leap of understanding, Rob said, "We can't do anything to help Jack now. He made sure we got here and we have to get home for him."

Christy shook her head no and just stood there, defiantly staring at both of them.

Danny saw her uncertainty and anger, and he spoke and signed slowly, "Christy, your grandfather is okay. I just know it. And Rob is right."

Christy shook her head again, but her shoulders relaxed as she finally admitted to herself that they were right. She looked Danny in the eye and nodded as he smiled at her. Rob watched the exchange of stares and stood up, followed by Danny.

When they were standing together, Christy signed and spoke: "Well, let's see if we can get inside. I want to go home."

They looked over the massive doorway in front of them. It was actually a set of double doors. They could discern the seam between the two doors. The doors were carved with intricate designs and figurines, as they'd thought when they saw them from the distance. There were dozens of designs and figures overall. Each design was contained in a square frame, so that the whole doorway looked like it was made up of square blocks. They all searched for some type of doorknob or handle, but nothing stood out. There was no way they could pry those doors apart. Rob even broke the tip of the knife Jack gave him trying to pry the doors apart. They were going to have to figure out some other way.

After a frustrated hour or so, Christy sat back down and began to cry again. She cried for both her grandfather's unknown plight and for their stymied attempts to get into the portal. Danny finally gave up looking too and slid down beside Christy, giving her a hug as he did.

While they were slumped in front of the doors, Rob stood, looking intently at some of the carvings, and eventually he ran his hands over some of them and then took a step back and looked at the doors again.

Smiling, he approached Christy and Danny and kicked them gently to get their attention. When they looked up at him, he said, "It's a puzzle! Who would ever believe it? I know how to solve it."

Christy and Danny stood up, and Christy signed, "How?"

Before Rob answered, he took hold of one of the designs, running his hands around some of the ridges. Then, finding a grip, he pulled. The block slid out, and bracing himself against the weight, he put it down on the ground. Christy and Danny scrambled to peek at the opening where the block had been. It was more solid wood behind, but flat and without any carvings or designs like the block they'd removed or like any of the other, what they now assumed to also be, blocks that could be removed.

"I don't think it will open up by just removing the blocks," Rob said. "Let me explain. I play computer games—not the 'shoot 'em up' ones. What I play are called adventure games. They're really a series of puzzles wrapped around a story. Almost half of them have some variation of this very puzzle. We've been concentrating on the seam between the doors, but I think if we solve the puzzle, the doorknob or handle will show itself."

Christy gave a shrug and said, "Okay."

"I just can't believe that this puzzle exists here," Rob said. "We have to look at the doorway from a few feet away. Notice that the blocks with designs form no pattern. At first glance, nothing makes any sense. We have to make sense out of the blocks. We have to remove all the squares and figure out the pattern and then place them back into the correct pattern. Somehow that will enable the door to open if I'm right. I don't know what that pattern will be, but it's there somewhere."

He then returned the block to its spot in the door.

"Christy," Rob said, "give Danny and me a piece of paper from the notebook and one of the pens you have. We should all step back, sit down, and look at the doors. See if we can determine what the pattern might be. They're usually a picture, or recognizable design pattern. It's always easier if you know what the pattern, when assembled correctly, looks like, but we don't have that luxury."

It took over an hour, but Rob finally saw it.

He stood up, looked down at his paper, and then went over to the door. He used his nimble fingers to search another of the blocks. He found a hold and pulled. The block came out and he placed it on the ground. Then he located another block based on something he'd put down on his notepaper and pulled that out too, this time finding the hold much faster. It seemed that all the blocks had been designed so that a handhold could be built into the same spot on each one.

Once he had them out side by side, Rob motioned for Christy and Danny to look at them. "See," Rob said, "these two blocks fit together, I think. See that figure in the first block, how it isn't complete, sort of continues to the edge of the block? It continues on the second block. It's a little difficult to see because the pattern or picture on each block doesn't just blend into another block; there's a border around each one. It makes it more difficult until you look past that. It's like each picture on each block is in a frame but, despite that, is still a part of the bigger picture that is the whole doorway."

The three of them began to remove blocks one by one. Being solid wood and almost a foot square, the blocks were heavy, but the three of them went about it enthusiastically. It soon became apparent as they removed blocks that the doors behind had been prepared expertly and meticulously for the removable blocks. The heavy wood of the doors behind the blocks was cleverly sculpted, almost imperceptibly, to contain ridges that indicated where to place a block. By that elegant design, when one block was removed, the one above didn't slide down into the open spot below. That meant that when they were solving the puzzle, they could place a block anywhere they thought it belonged, regardless of whether a block was already in place below it, and it would stay put.

It took a bit of time, but they finally had all the blocks removed and placed on the ground at their feet. The door was massive yet no taller than a normal door back home, but reaching the top tier of blocks was problematic till Rob took two removed blocks and stood on them.

Rob, who had the clearest idea of what the design might be depicting, got right to work trying to match up the blocks by rearranging them on the ground side by side and one above the other as the design dictated.

Christy watched Rob without interfering as he went about trying to solve the puzzle, but Danny was intent on inspecting the doors, now bare of the removable blocks. Danny took his hands and ran them across and over the full surface of the doorway, stopping if he felt something and then continuing on till he'd inspected the doors completely.

He walked over to where Christy and Rob were placing blocks together and stopped them for a moment. "I don't see what difference it will make even if we put the blocks in the correct spots," Danny said. "You'd think that near where the doors join together, they'd have some indentations other than the ridges, so that when the correct blocks were placed there, it somehow would allow the doors to open. But I don't see anything even when I feel the area with my hands. Did you find anything on any of the blocks that might show us which ones could be the ones that will act as the door handles?

Rob saw that the question had been to him, but he still had no skill at reading lips and shrugged his shoulders in a questioning gesture. Christy quickly scribbled on the notepad and showed it to Rob.

Rob shook his head. "I don't see anything different about any of the blocks except their different designs. The back side of each is no different than any of the others. But I agree with you. If we could see something sticking out of the back of a couple of the blocks or maybe some signs of a hole or two in some of them, we'd know. All we can do is finish solving the pattern and placing the blocks back—and hope that my idea is correct. Hopefully they were as ingenious with their woodwork as they were with their metal."

They only had a rough idea of the pattern. But it was solvable because it depicted buildings and statues that, even though completely of alien design, were still buildings and figures. When some of them were put next to each other correctly, the rest began to fall together like the giant jigsaw puzzle it really was. But it went very slowly.

Darkness came before they could finish. And they really were too tired to continue on even if they had a light to see by. So they huddled out of the wind and made the best of the poor sleeping conditions.

The next morning, Christy woke up with bright sun in her eyes. She reached over and shook Danny awake. Rob was already up and bending over the blocks all resting in various spots on the ground. Since they had very little left to eat, Christy's grandfather had carried most of the dried fruit and other food, so they got back to trying to solve the design.

It took them several hours more, but once they had them all in what they thought was the correct order on the ground, they began the process of putting them back on the door.

As they were putting the final blocks into place, still unsure if they had it exactly correct, Christy heard the rumble of what sounded like thunder from behind the doors.

"Oh no! I bet that's a storm from Earth!" Christy said. "Please be right! If we hurry, we can get home right away."

Rob had the final block in his hand, and even though he couldn't hear what Christy said, he saw her concern and hurried to put it in place. He gripped the handhold spot as he pushed the block tightly in. Something happened under his hand.

"Something moved inside the block! I don't know what or how, but I felt it." Rob put his ear to the door and said, "Something is grinding inside the door! I feel the vibration."

Christy didn't waste time trying to hear the grinding or even feel for the vibration; she tried grabbing at the handhold areas in the blocks that she thought might be the doorway handles. Nothing happened, so she tried two blocks just below those two. The doors still didn't budge, so she tried the two blocks above the first two she'd tried. She finally felt a slight giving of the doors.

"Help me! I think the doors will open!"

She expected both of her companions to help, but only Rob grabbed the blocks with her, searching for a handhold. While they were tugging, Danny slapped them both on the back.

"Turn around!" Danny yelled. "Look!"

They turned and looked where Danny was pointing. Coming toward them rapidly but silently—and carrying menacing-looking spears—were three Ancients.

"No!' Christy screamed. "Please not now!"

She turned back toward the door and tried to pry it open. She had grabbed the right spot, and it started to open ever so slightly. Danny joined Rob in helping—but it was too late.

The three Ancients were upon them in seconds and had them surrounded, spears pointing at them. One of the Ancients roughly pulled the three of them away one at a time and flung them to the ground. All three lay sprawled on the ground together, dejected. Victory had been taken from them seconds before they would have been inside what they hoped would be the portal with the way home.

CHAPTER 23

Ginny Wentworth, Trevor Hanson, Detective Lockhart, and Katie Lake were all grouped in Katie's living room. Ginny and Trevor were sitting at the laptop donated by Connie Walker, and the detective and Katie were sitting in front of her desktop computer. The four of them were searching online for the elusive clues that could lead them to a working portal.

After about an hour, Ginny sat back, turned around, and looked over to Mrs. Lake and the detective.

"This is frustrating," Ginny said. "I've followed the same links that you guys have and come up with the same results but can't get anything else out of it.

It seems that because most of what we've found is so far out of the realm of reality, nobody has taken it seriously at all. Even that mention of a pond near Paris somewhere doesn't seem to help us much because nobody believes the stories surrounding it … so we don't have an exact location."

Katie nodded. "Detective Lockhart and I have spent most of the last hour following different rumors of other disappearances all over the world because we were at a dead end with the France search."

Ginny thought for a moment about Katie's comment and then blurted out, "I think I have another idea how to go about this! Mrs. Lake, do you know what it's like around Paris?"

Katie frowned. "What do you mean by 'around Paris'?"

"I realized that we've been focusing on searching for stories of missing people or strange disappearances and appearances," Ginny said. "Now that we have a hint about a place near Paris somewhere, we shouldn't be trying to see if there's more info about disappearances, etc., to narrow down our search to find the location of that pond. We should assume there is one and try to figure out where near Paris the conditions would be similar to here. Once we figure that out, we can search for specific ponds. I asked what it is like around Paris because I want to know if there's rolling hills and valleys like here. If thunderstorms are critical to our pond here, they must be critical to wherever that pond near Paris is too."

Katie was grinning at the young girl and nodding. "Yes, of course! Although not right around Paris, but within a couple of hours to the southeast, there are hills similar to here. That's where the Alps begin. As you approach them, the terrain is very much like here, with hills and valleys and hot muggy summers."

Ginny nodded and smiled back at Katie. "Great! Then that's it. I'll pull up topographical maps of the area and go from there."

Ginny really was an intuitive researcher, and her fingers flew over the keyboard. Trevor was relegated to being a mute witness to her quick researching. All he could do was try to follow as best he could, but since it was all in French, he had no chance.

Finally Ginny gave a cry of triumph.

"What is it?" the detective asked.

"Trev and I pinpointed the place. It's a pond just like here!"

Trevor grunted at the mention of his name and just smiled in admiration at Ginny. "I had nothing to do with it. Ginny's the wizard, not me."

Katie and the detective came over and stood over the two youngsters' shoulders. Ginny pointed out a picture and description.

"Once we identified an area that has similar weather patterns to here, we searched for bodies of water. Eventually it led us to a pond. It was two different ones actually, but from there, we searched using the names of the ponds and one has this weird Facebook site dedicated to it. The stories are bizarre, but if you cut through the alien abductions and other wild theories, you still get to the fact that this pond has unexplained happenings just like ours does. The person who created the page actually has some photos and the town's name that the pond is close to. The area is very much like here. It can be muggy with severe thundershowers in summer."

Katie Lake began to cry. "So this could be it? Where we can go and try to find the kids?"

Trevor nodded, and he and Ginny grinned at the two adults.

"But," Trevor said, "are we sure that Christy, Rob, and Danny will be at this portal on the other side?"

Detective Lockhart shook his head. "No, sadly we don't know. But we've discussed that with what meager information we have, and if Christy's grandfather is alive and the kids are with him, we hope that he's trying to get the kids home. And he's even written in some of the stuff he sent over here after being stranded that he's heard of at least one other portal and that it possibly came out in France. So we've found what we hope is that portal, and all we can do is go on the assumption that Jack will try to get the kids there. If not, and we succeed in going through the portal in France—if it is one—then some of us have to go searching in the Empty World and find them somehow."

Then the detective grabbed his cell phone, but before making a call, he said, "I'm calling in every favor I can to get us tickets on a flight to France as soon as possible. Katie and Ginny, you can both speak French, so you're definitely two who need to go. Trevor, I'm afraid that your parents don't want you to go, but when we started this search, they told me you've already had that conversation."

Trevor pouted, remembering that conversation and couldn't look at Ginny. He couldn't bear to see that she was probably grinning from ear to ear.

With determination in his voice, Detective Lockhart said, "We don't know what we'll find when we get there. But those of us going should pack as if we're going to have to go to an unexplored land, and Trevor can help us with that since he and Christy packed based on Jack's letters. Okay ... Ginny, although you're going with us to France, only some of the adults will go into any portal we may find. Connie is coming too. She convinced Doug that if we are going, she should go to stay back in France if we do somehow find the portal and some of us go into it. So it's Doug and I, Katie and Ginny and Connie going."

Trevor frowned. "What about the Uptons?"

Detective Lockhart shook his head negatively. "I don't think they will go with us. Bob was very uncooperative when we all saw the pond being struck by lightning."

Just then, they were interrupted by a loud knock at the front door. Katie jumped up and opened it. Without so much as a nod hello, Kim Upton stormed into the midst of the group.

"Nobody is going anywhere without me!" Kim said. "I heard some of what you said though the open window. If you're all going to France, I'm in."

"Not everyone here is going," Trevor said.

Despite the seriousness of the situation, they all laughed, even Trevor.

When the laughter died down, Katie said, "Kim, we would have called you, despite Bob's getting so angry at us."

Kim acknowledged the comment with a nod and said, "Bob is going to drain the pond. I heard him on the phone pretending to be Wendell and asking someone—well, yelling at them actually—to drain the pond three days from now. I think he believes that the portal or whatever it is will be down there and visible for us to see."

Detective Lockhart grimaced, and Katie and Ginny both gasped.

"Well," Detective Lockhart said, "looks like I have a few more calls to make—not just trying to secure us plane tickets to France."

The plane ride was interminable. Ginny had never even been on a plane before and, for the first few hours, was wide awake and thrilled with the experience. But halfway across the Atlantic, she fell asleep.

Detective Lockhart spent most of the time sleeping after briefly talking out their game plan with the adults. That plan consisted of determining if it was possible that the pond they were heading to was in fact a portal. And that, they knew, would take observation and then waiting till the right conditions. If it displayed the same behavior as the pond back home, then they were hoping it was still working both ways. At that point, they would have decisions to make about what to do. Going home to talk out the situation was one of the possibilities, but the summer was getting along and none of them knew just how many chances they were going to get if this did turn out to be another portal. All five of the adults had pretty much made up their minds even before leaving New Hampshire that someone, perhaps several of them, would chance going through the portal.

Despite the long plane flight, except for the detective and Ginny, none of the others could sleep. They were too nervous for their children trapped in the Empty World and the thought that they might now have a chance to get them home.

When they landed, Katie was invaluable in renting the car and getting directions to the little hamlet where they were headed. Finding a car big enough for the six of them was a challenge, and the rental agency had only one that comfortably seated them all as well as had a luggage rack on the roof to accommodate all their things. Once they got on the road, the detective did the driving while Katie navigated, following the map they'd been given by the rental agency.

Connie, Ginny, and Doug sat in the backseat. Ginny was thrilled, as she had dreamed of going to France for years. Bolstered by her sleep on the plane, she was wide eyed and amazed at all the sights and sounds of the scenery, which was rapidly turning from cityscape to rural countryside.

Emboldened by her excitement of seeing France for the first time, Ginny asked the detective in a pleading voice, "I know you want me to stay back if there is a portal, but I really want to go, so can I, please?"

"No, young lady," the detective said. "You most certainly won't be going. If there is a portal, and it works, we won't know where it comes out in that other world. There's a good chance that it will be a long way from the portal the kids went through. That means that whoever goes will have to find their way to wherever the kids are. It will be a very difficult and dangerous task, I'm sure. Whoever goes will need to first go there and then come right back again to test the portal even before anyone sets off to search for the kids. Once we determine it works, we'll all make a decision and go from there. But ..." he emphasized, "... you won't be one of the ones going!"

There was no use arguing, and the conversation stopped as they all concentrated on the scenery of the French countryside.

Three hours after getting into the car, and more than twelve hours since boarding the plane in Boston, they pulled into the village and stopped their car in front of what Katie said was a general store. The weather was hot and humid.

Echoing everyone's thoughts, Ginny said, "Well, at least the weather is like home. That's a good thing. It feels like thunderstorm weather."

As they dragged themselves out of the car and began to stretch their legs, two elderly gentlemen came out of the store to greet them. They smiled and said in very good English, "Ah! Welcome, Americans. Come in, come in." He waved them toward the store.

"Thank you for the invitation," Detective Lockhart said, "but if you could give us directions, we really have to be on our way."

The man and his companion looked crestfallen. Then the one who spoke such good English smiled and said, "Can you forgive an old man his quirks? Please come in ... if only for a minute. You'll have your directions."

Resigned to it, the six of them followed the two men into the store.

Once inside, they were confronted with a very crowded area in front of an old-fashioned soda fountain complete with stools and polished countertop. There were six or seven strangers as well as the two old gentlemen. There was also one younger gentleman, probably in his early thirties, behind the counter lazily running a cleaning cloth over it. Everyone was grinning at them.

The Frenchman who had addressed them and ushered them into the store spoke again: "We have been expecting you."

That took the travelers by surprise, but Katie, recovering more quickly than the others, asked, "Expecting us? How is that?"

The old gentleman gave a small chuckle. "No mystery really. We got a call from the car-rental agent at the airport. She informed us that you had asked directions to our little village. We don't normally get many visitors, at least not sane ones. It was a bit unusual for someone to be inquiring about this small village, so she wanted us to be on the lookout for your arrival."

"What do you know about a pond, supposedly seven or eight miles southeast of here?" Detective Lockhart asked.

The Frenchman frowned slightly. "Ah," he said. "Maybe you aren't so sane after all."

Then he turned to the group of villagers and the man behind the counter and spoke in rapid-fire French. The man behind the counter replied in an angry tone, and the two of them stared at each other.

Katie interrupted their confrontation, addressing the older gentleman who had ushered them inside: "We aren't crazy. We're here because we think that what your friend just said is true. We have children missing. Please help us." She then explained to her companions: "The man behind the counter has a cousin who claims to have seen the phenomenon that we've all seen back home, in the pond outside this village."

The older gentleman bowed slightly, acknowledging the rebuke from both his countryman behind the counter and the Americans. Then he started again in rapid-fire French to argue with his younger friend.

The two went back and forth in sometimes angry tones. Ginny was way out of her league, her French nowhere near competent enough to understand the argument going on. Even Katie was having difficulty.

Finally the older gentleman turned and spoke to them, bowing again: "I am sorry for our bad manners. If you would be so kind as to wait outside for a few minutes, perhaps something can be done to help you." Then he gestured towards the door and said, "Please ... only a moment or two."

Once outside, they turned to Katie for an explanation.

"They speak a strange dialect, and both were speaking very quickly," she said. "Our English-speaking gentleman was against telling us anything. There seems to be a divide amongst the villagers here. Apparently they get ridiculed in the press and now online because of the few people who come here and claim odd happenings at the pond. But there are some villagers, like the cousin of the man behind the counter, who claim to have seen the strange portal open in the pond. That gentleman was trying to say that we, in fact, had validated what his cousin, and apparently some others in the vicinity, had witnessed. But there is something else going on between them. The younger man made some reference to something in the older man's past that I couldn't understand. Whatever it was, that's when we were asked to leave."

Just then, the older gentleman came out through the door and joined them, smiling slightly. "One question," he said. "Why do you wish to go there?"

Doug answered for the group: "We hope to rescue our missing children."

The man nodded, understanding and sympathy washing over his weatherworn face. "I will take you there," he stated. "I was reminded by my hotheaded young friend of something that I have tried for most of my life to ignore and disbelieve."

Sensing what the old gentleman was referring to, Katie asked, "Who was it?"

The man smiled sadly. "My great-grandfather. He went missing when I was only three years old. He was very old at the time, and everyone tried to say he drowned. But my mother was there and swore till the day she died that he jumped into the pond deliberately, aiming for an area that had just been struck by lightning and was no longer water as we know it. That is how she would describe it for the rest of her life: 'no longer water as we know it.'"

Their new French companion asked to pick up a few things, so all seven of them drove to a small cottage off the main road. The man hurried into his home, promising to only be a few minutes. When he came back out, he had a small knapsack, an umbrella, and a rifle.

"I want you to take this with you," the man said. "I'm sure you wouldn't have been able to bring something from the US to protect you."

"Thanks," the detective said with a grin. "I wanted to bring some sort of firearm but knew it would be difficult or impossible."

The ride to the pond was short but cramped with seven passengers in a vehicle designed for six. Their new friend was silent on the ride, the argument with his companion and the quest of the Americans apparently bringing up old memories. When they got to a fork in the road that branched off to their right as a dirt road, the Frenchman nodded and pointed, and they took that right branch.

Despite being a dirt road, it was surprisingly smooth, and after only a few minutes, the Frenchman directed them to pull off into a large field.

After they all stepped out of the car, the Frenchman pointed off into the distance, his gaze following a faint path cut into the tall wildflowers of the field.

"Just over that rise," he said, "we'll be able to see the pond. I see you have brought two tents with you. We should perhaps get where we're going quickly and set them up. It looks like the clouds have rain and worse in store for us. But that is what you are hoping for, I believe." He grinned at his new companions and started to help them take down the luggage from the roof.

A gentle rain began even before they got to the pond, but it stayed gentle and there was no wind. The detective and Doug were both experienced at camping. They had the tents, and a rain fly that they all could gather under, set up in no time and situated about fifty yards up a small slope from the edge of the pond.

As the rain intensified and the wind began in earnest, the seven of them grouped together under the relative protection of the rain fly.

"Okay," Detective Lockhart said, "it looks like we need to make a decision quickly. If this is going to be a thunderstorm, we need to be ready."

"Well," Doug said, "I think we have almost decided that one of us going to test it is not the best idea, since we think that the portals on that side are not like here—going both ways. Based on Connie's experience, the portals on that side are separate, one for coming, one for going. So whoever goes from here may have to find the return portal. Hopefully, like the one Connie found, it won't be far away."

The detective nodded and all the others did the same. "Good!" he said. "I think that only Doug and I should go. Not that I think the rest of us can't handle whatever we find there, but he and I have a lot of experience camping—and I have extensive firearms experience too. And the fewer of us who go, the better it may be trying to come back."

Doug nodded, but Katie, Connie, and Kim were a little reluctant. Finally, with the help of the clearly chauvinistic Frenchman arguing for the two men, the three women also agreed.

Once they had the plan finalized, Kim looked down at the pond with the others and, echoing what some of the others were thinking, asked, "There's no dock, so where is the portal going to open if lightning strikes?"

"That's where it will open," the Frenchman said, "wherever the lightning strikes. I don't know where that will be, but hopefully you will be close enough when it happens."

The group helped Doug and the detective gather their things just as they heard the first rumblings of thunder in the distance. Doug gave Connie a hug and kiss, and then he and the detective separated themselves from the group by heading to the shoreline as the rest of them stayed under the rain fly.

"What do you think?" Doug said. "Should we split up—you get halfway around the pond from me?"

The detective thought for a second then said, "No, we should stay together. Just one of us getting through might not be a good idea if there are any complications. I know that it might cut our chances in half depending on where it opens up because we have to assume this portal will be the same size in circumference as the one back in New Hampshire. And judging from the size of this pond and how long the portal stayed open for back home, we both could miss this if it opens up way across toward the other side ... but I still think we take our chances with sticking together. Do you agree?"

Doug nodded and the two of them walked right to the edge of the pond directly down the slope from the rain fly and the rest of their group.

Choosing a spot at random, they stood there tolerating the rain and wind that had now picked up. The thunder and lightning came rapidly in succession. Lockhart had the rifle wrapped against water, and he was clutching it close. It took more than ten minutes of withstanding the downpour and the constant flashes of lightning, but finally one flash hit the pond almost right where they feared it might, all the way across from them. For a split second, they had hope that it was a false alarm, but then almost immediately, they saw the beginnings of the yellow swirls that signaled a portal was about to open up.

Doug let out a groan, and the detective turned toward him even as he started to sprint while shouting: "Go around the other way! Maybe one of us can make it."

In an instant, they had abandoned their plan to stick together. They both sprinted in opposite directions, heading as fast as they could toward the spot on the shore where the light was swirling and coalescing a few feet out in the water. Doug was faster around, and his way was slightly shorter than Detective Lockhart's, but even at that, he was thirty yards from where he might have chanced a leap into the water when the portal closed. The detective slowed down and flung his pack off in frustration when he saw the water close in and the eerie swirling colors disappear.

Detective Lockhart stood for a few seconds catching his breath before swiping at his pack to pick it up again. He walked slowly toward Doug, who had crouched down sucking air almost immediately when the portal closed. Doug slowly rose to meet the detective.

When they were standing facing each other, the detective cursed under his breath and then said, "This was my fault. I blew it big time."

"No, you didn't. We both agreed to stick together," Doug said.

"Yes, till push came to shove. And then we were late anyway," Lockhart snapped.

From across the pond, they heard Connie's clear voice, even though the rain that was still pelting the pond: "You'll get it next time."

Doug waved weakly and the two of them started to circle back around the pond. The thunder and lightning had moved past them and headed farther down the valley.

CHAPTER 24

Christy, Rob, and Danny were seated on the ground in front of the door with one of the Ancients guarding them with his menacing spear and an equally menacing stare. The other two Ancients were talking together in an unknown language, and one of them was pointing off toward the now crumpled glider that was sitting just off the smooth runway less than a hundred yards in the distance.

Christy tried to speak but was rudely cuffed on the side of her head with the butt end of the spear. Only her quick reflexes in bringing up her arm to soften the blow kept her from being really hurt by the hefty spear handle.

One of the two Ancients who were apparently discussing the glider turned to his companion standing guard and said something. The Ancient guarding the three companions replied and nodded. As soon as that exchange ended, the two not guarding the companions started off in the direction of the glider.

Their captor was content to stand over them, silently brandishing his weapon. Christy, Rob, and Danny didn't dare move or chance any sort of conversation. From behind the door, another rumble disturbed the uneasy silence. The Ancient standing over them mumbled to himself and momentarily got down on one knee, placing his spear on the ground and then bowing his head. It was only for an instant and then he was back up standing over them, spear in hand again.

When the two other Ancients returned, they began a heated discussion with the guard. The three Ancients raised their voices and made all sorts of gestures with their hands and pointed several times back toward the glider. Soon it became clear to the three companions that there was not just a heated conversation going on, but an argument. The argument seemed to be pitting the two Ancients who had walked over to the glider against the one who stood guard over them. The one who had guarded them and cuffed Christy with his spear was clearly talking negatively about something. His hands several times came down and out in front of him in a universal gesture of no. He also shook his head side to side.

Christy was frustrated that they were just sitting there, unable to do anything even though a storm was obviously going on back home—and echoing behind the door and out through the hole on top of the hill. She chanced moving from beside Danny to facing him and Rob, with her back to the arguing Ancients. They ignored her as they continued their back-and-forth heated discussion. In her mind, she began forming a desperate plan.

Just as she was about to signal Danny with sign language, another louder rumble of thunder emanated from behind the door. The slight crack, which they had created trying to open the door before being captured, contributed to the heightened sound.

Instantly the three Ancients faced the door and went to one knee, mumbling and placing their spears on the ground. Christy turned her head, frightened that they'd see she'd changed position and get angry with her. It would ruin any chance she had of executing her plan. But the three Ancients had their heads bowed. One lifted his head up, and his and Christy's eyes met. She tried to turn away, but something in the Ancient's gaze stopped her. He said something directly to her and raised his now empty spear arm and extended his open palm over her head. It was only for an instant, but Christy, Danny, and Rob saw it. It happened too fast for the other two Ancients, who were still bowing their heads, to see it.

Their guard was one of the two who still had their heads bowed, and at the sound of his companion's quick words to Christy, he grabbed his spear with a grunt and stood up. Even though he hadn't seen the gesture, he knew what was said to her and clearly didn't like it.

The Ancient who had gestured over Christy stood up, facing his companion as the third Ancient also stood up to join them. Another argument was beginning. This one was more heated than before the thunder had interrupted them.

They completely ignored Christy, Danny, and Rob. Christy immediately inched closer to Danny and Rob. Keeping her hands low and hidden from the Ancients, she signed, hoping that Rob might also get some of it: "Do you have a ziplock bag?"

Danny gave an almost imperceptible nod and then tilted his head toward his backpack, on the ground within inches of him but within view of the Ancients if they were paying attention. Christy very slowly reached into her jeans pocket and fished for a loose piece of paper she'd ripped off from the ubiquitous notebook that had traveled the whole way with them.

Danny saw what she had, and even though he wasn't quite sure what she was up to, he knew it involved writing something. He reached into his shirt pocket for the pen Christy had given him to write explanations to Rob, and then gave it to her.

Then he tilted his head again toward his pack and signed: "Should I chance it?"

Christy nodded and signed: "No choice."

Danny slowly moved his hand till it was resting on the backpack. Instead of moving the pack and maybe causing one of the Ancients to notice, he groped slowly over the surface till his hand disappeared inside. Several seconds later, he slowly withdrew his hand, now closed around a small ziplock baggy. Extending his hand with extreme care, all the while never taking his eyes off of the arguing Ancients, he passed the baggy to Christy. She set it in her lap, nodding to Danny.

Cradling the paper in her left hand, she wrote with the pen, moving her right hand as slowly and as little as necessary to say what she had to say. Then, being just as careful, she placed the paper in the plastic bag. Before closing it, she glanced behind her at the arguing Ancients and then lowered her head, blowing into the bag and sealing it inflated as best she could.

Once she closed the bag, she signed her intentions: "Danny, I need you to run away. Even though you're smaller, you're faster than Rob or me. I'm going to try to open the door when another rumble of thunder comes—if it does. I want to send this message through the portal. Okay?"

Danny nodded yes and smiled.

Christy teared up and signed: "Please, if it looks like they're going to hurt you by throwing one of those spears, give up. I couldn't live with myself if you were hurt because of me."

Danny turned away for a second, then locked eyes with her. She broke the stare and got Rob's attention.

He had seen the note-writing and the baggy but wasn't sure what was going on, so had just sat trying to understand it all.

Christy mouthed the words: "Help me open the ..." and she pointed to the door. In case he didn't quite get it, she pointed at it again and then pulled her hand into her chest. Then she lifted up the baggy and pointed to it and dropped it down onto the ground in front of her. Rob's eyes showed understanding and then he nodded. Christy mouthed: "Wait." Rob nodded again.

They were finished with their plans just in time, as the argument was slowly coming to a close. The two Ancients, who seemed to be standing against the one who had guarded the three companions, were lowering their voices and almost smiling. The angry guard, although calmed down considerably, was still not happy. Without the conflict, he focused his attention on the three sitting a few feet away. He noticed Christy was facing Danny and Rob, and he grunted and gripped her shoulder, turning her rudely around.

One of the other Ancients, the one who had gestured over Christy's head, let out a stream of words. As he did so, he grabbed his fellow Ancient and pulled him away from Christy. The two stared at each other, but before it could escalate again into a further argument, another rumble of thunder stopped them in their tracks. They all went to the ground, dropping their spears and bowing their heads.

This was the chance Christy was waiting for. She gave a thumbs-up to Danny, who was already jumping up when he saw the Ancients go down to the ground.

Danny bolted away, taking the Ancients by surprise. He'd had a few minutes to plan his route and had rightly figured that the best direction was directly out from the door, so that the eyes of all three would be completely turned away from Christy and Rob. As he started to put a few yards between him and the Ancients, they grabbed their spears and jumped up. The one who had guarded them took off after Danny while the other two stood watching the chase.

Christy jumped up and immediately grabbed the door. Rob joined in and they pried it open just enough for Christy to slip inside. She tried to pull Rob in too, but he shook her off and, to her surprise, signed "Close."

Christy let go of him reluctantly, and the door closed behind her. She heard the angry shouts of the Ancients and the sound of a block being pulled out of the door, then another and then another. She smiled to herself. Rob had maybe given her a minute or two more by that act.

Quickly looking around, she immediately saw the pool. The loud thunder reverberated and echoed off the walls, and the flashes of lightning illuminated the whole cavern. It looked so different than her pond. Over the sound of the thunder, she heard blocks being put back in the door.

"Please, please, please, happen quickly!" she mumbled to herself.

The message was clutched in her hand as she stood waiting, but she knew she had little time!

CHAPTER 25

Detective Lockhart and Doug were slowly walking back to the rain fly to join the rest of the group. The wind had already calmed down, but the rain was still coming down at a good clip. They had got about halfway back when the whole group under the rain fly came running toward the pond, shouting and pointing.

The commotion stopped the detective and Doug. They at first couldn't understand what any of the others were saying, but then as the group got closer to the pond, they heard Kim Upton.

"Look!" Kim said. "Something just came floating up through the water."

She was pointing back where the two men had stopped when the portal closed.

Doug saw it first and sprinted back the way they'd come. The detective was rooted to the spot, searching where Kim and the others were pointing. Finally he saw what they did. A small balloon, or something like one, was bobbing on the water where the portal had been.

Doug was already wading in almost chest deep when the detective sprinted after him. He arrived at the spot where Doug had gone in the water just as Doug was retrieving whatever it was, so he waited for him.

Doug came out of the water holding what they now knew was a plastic baggy inflated to float. Inside was a crumpled piece of notebook paper. Doug held it up for the detective to see.

"Are you going to open it?" the detective asked.

"Let's wait till we join the others," he replied.

The group all met up almost at the shoreline where Doug and the detective had mistakenly waited for the portal to open. Ignoring the heavy rain, they gathered around Doug, who held the inflated baggie.

"What's in it?" Connie asked.

"I don't know. We wanted to wait till we were all together," Doug answered.

"Open it!" Katie Lake said, and everyone nodded agreement.

Staying beneath the one umbrella they had among them, Doug pried open the seal to a small rush of air.

and took out the paper. As he was unfolding it, Connie, who was standing at his shoulder, gasped and began to sob.

She grabbed the paper from Doug and read it aloud: "'Call our parents in US. We're alive.'" Then she said. "It has our home phone number, Doug! This must have been Christy writing this. I wouldn't have guessed it by the writing. It's so shaky and almost illegible."

Despite Connie's concern about the writing, they all shouted and slapped each other on the back and hugged for joy. Their kids were alive! And they were at a portal in the Empty World that was connected to the pond in front of them.

"What do we do now?" asked Kim Upton.

The Frenchman was grinning and hugging along with everyone else, but he stopped to answer her: "I would suggest that you wait for another storm. This week is going to be hot and oppressively humid. Thunderstorms are predicted for the next three or four days. You can all stay at my house, and at a moment's notice, we can be back here as needed."

"But why didn't they come through? Why send this message instead?" Katie asked, turning the mood somber from the jubilation of the previous couple of minutes.

The whole group was silent, contemplating possible answers to Katie's question, when Detective Lockhart said, "You all go. I'm going to camp here like we planned just in case they do come through when we don't expect it."

Doug nodded. "I'll stay too." Connie was about to protest, but Doug said, "No, we all shouldn't stay. There's a good chance that nothing will happen, and the rest of you will be close if the right conditions happen again."

The Frenchman nodded. "We'll have plenty of time to get back here before any storm comes through."

"It's settled," the detective said. "Doug and I will stay ... just in case. And if a storm does come up unexpectedly, Doug and I will be ready to jump in this time. If they couldn't come through just now, maybe we have to go get them just like we planned. But now we know they're close." Then he hesitated and said, "Well, as close as can be considering they're in another world."

CHAPTER 26

Christy and Rob were crumpled on the ground in front of the door again. Both of them were being held down at spear-point, although their two captors didn't seem to have much heart for it. Off in the distance, they saw Danny kicking and banging the back of their original guard who had slung the little boy over his shoulder and was carrying him back.

When the Ancient carrying Danny came back to the door, he dropped the boy unceremoniously onto the ground and gave him a vicious kick. That violence again elicited an immediate response from the Ancient that Christy was coming to call their protector. He stepped in between Danny and the Ancient bent on doing them harm and gave a shove as he let out a string of words. The two of them went back and forth again with angry words.

Finally the Ancient who had captured Danny spit on the ground and turned his back on everyone. He stood for a minute then walked off toward the glider, which hadn't been moved and was still leaning on its side just off the landing area. When he'd been gone for a few minutes, Protector Ancient spoke in a soft tone to the three companions on the ground. Christy shook her head and spread her hands in a universal gesture of non-understanding. The Ancient tried one more time then gave up and went back to standing with his companion.

Christy had mentally begun calling their second captor "Neutral Ancient," since he seemed to be not for them or against them. Christy was glad that he didn't seem inclined to hurt them like the violent one who Christy was now calling "Angry Ancient."

After a few minutes, Christy chanced speaking to Danny. She decided not to sign yet since she knew that many Ancients understood a rudimentary form of sign language and she didn't want either of the Ancients to understand any of what she was saying.

"Danny?" she said. "Are you okay?"

Protector Ancient glanced at her but ignored the conversation. Apparently he was going to let them talk.

Danny also saw the disinterest from the Ancient and said, "Yes, my side hurts but I'm okay. Did you get to the portal?"

Christy nodded and then spontaneously leaned over and enveloped Danny in a big hug. He clung onto her, and she felt him sobbing. At that moment, she knew he was more injured or afraid than he was admitting.

When she released him, she said, "Thank you! Without you running away, I never would have had time."

Then she grabbed Rob by the sleeve and pulled him to her in a hug. It startled him, but he hugged her back. Christy let him go and mouthed to him, gesturing as she did in hopes he would understand: "And thank you. Without you pulling the blocks, I would not have had time, either."

Rob smiled slightly in acknowledgement, then asked her, "Christy, why didn't you jump into the portal when it opened?"

Danny was watching Rob's lips and said, "Yes, Christy, you should have gone!"

Christy teared up and spoke slowly, hoping Rob would catch some of her meaning: "I wouldn't have done that. I couldn't leave without both of you."

Tired and dejected, they fell silent till Danny finally asked, "Christy, do you think these three are the ones who were at the glider trying to stop us?"

Christy nodded yes, and then Danny said, "Then I think that Jack is definitely alive."

Christy brightened up. "Why do you think so?"

"Well," he said, "there were four Ancients who tried to stop us at the glider. If they had killed your grandfather, all four would have followed us. But only three came. One must have stayed back to guard your grandfather. Anyway, that's what I think."

"Thank you, Danny," Christy said, then sighed. "I hope you're right."

Christy sat thinking for a while then ventured a conversation again. "Danny?" When he nodded, she continued: "Would you try signing with Protector Ancient? I think you'll have the best chance of understanding any sign language they may have."

At Christy's naming one of them, Danny smiled, knowing which one she meant.

"What do you call the other two?" he asked with a grin.

"Angry Ancient and Neutral Ancient," she replied.

Danny's grin spread even wider. "Why do you want me to try to communicate with him?"

"They don't seem to be doing anything with us, even after we tried our stunt to get inside and send a message. I wonder why. We know they got here somehow, probably by a boat hidden somewhere close, and there's that big boat way down the coast that we saw from the cliff. Why aren't they taking us to one of those boats and back to their village? What are they going to do with us?" She paused for a moment, then said, "When those two finally opened up the door and got to me, I had just thrown the note into the portal. We were really lucky that it opened up just after I entered. But what surprised me was they weren't angry at me. Protector Ancient actually bowed to me and took me gently by the arm and led me outside. He was speaking all the while, but of course I couldn't understand him."

Danny nodded. "And I think Angry Ancient might actually have killed us by now if not for these two."

"I agree," she said.

The two Ancients were now facing the direction their companion had gone. They were watching him struggle to do something to the glider. Danny stood up and tapped Protector Ancient lightly on the shoulder. He turned and surprised Danny by bowing to him.

Danny didn't know why, but he bowed back before signing: "Why are we waiting here?" What he actually signed and hoped would be understood was, "Why" and "wait here?"

Protector Ancient was taken aback but smiled and grunted. He let loose with a flurry of signs then hesitated, searching for the right sign, then continued. When he was done, he bowed again.

Danny turned to Christy and Rob, and tried to explain. "I think he said 'Ride Honor Bird, journey start, must finish. Must pass through.' And then he struggled to come up with a sign. I think he said 'law' or maybe even something stronger like 'taboo,' but he distinctly told me 'not go, wait here, storm.'"

"Ask him about his friend who's angry at us," Christy said.

Danny turned again to the Ancients and pointed to their companion in the distance, signing: "Why hurt us?"

Protector Ancient replied in another stream of signs and grimaced.

Danny turned again to Christy. "He signed 'no' and then I think 'believe,' then I'm pretty sure of what he signed next. It was 'eat soon,' and 'sleep.'"

Christy pondered the answers Protector Ancient had given Danny. Finally she said, "Do you think that what Protector Ancient meant about Angry Ancient was that he is a nonbeliever in something that has to do with us? But then, I wonder why these two don't seem the least bit angry at us."

Danny shrugged his shoulders and tried to reason out loud for the three of them: "We're not going anywhere by the sounds of things. I mean, 'not go' and 'wait here, storm' as answers to my question seem cut and dry. They are waiting for another storm."

Christy frowned. "Waiting for another storm ... but why? Who must pass through? Us? If so, then why didn't they just let us go in the first place?"

Danny shrugged. "Maybe the Angry Ancient is the boss, or at least they have to listen to him. That makes some sense. These two are doing one thing ... being nice to us and almost ... what's the word?"

He couldn't think of what he meant, so Christy chimed in, "Deferential?"

"Yes, that's it. Bowing to us and everything ... deferential. But bad guy over by the glider, he clearly has it in for us. If he's in charge, then maybe these two are afraid to let us go, even if we interpret what those signs meant, and they want to let us.

"But then again, maybe even if he is the boss, he can only influence the others so much. He could be so angry because he doesn't agree with his fellow Ancients about us and can't do anything about it. What if because we rode the glider, they have to let us finish the journey through the portal?"

As their discussion petered out for lack of real answers, their captors sat down next to them, offering the three companions dried meat and some kind of thin bread. After they had eaten and were given water to drink, the Ancients threw each of them a woven blanket from one of their packs, and it was clear that they were to get settled for the night. Out in the open, fires were impossible, and unless they were permitted to open the door and sleep inside, there was no place out of the wind to build one even if they had the fuel to do it.

As the sun set, they lost sight of Angry Ancient, who, all the while they were eating and settling down, hadn't returned.

The woven blankets proved surprisingly warm. On their first night together on the search for the portal, Danny had shown Christy and Rob how to scoop out shoulder and hip indentations in whatever ground they were forced to sleep on, piling up the material for a sort of pillow. Tonight it was the crushed shells of the hard packed runway area. After preparing their sleeping spots, they settled down for the night.

The next day was more of the same waiting with the two Ancients standing guard over them, all the while constantly looking at Angry Ancient, who was still with the glider off in the distance. Christy, Rob, and Danny were given more water and dried meat but weren't permitted to go anywhere. All they were allowed to do was talk and watch the Ancients occasionally conversing in their undecipherable language.

Late in the day, Angry Ancient returned, and the three Ancients sat down a few yards from their captives and held a quiet conversation for several minutes. After that quiet start to their conversation, Angry Ancient began to raise his voice and point to the glider and gesticulate wildly. It soon became apparent that Angry Ancient was continuing to try to make some sort of case against Christy, Rob, and Danny.

He looked their way once in a while and pointed at them, all the while arguing with his companions who were shaking their heads, not accepting whatever it was he was saying. When the argument reached a particularly loud point, Angry Ancient drew out a knife and made a cutting motion across his own throat, then pointed at the three captives. His intention was obvious. Protector Ancient swatted down Angry Ancient's arm, the knife flying out of Angry Ancient's hand.

"Did you see all that?" Christy asked Danny, hearing the panic in her own voice.

Angry Ancient heard the whisper and stood up, taking a step toward the three of them. He grunted a few words and was about to strike Christy when Protector Ancient again intervened by jumping up quickly and standing over Christy, his arms folded across his chest.

What might have happened next didn't, because at that moment, rumblings of thunder emanated from behind the door. Neutral Ancient and Protector Ancient immediately dropped down to one knee and bowed their heads. Angry Ancient also got down on one knee, but he didn't bow his head.

He kneeled there staring at the captives and catching Christy's frightened eye. When his fellow captors rose up again, he did so too, saying something and walking away from where they all were waiting by the portal doorway. As he walked away, he picked up his knife. After tucking it into his leather belt, he pointed his spear at the three frightened captives, said something to them, and turned his back.

Protector Ancient looked at the three frightened faces sitting below him and pointed toward the door. He signed and waited, clearly expecting something.

Danny signed back, and the Ancient nodded.

"What did he say?" Christy asked. "I think he signed, 'soon, wait over.' Was that it?"

Danny nodded. "Yes, and I told him that I understood."

"But ... whose wait is over?" Christy asked. "Ours or theirs?"

Shrugging his shoulders, Danny answered, "Not sure, but I sure hope he means our wait is almost over."

More thunder sounded on the other side of the door, and instead going to the ground on one knee,

Protector Ancient gestured the three captives to stand up, and then he again pointed at the door.

"Come on!" Christy said. "Let's get up like he wants us to."

Danny nodded, and even Rob understood what the Ancient wanted them to do. So when Christy started to rise, he got up also.

Protector Ancient stood facing the three of them. On the other side of the door, the thunder was coming more rapidly. Neutral Ancient looked frightened but stood out of the way and didn't go back down on one knee. A few paces off, Angry Ancient stood with his back to everyone else, staring out toward the glider.

Protector Ancient then proceeded to sign again, then smiled and waited with his open hand pointing at the door.

"Is he inviting us to go inside?" Christy asked Danny.

"Yes, I think so. What he just signed was, 'You who rode Honor Bird, continue journey. Go through entrance now.'"

"Then he's letting us go!" Christy shouted, almost crying for joy.

Protector Ancient saw the relief on their faces and smiled. He stepped to the door and gripped the exact spot needed to open it and pulled.

Angry Ancient heard the door open and turned with a yell. He reached Neutral Ancient first and felled him with a quick blow of his spear. Protector Ancient turned toward the commotion just as Angry Ancient swung a vicious blow at his head. Because Protector

Ancient didn't have his spear ready to parry the blow, it caught him square on the side of his head. He staggered back into the edge of the open door, and he, too, crumpled to the ground.

Christy screamed just as Danny grabbed her hand and pulled her into the open doorway. Rob stood there, too shocked and afraid to move. Angry Ancient turned from his fallen companion and pointed his spear at Rob. The raging Ancient said something to Rob and grinned viciously at him, waving his spear. He was about to thrust it into Rob, but the Ancient's needless act of boasting had shaken Rob out of his paralysis of fear.

Quick as a cat, he turned and bolted through the door. Startled at the boy's quickness, Angry Ancient hesitated—but only for a second, then he followed Rob through the open door. As Angry Ancient crossed the threshold of the doorway, he went sprawling on his face, his spear flying ahead of him right into the pool of water.

"Ouch!" Danny yelled, then rubbed his leg.

He had positioned himself behind the closed half of the door, and when the Ancient came through, he stuck his foot out, taking the Ancient by surprise.

Christy quickly pounced on the winded and surprised Ancient, who, with Christy's added weight and the force of his fall, was struggling to get up again.

Rob turned around in time to see Christy jumping on the Ancient. When he saw that, he stopped and reached down on the ground for a fist-sized rock.

Going quickly over to the two figures on the ground, he took his rock and hit the Ancient on the head with it. Immediately the Ancient stopped struggling.

Christy was panting from her exertions but got up off the now still Ancient.

"Did I kill him?" Rob asked. "I hope not."

Danny kneeled down, looking closely at the Ancient. "He's still breathing!" And for Rob's sake, Danny then shook his head.

"Good!" Rob said. "But what do we do with him?"

Danny ran out, gathered their packs, and dragged them inside the door.

"Do you think the other two are dead?" Christy asked, signing.

"Probably not, only knocked out like this guy here," Danny replied as he was rummaging through his pack. Pulling out a couple lengths of rope, he tied the Ancient's hands behind him and then tied his feet too, using knots he learned as a scout. "That should keep him from doing anything even if he wakes up." Danny then pulled the knife out of the belt at the Ancient's waist and threw it into the water.

Christy hoped Danny was right. But, still not feeling right about abandoning the Ancient who'd helped them, she grabbed a rag out of her pack and dipped it into the water of the pool before bolting outside again.

Christy sprinted over to Protector Ancient. Kneeling down beside him, she used the wet rag on the Ancient's face. She didn't dare wait too long, but she was rewarded within a few seconds by the Ancient opening his eyes. He woke up, momentarily disoriented, but Christy smiled at him and signed, "Thank you."

She thought she saw understanding come into his eyes. She handed the wet rag to her protector and motioned toward the other Ancient who was still out cold. He nodded understanding again and then signed, "How?"

Christy wasn't sure of his meaning but assumed he meant something about the one who had hit him and had been against the three kids using the portal. She smiled and hit herself over the head with her closed fist and mimicked falling down.

That brought another smile from the Ancient, and he pointed to the portal and said something in his own language.

Christy was pretty sure he'd said "Thank you," but she didn't dare wait to be sure. She smiled and bowed to him, and then jumped up and sprinted back through the portal door to join her companions.

Now that they were all inside, peals of thunder echoed and the flashes of lightning lit the inside of the cavern. The water, though, remained just water. With the Ancient no longer a threat to them, they stood on the edge of the water and waited.

Just after another loud thunderclap, Christy tapped Danny on the shoulder, and he turned to face her.

"It's eerie to think that the thunder we're hearing is coming from back home on Earth," she said.

Danny nodded. "I hope we didn't miss it."

Christy never heard him because he was drowned out by a deafening clap of thunder. The cavern brightened, and the water began to swirl and change colors from beneath.

Christy was standing between the two boys, and without taking her eyes off the water, she grasped each of them by the hand. Despite knowing that without signing or without either of them looking at her, they wouldn't hear or know what she was saying, she said, "You guys are the best. Let's go home!"

CHAPTER 27

The next day saw the group gathered at the pond again. The night before, they had watched the weather reports and hoped that they were going to have another chance.

Their French host was true to his word. He was gracious and as helpful as can be. Early that morning, he even made a marvelous breakfast for them all, saying he hadn't cooked for so many in years and it was a pleasure to entertain them. Although his house was small, there was a sense of purpose and urgency that made the overcrowded situation seem trivial by comparison.

The detective and Doug spent the night in one of the tents they had set up the day before. Early in the afternoon, the weather was clear, but by later, the clouds thickened and thunder could be heard off in the distance.

Grouped together under the rain fly, they all tried to hide their impatience with the weather by going over their plan again and again. Since that plan consisted of waiting for the portal to open again, which was out of their control, it became redundant and old very quickly. Detective Lockhart and Doug at least had more to think about since they were going to jump into the water when and if the portal opened.

It was still a couple of hours before dark when the rain began and the wind started to blow the trees in earnest. Doug winked at Connie as the thunder and lightning began to move overhead, and he and the detective picked up their packs to head out from under the rain fly to where they hoped they'd be able to jump in at the right time.

As they walked around the perimeter of the pond toward where the portal had showed itself the day before, Doug said, "This time, even if I can't get there in time for some reason, you make sure you jump in, okay?"

The detective nodded. "Likewise, okay?"

Doug nodded back. "Although, hopefully, if we're close enough, we won't have to make any decision like that. As long as the portal opens up in the same spot as yesterday, whenever it opens again, both of us should make it."

They stood on the shore within yards of where the portal had opened up in the water the day before and withstood the driving rain and wind, praying with each new series of thunder and lightning that this one would be the one!

As the sky turned almost black and the wind was ripping leaves off of the trees and sending them swirling around in all directions, the right combination of thunder and lightning finally occurred. Doug and the detective watched in near horror as lightning struck the pond—almost completely on the other side. Unlike the portal back home, this one seemed to be more fluid, less anchored to one spot. The cries of the group watching from under the rain fly were echoed by both Doug's and the detective's curses.

Off in a flash, they both sprinted toward the coalescing, color-changing spot where they knew the portal was opening. Within two seconds, they both knew they again weren't going to make it, but they kept running toward the spot anyway.

As the portal was closing and the two men began to slow down out of frustration and anger, three heads bobbed to the surface of the pond. The screams of joy from the rain fly were mingled with shouts from Doug and the detective as the three heads turned into three figures swimming toward the shore.

By the time the three kids had walked out the last few feet of water to stand on the shore, everyone was there to meet them, shouting words of greeting and crying unashamedly.

"I can't believe it! How did you get here?" Christy said to nobody in particular.

"You can thank Ginny and Trevor," Detective Lockhart said with a grin. "They found this portal."

The detective wasn't sure that anyone was listening, though—even Christy, who had asked the question. Everyone was hugging and crying.

Connie and Doug clung to Christy, holding on for dear life. Katie Lake had her son Danny surrounded in a big bear hug, twirling him around off his feet. Rob was clinging to his mother, who was crying like a baby. Ginny, the Frenchman, and the detective took turns hugging everyone.

After what seemed like an eternity, the tears of joy stopped, and then everyone tried speaking at once. Ignoring the growing chaos of voices, the detective let out a loud whistle that quieted things down for a minute.

He grinned and then spoke: "Let's get everything packed and get out of here before we get really soaked."

Everyone laughed and then returned to their catching up.

During the continuing confusion and voices, Connie leaned into Christy and whispered in her ear, "Let's go home."

Christy shook her head and pulled away from her mom. It startled Connie, and she stared at her daughter.

"Please listen, everyone!" Christy shouted.

It took a second or two, but then all eyes were on Christy.

Once everyone was quiet, Christy said, "Mom, Grandpa's alive! I have to go back to get him."

Thanks for reading!

You made it to the end! This may be the end of one story, but if you like reading the Empty World Saga, there's more to come. Don't want to miss a release?

Perks of being an Email Insider include:

- Notification of book releases (1-2 times per year)
- Inside track on beta reading
- Access to Inside Exclusive bonus extras and giveaways

Sign up for the my Email Insiders list at: www.davidkanderson.info

Books by David K. Anderson

Empty World Saga

The first 4 books of the Empty World Saga are available in ebook and paperback.

1. Portal Through the Pond
2. Beyond the Portal
3. At the Portal's End
4. The Lost Portal

Read about the Empty World Saga and discover where to buy at: <u>emptyworldsaga.com</u>

About the Author

Growing up, David K. Anderson was mentored by his Uncle Ralph, a gifted artist who taught him to express himself in creative ways: writing, drawing and sculpting.

David is married and has three adult children. Throughout his adult life, he has volunteered countless hours with children with disabilities involving creative activities. His lifelong passions for art, sculpting and storytelling have helped him combine his talents to create enjoyment for hundreds of children of all abilities. His family's mutual love for fantasy, fiction, and fun along with a desire to ensure that children of all abilities can be heroes, has motivated him to write stories that engage us all.

Made in the USA
Middletown, DE
12 December 2018